Also by Ed Hamilton

Legends of the Chelsea Hotel: Living with the Artists and Outlaws of New York's Rebel Mecca

The Chintz Age: Tales of Love and Loss for a New New York

Lords

of

the

Schoolyard

Contents

Part One

The field where we played football in eighth grade was across the parking lot from the church and the school. Mother of Good Council, affectionately known as Mother Goose. Maybe not so affectionately. There were woods on the other side of the field, where we had our bench. The woods were still thick and green at the beginning of fall.

There was a kid named Chip on our football team. He was just a scrawny, little kid, uncoordinated and not very strong. I don't know why he played football. He never got into the game, not until the final seconds, and then only if we were ahead by fifty points or so. Maybe his dad made him play. That was the reason I played, because my dad made me play.

Chip looked like an idiot in his uniform. It was too big for him, and Coach Johnson had given him all the worst equipment, the old-time equipment, shoulder pads made of cardboard and a helmet with the ears sticking out, and pants that were a sickly yellow-brown instead of white. The coach wasn't going to waste good equipment on somebody who was never going to play.

Neither me nor my best friend Johnny was so good that we played all the time. Neither of us really cared about football. When we were over on the sidelines during the games, we just hung out looking for something to do. When we were bored we picked on Chip. We punched him and threw him around. One time Johnny grabbed Chip by his face mask and wrenched his head around and flung him to the ground. Chip went sprawling.

Once Chip got back up, I said, "Hey, let me try that!" I grabbed him the same way and twisted him around by the face

3

mask and threw him to the ground. He went rolling along the ground. Well, at least he rolled once. I thought I had got in a better toss than Johnny. There was always a healthy spirit of competition between us.

We may have been outcasts, me and Johnny, but we never took it lying down. We took it out on others instead.

Chip didn't complain. Well, at least not much. He didn't exactly like it, but what could he do about it?

Johnny worked up a hocker. He told Chip to hold out his hand.

"Come on, Johnny!" Chip whined.

"Hold out your hand!" Johnny said.

"No, I don't want to."

"Hold out your hand!!!"

Chip held out his hand slowly, timidly, and turned it palm up. Johnny spat in it, and Chip wiped the spit on his pants.

I could do better! I grabbed Chip by the face mask and spat in his face. The hocker strung between the face mask and his face. Chip struggled to get away from me, and when I let him go he wiped at the hocker with his hand and his sleeve and then with the ragged tail of his jersey.

One time we found an old sock in the leaves and dirt back by the edge of the woods. It was an athletic sock, but it was filthy and brown, and matted down into the ground. We decided to tie the sock to Chip's face mask.

Johnny held him while I tied knots. I got the first knot in, and was working on the second, when Chip jerked his head away from me. "Hold onto him!" I told Johnny.

"Hold still!" Johnny knocked him upside the head. "Quit struggling!"

"Come on guys, leave me alone," Chip whined.

I knotted the sock up good. We looked around on the ground some more. When we found another sock Johnny knotted that one on there too while I held onto Chip.

When we finished, Chip looked stupid as shit. He had looked stupid before but now he looked like a retard. We stood back and looked at him and cracked up laughing. Everybody who saw him cracked up laughing. The guy who was our starting quarterback and the best athlete in the school came by and saw him. "Nice decoration," he said, rolling his eyes. We were proud of our handiwork.

We had to keep an eye on Chip to prevent him from untying the socks. I usually played on defense and Johnny played on offense, so we took turns watching him, and looking for more shit to tie onto his helmet. We found another sock, and a brown, maybe bloody rag, and we knotted those on Chip's face mask as well.

As the game wore on, Chip quit whining about the socks. He knew it just called attention to him. He kept trying to slip away so he could get the socks off his helmet, but it took him a long time to untie them. He would get one or two of the knots out, but then one of us would catch him and retie them, and hit him a couple of times as punishment.

Eventually, Coach Johnson came walking by. He was a young guy, just out of college, but still big and fat, with thick, hairy legs. He had long black hair and a mustache.

"What the hell?!" Coach Johnson said when he saw Chip. "Goins, you think that's funny?" Chip's last name was Goins. "Get that shit off your helmet, you idiot!"

Me and Johnny were standing there trying our best to keep from laughing.

"He thought it would protect him from blows to the head," I said.

"I'm not talking to you, Donaldson," the coach said. "When I want your opinion I'll ask for it."

"They made me do it!" Chip whined.

"Spare me, Goins. I don't want to hear it."

"But coach!"

"Shut up!!!" Johnson yelled. He smacked Chip upside the head. "Nobody can make you do anything you don't want to do!" He grabbed Chip by the face mask and shook him vigorously. "You hear me, Goins?!"

"Yes sir! Yes sir!" Chip stammered. He was terrified.

Pulling Chip up on his toes, Johnson got right up in Chip's face and yelled in his face. "You stand up for yourself! You hear me?! Be a man!" There was spit in Johnson's mustache and he sprayed it as he spoke.

"Yes sir!"

The coach shook Chip once more by the face mask and then flung him aside. Effortlessly. You had to admire his technique.

We were trying our best not to let the coach see us laughing as he walked away. But then when he got far enough away we really cracked up. When we turned back to Chip we saw that he had walked off a ways and was trying to untie the knots.

"Hey!" Johnny called after him.

"What do you think you're doing?!" I said.

We rushed over to where Chip was standing. He stopped trying to untie the knots and said, "Come on guys. You heard the coach. Enough is enough." Apparently he was trying to stand up for himself like the coach told him to. He said, "I've had enough." He thought now we were going to give him a break.

After careful consideration, we made him keep the socks on his helmet. We figured eighth grade was too late for him to start being a man. Johnny found an old ripped-up jockstrap and pried it up out of the dirt. We tied it onto the front of Chip's face mask, and twisted his mouthpiece up in it. We left some of the main part hanging off, the part that held your nuts, so that people would know what it was instead of just thinking it was another sock.

Football was very important to my father. When I was ten years old, he decided it was high time for me to play. I wanted to please him and I was too young to refuse anyway. So one weekend in the late summer before fourth grade, he took me to the football field to show me what the sport was about and to see if I could get on a team.

When we got there, the kids were in the middle of a drill where they had to scramble up a hill on all fours and slam into a blocking sled, over and over. They were all breathing heavily, and seemed to be in agony. They were in full gear, and it must've been ninety-five degrees out.

I was uncomfortable just standing there in the sun. The last thing I wanted was to sweat and strain like that. I wanted to be at home in the AC reading a comic book or watching TV. But when my dad asked me if I wanted to do what those boys were doing, I said yes, because I knew that was what he wanted to hear.

In fact, I didn't like anything about it. I didn't like the uniforms, which looked bulky and cumbersome. The helmets looked hot, heavy and uncomfortable. I didn't even like the ball, which I was already familiar with from playing catch with my father. It was a huge, rock-hard ball with a point on both ends that came flying at your face like a missile, and if you didn't catch it properly it would hit you in the teeth and hurt like hell.

The guys in charge of the league said I couldn't play. I was only ten and you had to be twelve. I think my dad would have lied to get me on the team, but it was obvious I wasn't old enough because of my size, so he didn't bother. It's hard to express just how happy I was. I could put it off for another year, maybe even two. I was overjoyed.

But my dad was not one to give up easily. He felt I should start playing right away, the sooner the better. If I had to play with kids older and bigger than me, then that would just make me stronger. After wrangling with the officials for a while, he was able to convince them to let me play. Their condition was that he coach a team. He had been a star, or an actual pro anyway, with the Cleveland Browns, and so they were willing to bend over backwards to have him associated with their program. Plus, they figured he knew what he was talking about when he said I was ready to play.

In a way, I liked the idea of playing football. I dreamed of being a big star and making my father proud. And I loved spending time with my dad, who was otherwise kind of unapproachable. I loved the drives to practice, when me and my dad would talk and listen to the radio.

But the drives were over all too soon. I was in love with the idea of football, but not the reality. I was too slow to be a running back, which had been my father's position, and so he reluctantly decided that I would have to play on the line. This was less glamorous, but it took the minimum of running, so I liked that part of it. But the big linemen were always knocking me flat. Half the time my head was ringing from the blows of the other kid's helmets. Several times I was knocked senseless. I thought I would learn to be a better player, maybe even grow some and be bigger, but it just got worse. It didn't take me long to figure out that I wasn't going to be able to live up to my father's ideals.

And that was just the physical part. On top of that, the other kids made it hell on me, saying the only reason I got to play was because my dad was coach. I would have told them to fuck off, but they were bigger than me, and anyway I knew they were right. Fortunately, they liked and respected my dad, or else I think it would have been worse. Still, it was bad enough.

Halfway through the season I had about reached my limit. So one Saturday I refused to get out of bed, claiming I was sick. My mother took my side, as I figured she would. She didn't have so much invested in my playing football. She felt my forehead and put a cold rag on my head. She took my temperature, and even though it turned out normal, that was no proof I wasn't sick. I said I had a sore throat, and acted like it hurt to swallow. I put on a good show. I almost even managed to convince myself.

Practice wasn't until the afternoon. I could hear my mother and father discussing my illness downstairs. My mother could usually be counted on to win an argument with my dad, but this was a special case. My father only felt strongly about a couple of things. Religion was one, and football was another. It sounded like my mother was winning him over, but that was just because he wasn't saying much. The idea of me staying home from practice was so absurd that he refused to take it seriously.

About an hour before it was time to go, my father came upstairs to check in on me. "Better get up now so you can have something to eat," he said.

"I'm sick," I said.

He didn't say anything, but turned and went downstairs.

A half an hour later he was back. "I've had enough of this! Get up!" he said, and grabbed the bed covers and ripped them off of me.

"I'm sick! I'm sick!" I whined. I tried to grab the covers to pull them back over me, but my father grabbed me by the arm and flung me to the floor. Crawling in my underwear, I struggled to get out of his way.

He kicked me in the ass. "Get up and get your uniform on!" That day we didn't listen to the radio. We drove to practice in silence.

My dad must've been a good coach, because we made it to the championship game that year. He yelled, and he was tough, but he wasn't a slave driver like most coaches. Like Coach Johnson, for instance. He just had a way of making you want to be like him. He also had a way of making you feel like a complete failure if you didn't live up to his standards. He had a sort of charisma that allowed him to motivate everyone on our team to give their all for him.

Still, since he couldn't get what he wanted out of me, my father didn't consider himself a good coach. To my father, it was what was inside the player that mattered. And I had proved that there wasn't much inside of me.

The championship game itself was the realization of my worst fears. I don't remember much of the first part of the game, except that it was a defensive battle. Going into the final quarter, the score was tied zero to zero. I hadn't been playing much, but to give one of the other guys a breather, my dad sent me into the game. I was playing defensive guard.

They hiked the ball and the play went off. Usually I was stopped cold at the line and either driven back or knocked to the ground. But for some reason, not this time. I slipped through the defense and, to my amazement, found myself in the backfield, alone with the quarterback.

I couldn't believe my good luck. I was going to get the big tackle and save the game. Then my dad would really be proud of me. The quarterback was a big, tall kid, but he couldn't get away from me now. I had rarely had a tackle all season, never one unassisted. Still, I knew how to tackle. I knew how to grab hold and hang on.

Then, just as I was reaching out to grab him, something hit me from behind, in the foot. It wasn't much, maybe a leg or an arm, but it caused me to stumble, and to lose my footing. As I was falling I reached out and made a desperate grab for the quarterback, but all I got was the tail of his jersey, and he squirted out of my grasp and ran around the end of the line for a touchdown. Reluctantly, wishing I had been injured, I picked myself up from the ground and trotted off the field.

I wanted to face my punishment and get it over with, so I ran right up to my father on the sidelines. I expected him to hit me, or at least to yell at me. I don't think I would have minded that so much. Instead, he just said, "I don't even want to look at you."

They missed the extra point, but it didn't matter. We went on to lose the game, 6-0. After the ref blew the whistle for the end of the game, and the end of our season, we stood milling around on the sidelines, unable to believe it was over, looking on dejectedly as the other team celebrated.

Finally, my dad called us all together in a huddle. "We had a great year," he said. "And we played them tough. They beat us fair and square, and we have nothing to be ashamed about. Another day, it certainly could have gone the other way." I was feeling dazed, almost too shell-shocked to listen. "Let's show them we're bigger men than they are," my dad went on. "Let's show them we can snatch victory from the jaws of defeat!"

My father grew quiet for a moment. Then he said, "Men, I want you to do something for me. I want you to lift me up on your shoulders and carry me across the field." He pointed to the bleachers on the other side of the field, where our friends and families were gathered. "I've always wanted to go out that way," he said. "So what do you say? Can you do this for me?"

My teammates cheered, their spirits suddenly lifted. I cheered along with them. We knew we could do it.

My father was a big man, and it took several of us to lift him up, supporting him by the legs and ass. Maybe ten or a dozen of us had a piece of him. We ran with him across the field, cheering wildly, as my father pumped his fists in the air. The other team was silenced, and our friends in the bleachers took up the cheer. We were a team once again, for one brief, final moment. We were going out on top after all.

In the middle of all this excitement, I looked up at my father and he looked down at me. And then he reached down and grabbed my face mask. The helmet came off easily in his hand. He held it for a moment, and then he dropped it into the crowd. Reflexively, I bent to retrieve it, but it was kicked out of my grasp and I was shoved from behind. I went after it again, but it was kicked again, and I was shoved again. The other players kicked my helmet all around, as I stupidly chased after it. Finally, just as I had the helmet in my hand, somebody crashed into me and I fell, sprawling out face first as the rest of the team surged over me, trampling me, stomping on my legs, my arms, and my fingers with their cleats.

3

My friend Johnny was just like me. We met in the fourth grade, when both our families moved to town. Being the new kids in town we were thrown together naturally, first defensively, and then for more offensive purposes. We were both tough kids, and we didn't get along well with too many people except each other. This is the story of how we grew up, discovered girls and liquor, and grew apart. It's also the story of how we terrorized quite a few people along the way.

After school and before football practice we usually had a couple of hours to fool around before we had to get into our uniforms. So one bright autumn day we all went out into the woods behind the school and held a contest to see who could kill a squirrel first by throwing a rock at it.

The squirrels weren't used to people since they lived in the woods. A big crowd scared them away, so we split up into teams of two or three and went off in different directions. I teamed up with Johnny. It didn't take us long to figure out that it's not as easy as it sounds to hit a squirrel with a rock. They seemed to know what we were up to. They would scamper off up a tree just as we got ready to throw. It was frustrating. Johnny soon lost interest, but I wasn't one to give up that easily. I was determined to bag one of those cute little suckers.

While Johnny hung back, I crept up on a squirrel that had its back turned to me. I tried to be as quiet as possible as I inched closer, step by step. The squirrel was busy rooting around in the grass. From about five yards away, I cocked my arm back ready to throw. Then I stepped on a twig and the twig snapped. The squirrel sprang and ran for the tree. I threw the rock out in front of the fleeing squirrel, missing its head by a fraction of an inch. The squirrel pulled up and wheeled around in my direction. He stood there for a moment, confused, then turned back toward the tree and darted up it.

It seemed like I was really getting the hang of it. Next time, surely. I started looking around for another good rock. But just when I found one, Chip came marching through the woods, swinging a plump squirrel by the tail. I couldn't believe it. The biggest sissy on the team. Amazing.

"How the hell did you do it?" I asked.

"I used a brick," Chip said. He was quite pleased with himself. He was smiling.

"That's cheating," I said. But of course I would have been the first to use a brick if I could have found one.

The rest of the guys from the team gathered around and we examined the squirrel. It was dead alright. Its eyes were open and fixed. But it didn't seem to have been damaged much by the brick. Its coat was tan, healthy and sleek. Its tail was full and bushy. There was only a trickle of blood coming from its mouth.

We carried the squirrel around in the woods for a while, swinging it by the tail. Mostly Chip carried it. He wouldn't even let me touch it, since he was afraid that I wouldn't give it back.

But eventually Chip got sick of toting around a dead animal carcass. "What should we do with it?" he asked. "Should we bury it, or just throw it in the trash?"

"That's a waste," I said. "Give it here."

Somewhat reluctantly, Chip let me have the squirrel. I carried it through the woods as the other guys followed. I carried it, swinging at my side, over to the edge of the four-lane highway.

"What are you gonna do with it?" Chip asked.

Johnny had figured it out, and was smiling in anticipation. If there was a leader between the two of us, it was me. I was the one who would do anything. But Johnny always egged me on. A lot of the times I wouldn't have been so bold if not for him. We needed each other in that sense. I thought up the crazy, absurd things to do, and Johnny convinced me it was OK to do them.

The cars were whizzing by at about fifty miles an hour. I hesitated for a moment. "Go on. Do it!" Johnny said. I whipped the squirrel around over my head by its tail and then flung it into the windshield of a yellow Nova. It landed with a splat and some guts flew out of its mouth onto the windshield. It bounced over the top of the car and into the road, as the driver slammed on his brakes and nearly got rear-ended. He pulled off onto the shoulder of the road.

The other guys took off running into the woods. I retreated into the woods as well, but not too far. I wanted to see what the guy in the car looked like, and what he was going to do. I figured I could outrun him since I knew the paths. Johnny hung back right behind me, a little bit further into the woods.

The driver got out of his car. He was a big guy of about eighteen or twenty, heavy and lumbering. I was no match for him. He came a little ways into the woods and spotted me, but he was reluctant to come any further. He pointed his finger at me and yelled, "Hey, you asshole! You could've got me killed!"

"So what?" I yelled back. "No big loss!"

"You can't just go around doing things like that!"

"Oh yeah? Who's gonna stop me?"

"Come here!" he demanded.

"Fuck you!" I said, and gave him the finger. "Come and get me, fat boy!"

This really burned him up. His face got red and he clenched his fists. He started after me a few steps into the brush, then he thought better of it. The going was tough through the woods, and he was slow and clumsy. He knew he wouldn't be able to catch me.

"I'm gonna go get my little brother to kick your ass," he said.

"What's the matter, fat boy? Can't do it yourself?"

"You wait right here, you little shitass!" he said. And he got in his car and drove off.

Johnny was laughing his ass off. "Come on, you lunatic! Let's get out of here!"

4

That was about how it went all through the football season, cutting-up and playing pranks, that is, not the squirrel thing. That was a one-time thing. And teasing Chip. When we were really bored we had that to fall back on. In one two-week stretch of rainy weather, one or the other of us gave him a wedgie almost every day. It was a technique we had just picked up, don't ask me where. But hey, Chip must not have hated it too bad, because he continued to hang around with us. He could have just as easily avoided us. It was easy enough to think that on some level he actually enjoyed the abuse.

One day not long after the squirrel incident me and Johnny were sneaking a smoke in the bathroom at school, passing a cigarette back and forth in one of the stalls. The other kids had cleared out. Johnny had a magic marker and was drawing a picture of a big long dick on the wall of the stall. Johnny had a talent for art.

The dick turned out to be attached to one of the priests, and Johnny was getting set to draw the nun who would receive it.

For reasons I'll get into soon, I didn't have much interest in art, especially not this kind of art. I was taking a long draw off the cig when the bathroom door swung open. I flung the cig into the bowl and kicked the handle, flushing it down. I fanned at the smoke as I exhaled. The whole place was filled with smoke.

It was Chip. He had come after us to see what we were up to. He must have smelled the smoke right off, but he came far enough into the bathroom to see us standing there in the stall.

He looked horrified. He didn't even piss. He just turned around and ran out of the bathroom.

We already had the window open, and we tried to fan the air some more. It seemed to do some good, though not much. We were already late, so we figured we'd better get back to class.

Chip had run and told the teacher. As we were walking down the hall, she came charging out of the classroom toward us.

"What were you boys doing in there!?" Mrs. Bream shrieked. "Chip tells me you were smoking!"

"Chip doesn't know what he's talking about," I said. "We were just burning a stick of incense."

Mrs. Bream believed me. Or pretended to anyway. Smoking was such a serious offense that she just didn't want to deal with it. She didn't even bother to check the bathroom.

"Chip just gets excited sometimes," she explained as she walked with us back to class. "I'm sure you can understand his concern."

Sure. Dumb as he was, Chip knew better. And he had to know that we would retaliate. We gave him dirty looks all through the class period. Then at recess we waited for him outside. As soon as Chip came out the door, he saw me coming for him and ran the other way.

Johnny headed him off. He got Chip in a bear hug, lifting him off the ground and squeezing the wind out of him. "Where are you going, Chipper boy?" Johnny said.

Johnny let him go. Chip stood there shaken and out of breath. He said, "What did I do? Let me alone!" He didn't try to run. He knew we would have run him down. "I'm glad you could come out and play," I said.

We led him along, each with a hand on one of his arms. We led him around the side of the school. Chip started getting really scared now, since we were taking him to a place where nobody could see us. He would have broken and run if we hadn't been holding him. "What did I do?!" he whined. "What did I do?!"

"You know very well what you did," I said.

"But… but smoking is bad for you!" Chip said. It began to look like Mrs. Bream had been right. Maybe Chip had told on us out of some misguided concern for our health.

"Yeah, yeah," Johnny said.

"And you could burn down the school!" Chip said.

We led Chip around to the garage behind the school. Mr. Blount was in front of the garage fooling around with the lawn mower and cursing to himself. Mr. Blount was the janitor. He was an alcoholic and a crazy motherfucker. He'd been in prison, it was rumored, and maybe even in a mental hospital. He was wiry and mean-looking, with long brown hair hanging in greasy curls, and self-inflicted tattoos on his arms.

We stopped a ways off from Mr. Blount. He didn't notice us. "We'd been thinking about kicking your ass, but we figured we might give you a break," I told Chip. "That is, if you do something for us."

"What is it?" Chip asked. He was suspicious. He knew us well.

I said, "You see that guy standing over there in the garage?"

"You mean Mr. Blount?"

"That's his name," Johnny said.

"So?" You could see the apprehension in Chip's eyes.

"So, you're gonna go up to him and tell him you want to suck his dick," I said.

"No way, man!!!"

"And you'd better say it loud enough so we can hear!" Johnny added.

"He'll kill me!"

"Either that or he'll whip it out," I said. "You know you want to anyway."

Chip was kind of effeminate, and that was part of the reason why we targeted him. Neither Johnny nor I had ever had any experience with girls. Neither of us had ever had a girlfriend, so we were sensitive on matters like that. I guess picking on Chip made us feel more like men.

"If you don't do it, we'll kick your ass!" Johnny said. He punched Chip hard in the arm. "Get over there!"

"Owww! Cut it out!" Chip said, rubbing his arm. "You can't do anything to me. Mr. Blount is right there. You'll be in big trouble!"

"You think he gives a fuck? You're even dumber than I thought. Now get over there!" I said.

"No. I don't care what you do to me. No way. Please guys, I'll do anything, just not that." No amount of threatening would make him change his mind.

By this time Mr. Blount had seen us and was standing in the entrance of the garage watching us sling Chip around. He was smoking a cigarette and laughing. We waved and called out to him. We thought Mr. Blount was a pretty cool guy. He was an unrepentant outlaw, a guy whose crimes had caught up with him, but who seemed unconcerned by that fact. I think we realized on some level that that could be us in twenty years.

We led Chip back around the school to the parking lot. By this time lots of kids were out, playing games or else standing around in groups. When we stopped, I said, "You see that penguin over there?"

I pointed to Sister Mary Catherine. She was the art teacher for the whole school. She had her back to us and was talking to some girls. Mary Catherine was young, in her twenties. She had a mustache and wore coke-bottle glasses. She was easygoing, but like all nuns she had a mean streak. "We want you to go up to her and pull off that rag she's got on her head," I told Chip.

"It's called a veil," Chip said. "You know, like a wedding veil. Because she's married to Jesus."

"OK, Mr. Know-it-all."

"We're gonna marry you to Mr. Blount if you don't do it," Johnny said.

Surprisingly, it didn't sound that bad to Chip. "If I do it, then you'll leave me alone?"

"I swear to God," I said. "That's all you need to do."

We didn't think he would do it. We thought that he would probably get close and then run, or else just hang around close to the nun for protection.

But Chip walked right up behind her and without ceremony just yanked the damn thing off. The nun let out a little shriek and her hands shot to her head. It was pretty damn funny. Mary Catherine had short, spiky black hair.

Chip stood there with the veil in his hand, looking like a dope. "Oh, I'm so sorry," he said as he handed the thing back to her. "I'm really, really sorry, Sister. I didn't do it on purpose."

Mary Catherine didn't think it was that big a deal. "That's OK, Chip. I know you wouldn't have done it on purpose," she said.

"I can't believe it!" Johnny said.

Neither could I. "Damn. She thought it was an accident." As the nun was fixing her headdress and the girls around her were whispering to her excitedly, probably telling her it hadn't been an accident, Chip came strolling back over to us. He was smiling. "See, I did it," he said, proudly.

"That sucked, man." I shook my head in disgust. "She just thought you did it accidentally."

"So?"

"And then you just handed it back to her. I can't believe that shit. And apologized! What a pussy."

"What was I supposed to do?"

"You were supposed to throw it in her face!"

"Yeah! And tell her to fuck off!" Johnny added.

"Well, you didn't tell me that."

"We're telling you now," I said.

"I'll remember it next time," Chip said, like a little smart-ass.

"No. This time," I said. "You have to do it again."

"Oh no, I'm not doing it again."

"Yes, you are! Or else we'll kick your ass!" Johnny said.

"You said you wouldn't touch me if I did it. And I did it. You swore to God."

Johnny grabbed Chip by the collar and shouted in his face, "You did it wrong! Now get over there and do it again! Throw that hat in her face and tell her to go fuck herself!"

"Please don't make me do that," Chip pleaded. "I can't do it like that!"

"Yes you can!!!" Johnny yelled.

"Wait a minute," I said. "What part about it don't you like?"

"I don't like any of it!"

"Hmmm. Alright, I guess we can compromise. Here's what you do. Snatch the hat, run away with it, and throw it up in that tree." I pointed to a big oak that stood in a grassy area on the other side of the nun. "You got that?"

"OK," Chip nodded his head. "And then you'll leave me alone?"

"Swear to God," I said.

"At least call her a whore," Johnny said as Chip turned and walked toward the nun.

The girls around the nun saw Chip coming this time, but they didn't bother to warn her. This time the headdress came off a lot easier. Mary Catherine wheeled around, her face red with rage.

Chip hesitated when he saw her face. Then he tried to get by her to get to the tree, but she jumped in his way and made a grab at him with her claws. He turned and fled in the opposite direction, back around the building, with Mary Catherine hot on his heels. We ran after them, and so did the girls and everybody else who had watched the action.

Chip headed straight for the dumpster, and when he got close he winged the head rag toward its open mouth. Good idea! But he screwed it up. The rag hit the folded-back lid of the dumpster and bounced off onto the ground.

Then Chip slowed down and let the nun catch up. It was a good thing too. Mr. Blount had come out of the garage and was ready to run him down.

Mary Catherine walked up to Chip as he was blubbering excuses. "I didn't mean to! They told me to! They made me do it!"

This time, the nun wasn't listening. She grabbed Chip by both his arms and shook him. Then she reared back her arm and smacked him with her open hand, right in the mouth. She marched him over to where the head rag lay crumpled on the pavement and made him pick it up and hand it back to her. With the rag in one hand and Chip's arm in the other, she hauled his ass off to the principal's office.

The nun knew that me and Johnny had something to do with the incident, but she didn't care. The funny thing was, the teachers usually let us get away with picking on kids like Chip. We were doing part of their job for them, after all, by showing that difference and weakness were prohibited. We were the classroom cops, the Law of the Schoolyard. And besides that, teachers are only human. They would rather identify with the strong than with the weak.

Chip would have his revenge. But the story is not about Chip, at least not primarily. Chip became less important as girls became more important. After all, me and Johnny were growing up.

It was a big status thing to have a girlfriend in eighth grade. All the popular kids had already paired off. And girls were looking pretty good to me even apart from that. I was just entering puberty and this was a new feeling for me, but one that I wanted to explore. I was definitely curious about girls.

Johnny and I discussed girls sometimes. We both wanted a girlfriend, but we didn't know how to go about it. We weren't bad looking. In fact, we looked kind of similar. We both had blond hair and freckles. Johnny was a little bit chubby, and his older brother had teased him about it growing up and that had made him self-conscious about it. He was worried that he might not be attractive to girls, and so he looked to me to show him the way. Since I was clever and sarcastic, Johnny figured I would know how to talk to girls. He was wrong about that. I was just as shy as he was. But I guess Johnny figured all I needed was a little encouragement.

There was a girl named Sheila in my class. She had big tits. Most of the girls weren't that well developed. Probably for that reason, some of the girls started the rumor that Sheila stuffed her bra. It got around to the boys and we talked about it. We had been looking at her tits for the last few weeks, since the beginning of the school year. We had all been wondering about them, but had never talked about them before.

Johnny said they were fake. "There's no fucking way, man. Last year she was in a training bra. Now it's like a fucking D-cup!"

He was exaggerating, but he had a point.

Some people even made wisecracks about it to her face. "Hey Sheila, how many boxes of tissues you got in there?" Johnny yelled across the class while the teacher was out.

They looked pretty good, the tits that is, pretty realistic. And I couldn't see why she would actually stuff her bra, since all it seemed to do was get her subjected to ridicule. "They've got to be real," I said.

"You must be in love with her or something," Johnny said.

"No, I'm not. You're crazy. But if they were fake they'd be all lumpy and shit."

I didn't see anything wrong with Sheila and I couldn't figure out why the other guys were giving her such a hard time. I had always gotten along well with her. I liked her. She was pretty, with long, dark, shiny black hair and big brown eyes. She was one of the girls I looked at while I was sitting in class and thought maybe I might have a chance with her.

But I wouldn't admit it. I didn't know about her status, whether it was OK to like her. It seemed like maybe not, since everybody was picking on her. And if her tits really were fake, I sure as hell didn't want to have anything to do with her.

"You seem pretty interested in her tits," Johnny said.

It didn't occur to me to mention that he seemed just as interested as I was.

"Why don't you go find out whether or not they're real?" Johnny suggested.

"How am I supposed to do that?"

"Reach down her shirt and pull out one of those tube socks she's got stuffed in there."

"I'm not gonna do that!"

"You must really like her," Johnny said.

"No, I don't."

"You're afraid of her."

"No, I'm not."

"Go on then," he dared me. "Only one way to settle this."

I didn't know how on Earth I was supposed to find out whether or not the tits were real. I thought about sticking Sheila in the tit with a pin to see if she felt any pain. But unless I did it so she wouldn't notice it, she could just fake the pain. And I couldn't figure out how to do it without her noticing.

Sheila was standing out by the water fountains after school. Sheila was the water fountain monitor. Her job was to watch the water fountains at breaks and after school. She got the job because her bus came later than the other buses and they wanted to give her something to do in the meantime. My bus came earlier, but I still had time to fool around for a few minutes.

Johnny knew I was going to do something. He was watching from around the corner as I walked up to her. "Hi, Sheila," I said.

"Hi, Tommy," Sheila said. She smiled.

"How are you doing?"

"Oh, I'm fine."

I just stood there. Maybe I'll just ask her, I thought. But I knew I couldn't get a satisfactory answer that way. "Water fountain monitor, huh?"

"Uh huh," Sheila said, nodding.

She was still smiling. She liked the attention. She was water fountain monitor every day, but I had never stopped there to talk to her or paid any special attention to her before.

I didn't know what to do. I said, "I was just wondering, why do we need a water fountain monitor anyway? Do they think somebody's gonna spray water out on the floor and flood the place or something?"

"I think it's mainly to watch the little kids, so they don't get hurt."

"Yeah, I guess they might cut their lip, or crack their skull open on it," I said.

Sheila laughed. "I guess it's possible."

I couldn't think of what else to say. I stood there for a few moments without saying anything. Then I reached out and grabbed her tit. I squeezed it good. It felt real to me. And Sheila didn't seem to mind.

Mrs. Bream came out of her classroom just in time to witness the whole sordid affair. She shrieked at me, "Tommy! Oh my God! What are you doing!?"

She spooked me, shrieking like that. I took off running down the hall.

"Tommy! You get back here!"

I sure as hell wasn't going back. It was time for the buses to leave, and I ran into the parking lot and got on my bus. I ran all the way to the back and slunk down in a seat, then popped my head up and peaked out the window. I half expected Mrs. Bream to come running out of the school and drag me off the bus. But she didn't come out of the building, and once everybody was on the bus we pulled out of the lot. I popped my head up a little more, craning my neck around to look back toward the parking lot. Mrs. Bream wasn't coming.

Johnny was on the bus, but he hadn't seen me. He was sitting about halfway back on the bus. "Oh, there you are!" he said when he finally saw me. "I thought you must have run off into the woods!" He came back and sat next to me. "What the hell are you hiding from?" he said. I was still sunk down in the seat.

"Oh, nothing," I said, sitting up straight. My heart was still pounding from the excitement.

"I can't believe you did that!" Johnny said, laughing.

"Me neither," I said. I was starting to relax and see the humor in it. "By the way," I added, "Sheila's tits are real."

"Oh, really?" He didn't seem surprised.

"I think so," I said.

"Of course they are, you idiot! I was just fucking with you!"

"Well, what about everybody else?" I asked, a bit puzzled.

"Those stupid bitches are just jealous. They just made that shit up. Nobody else believes it."

Johnny was proud of himself for having tricked me like that. I was supposed to be the clever one, after all. But Johnny had also been curious, just not in the same way. Or maybe in exactly the same way, once I think about it.

"I'm surprised she didn't smack you or kick you in the nuts or something," Johnny said.

I was kind of surprised too.

"I think she liked it," Johnny said.

"I don't know about that, but she didn't seem to really care."

"I think she likes you."

"Ah, you're crazy," I said. But I was beginning to think it might be true. "She's got a pretty good body," I said.

"Hell yeah! She's got a great body."

Still, there was the matter of Mrs. Bream. I thought I was really in for it, and I was scared to go to school the next day. But I went anyway, and it didn't stop me from telling everybody that I had determined that Sheila's tits were real. Johnny had spread the story around anyway before I could say anything.

Mrs. Bream didn't say anything to me. Sheila must have told her she didn't mind. Instead, she gave a talk to the class. She didn't mention any specifics, but just said, "A young girl's body is sacred, and not to be pawed at and treated like a piece of meat." She went into a little more detail, but that was the gist of it. She gave me a nasty look at the end of this message.

"And girls, you must have respect for your body. Your body is God's sacred temple," Mrs. Bream added. She didn't look at Sheila when she said this. She blamed me more than she did Sheila, who was a good student and a bit of a brownnoser. And, once again, she just didn't want to have to deal with a problem as troublesome as this. As I had known since at least the fourth grade, sex was a million times worse than smoking. Because of what happened in the fourth grade, Mrs. Bream had probably been wary of me all along. Now I had confirmed her worst suspicions. I noticed that from this point on Mrs. Bream showed an increased dislike for me. But I was just glad to be getting off so easy.

I was too shy to say anything else to Sheila about it. In fact, I purposely avoided her for the rest of the day. If I saw her looking my way in class I tried not to look back. Mrs. Bream had made me feel sort of guilty, or at least like I'd better steer clear of such offenses in the future. But by the next day the whole thing seemed to have blown over.

6

I wanted to be tougher than anyone else, and if that didn't work out, I wanted to be smarter than anyone else. It wouldn't impress my father, but it seemed like at least I had a better shot at that. Though I didn't like schoolwork, I liked writing stories. I was always able to write better than most people, without much effort. I found that I could be funny and entertaining and have people like me on my own terms, or at least like to hear my stories. Johnny liked my stories too, and he tried sometimes to produce his own, but they didn't quite work out. He didn't have the same knack for it.

The day after Mrs. Bream's lecture several of us read stories to the class. I read a story called "Massacre in the Mortuary." It was about people getting chopped up and killed in lots of funny and entertaining ways. Everybody laughed, or most people anyway. I don't think Mrs. Bream cared for the piece, though she was probably relieved, at least, that it didn't have any sex in it. The assignment was to write a story using all the vocabulary words for that week. I just wrote whatever I felt like, and then at the end I had the main character recite his vocabulary with his dying breath.

Sheila came up to me after class to tell me that she really liked the story. She said she would pay me fifty cents for a copy to save as a collector's item. "I'll keep it, and then it will be valuable if you ever get famous," she said.

I didn't want to give her my only copy, so I had to go home and copy it over again. On Sheila's copy I put drawings in the margins of people getting chopped up with axes, and hanged and burned at the stake, as a bonus.

A couple of days later some girls passed a note across the room to me. These were the same girls who were gossiping about Sheila's tits earlier. That is, the popular girls. They had been doing this a lot lately, sending around notes like this. But never to me, until now. Johnny saw me get the note and he tried to grab it out of my hand, but I wouldn't let him see it. The note said, Check here if you like Sheila, and it had boxes marked yes and no.

I thought about it. Then I checked yes. Like I said, she was pretty, and I was attracted to her. Plus, she liked my stories. Not everybody liked them. Some people didn't think it was funny to joke about people getting shot and stabbed and killed.

I looked across the classroom at Sheila. She wasn't looking in my direction. She was pretending to pay attention to Mrs. Bream, who was writing something on the blackboard. Johnny knew the note was something good. He made one more grab at it while I was distracted, but I held it away from him. I folded the note and handed it back to the girl next to me, and she sent it back the way it had come. I told Johnny what was in the note and told him to leave me alone at the break. I went up to Sheila at the break and we hung out together in the parking lot.

The next day I brought her some candy. Not a box of candy, but just some candy from the store, candy bars and penny candy. I couldn't think of what else to do. We were a little bit old to get excited over candy, but I didn't think she'd want any cigarettes or beer. Sheila acted like she didn't know what to do with the candy, but she tried to act pleased. Maybe she would have rather had the cigarettes and beer. Maybe that would have been a better idea after all.

The thing with Sheila was my first real encounter with the opposite sex. I had had at least one other experience related to sex, however, a significant one. It was in the fourth grade, when I created *The Sexbook*. My family had only recently moved to town and I had just transferred from another school at the beginning of the year, so I was trying to get attention, I guess, trying to be liked. I hadn't made a good impression to start with, showing up for my first day wearing a blazer and carrying a briefcase, and standing when I answered the teacher's questions. This was how they did things at my old school, but here it got me subjected to ridicule, and I had yet to live it down. This was before I met Johnny, who transferred to our school later in the year.

The Sexbook was no big deal as far as the production value goes. It was just made up of sheets of loose-leaf notebook paper, bound with yarn. I did the drawings in different colored magic markers. My drawings weren't exactly stick figures, but they weren't much better. I made the teachers as ugly as possible, with big hooked noses with warts on them, and jagged, busted-up teeth.

And of course they were all naked. I drew the nuns and the women teachers with large pendulous breasts hanging down to their knees, and huge, hairy bushes. The priests and the janitor and the P.E. teacher had thick, long wieners curling round and round.

There was only one actual sex scene in the book. In that picture, an old nun, Principal Pale Butt, lay prone as the drunken janitor, Blotto Blount, stood over her, guzzling from a bottle of hooch. His penis looped around twice before snaking its way down into the nun's vagina.

That, I suppose, was my *tour de force*, my *pièce de résistance*. But the main point was just to have a good laugh at the teachers' expense. And so the rest of the drawings were just satirical treatments of individual teachers. So, for instance, our homeroom teacher, Raunchy Richards, who was fat, was shown chasing a pig with knife and fork in hand. She was nude, of course. But then, so was the pig. And Sister Mary Margaret, a young nun who was short, was wandering around near a urinal while a priest, Father Hoodlum, pissed on her head. "Hey! Watch it!" the tiny nun, whom I renamed Sister Mary Suckoff, cried. "Oh, I didn't see you down there," the priest, who was tall, replied.

In another picture, the eighth-grade teacher, Buttbreath Bream, was taking a shit, and blowing the toilet off the wall. KAPOW! And, oh yeah, one more sex scene, if you want to count it as one. The P.E. teacher, Snotty Snaggletooth Snyder, had his whistle in his mouth, blowing it as usual, only this time it was shaped like a penis. TWEET!

I produced five copies of this masterpiece to start with, cranking them out at home one Sunday when I had nothing better to do. I brought these volumes to school the next day, hidden in a folder. Scarcely able to contain my excitement, I showed the book to some of my friends on the bus, and in the parking lot before school. But the boys I showed it to were barely awake, and so couldn't fully appreciate it. They chuckled a bit as they flipped through the pages, but mostly just yawned. It was starting to look like maybe I had wasted my time.

But as the morning wore on, my friends began to think about what they had seen, and the significance of it gradually hit them.

By the time of the morning milk break there was a big buzz about the book going around the class. I couldn't have been happier.

Still, I wasn't having much luck selling the book. Everybody seemed to like it, but nobody particularly wanted to own a copy. "I've already seen it," one boy told me, leading me to think that I should have demanded cash up front. "What would I do with it?" another boy asked. "I sure as hell don't want to get caught with it."

One exception was my friend Paul Verne, a fat kid with a good sense of humor. He, at least, bought a copy. As he flipped through the pages his belly rolled with laughter. "Wow, man! Look at that shit!" He was especially amused by the Raunchy Richards picture, though I don't know what he found so funny, since he was almost as fat as she was. "Put a bowl of spaghetti and meatballs on that bitch's head!" he said.

It sounded like a good idea. "Why don't you draw it for me."

"No, no," Paul said, nervously. "I don't know how to draw. You draw much better than me."

This was untrue. He just didn't want to get involved. I took out my markers and gave Mrs. Richards a big curly mop of hair like spaghetti, with sauce and meatballs on top. When I was done it didn't look much like spaghetti, but I was able to explain it with a caption. Paul was even more excited by the new version.

When I say that everybody liked the book, I mean all the boys liked it. As far as I knew, no girls had seen it. I was way too unsure of myself to show it to them. But once they heard of the book's existence, the girls all wanted to see it too. A group of the bolder ones, the pretty, popular ones, came up to me on the playground during recess and asked to see the book. I was helpless to refuse. They passed it around amongst themselves, giggling at the pictures, as I stood there shifting nervously from foot to foot. When they had all seen it, the leader herself, the girl who would be the head cheerleader in eighth grade, thanked me as she handed it back. Surprisingly, there was not even a hint of ridicule in her voice.

That made me bold, and gave me an idea. I thought I'd try it out on a girl I liked. Jennifer was a cute little girl with blue eyes and sandy blond hair. She was not one of the popular ones. She was about in the middle. "Hey, check this out," I said. At first Jennifer was eager to see the book. She was pleased that I had singled her out. But I could tell pretty quickly that she didn't like it. She screwed up her face in disgust as she flipped through the pages. Then she crumpled the book and threw it to the ground. Without a word, she turned and walked off across the playground. I was crestfallen. I bent to retrieve the mangled copy.

Paul wasn't as careful with the book as I was. There were some kids, boys as well as girls, who you just couldn't confide in, because you knew damn well they'd run and tell. Paul had no qualms about showing these people the book. I could understand why he did it. The best part was seeing people's reactions when you first showed them the book, and by the end of recess we were running out of new people. Harder to understand was why he showed the book to his mother.

Paul's mother was our school librarian. Mrs. Verne was an intelligent, educated woman. And though she was a Catholic, she didn't take religion too seriously. She was even divorced. Paul had grown up in a more open sexual environment. So I guess that's why he thought it was no big deal to show her the book. Still, there *are* limits. There is still common sense.

Mrs. Verne knew me well. Besides seeing me at school, she and Paul lived in my neighborhood, and I had been to their house. On my way back from recess she stopped me in the hall. I could tell she was pissed off. "I have seen your so-called book," she said. "And if you think that garbage is funny, mister, you are sorely mistaken."

"Well, other people seem to like it. For instance, Paul," I said.

"Paul is an idiot," Mrs. Verne said.

Since she was his mother, I didn't feel like I was in a position to disagree with her.

"You are both idiots," she added. "But up until now I thought you had slightly more sense than Paul."

I still didn't say anything. Mrs. Verne said, "Though I have always stressed that Paul can read whatever he likes, I have made my feelings clear to him in this matter. I'm just glad he didn't give you any money for it."

"He gave me baseball cards," I said.

Mrs. Verne shook her head in disgust. "The drawings are so crude, like the work of a two-year-old. And the most pitiful part of all is that you don't even understand human anatomy."

"What do you mean?" I asked.

"Well," Mrs. Verne explained, irritably, "for instance, you have a baby emerging straight from a woman's stomach. A woman gives birth through her vagina."

She was referring to my drawing of Fuckwad Ferguson, a teacher who had just returned from maternity leave. The baby was popping out of her stomach, and, what's more, reciting its multiplication tables. Mrs. Ferguson was a math teacher.

It was embarrassing to have my own ignorance revealed. "Oh, I knew that. I was just trying to be funny."

Mrs. Verne was not convinced. "Also," she explained, "a man cannot have sexual intercourse with a flaccid penis. The sex act requires that he achieve an erection."

So that's what that was for!

"I'm not going to say anything about this to anyone," Mrs. Verne said. "But you had better be careful who sees that thing. There are people around here who are not quite so reasonable as myself. If I were you I would collect all the copies of that piece of trash and burn them immediately."

Her words brought a huge sense of relief. I decided that what Mrs. Verne was chiefly concerned about was my stupidity. "OK, that's what I'll do," I said, and quickly made my escape.

On my way back to the classroom, I was already thinking about how I could use Mrs. Verne's suggestions to make the book even better. No matter what she said, I still liked the long, curling wieners. Though they may not have been anatomically correct, they sure were funny.

In the disorder before the period began, a girl named Jo Anne Haggerty came up to me. "I hear you've written a book," she said, maybe not quite getting the idea. "I'd really like to read it." Jo Anne was a tall, skinny, gawky girl. She was the studious type, and wore cat's-eye glasses. I hadn't seen her out on the playground at recess that day, but knowing Jo Anne, she had probably hidden somewhere in order to study.

After what had happened with Jennifer, I had made up my mind not to show the book to any more girls. But that really only went for girls I liked. I took a copy out of my folder and handed it to Jo Anne, figuring her reaction would be similar to Jennifer's, but not really caring one way or another.

But Jo Anne actually liked the book. The page she liked best had a picture of Sister Theresa, a stern old nun, getting her blackboard poker rammed up her ass by an unidentified student. Jo Anne let out a crazy cackle when she saw that one. She had a very unattractive laugh.

Still, I was flattered. Jo Anne wasn't much to look at, but she at least had a brain. I began to look at her in a more favorable light. Jo Anne even bought a copy of the book, though she wouldn't pay the cover price, which was a dollar. We settled on fifty cents.

If I hadn't been preoccupied in talking to Jo Anne, maybe I would have noticed that something strange was going on. Neither Paul nor our teacher, Mrs. Richards, had returned to the classroom after the break. Without a teacher present, the place was a nut house. Everyone was yelling and running around the room. But that changed quickly, and silence descended, as Mrs. Richards, and Sister Rose, Principal Pale Butt herself, came into the room. Sister Rose said, "Come with me, Mr. Donaldson." She took me by the arm and led me out of the classroom.

I thought I would be going to the principal's office, since that's where they usually take you when you're in trouble in the fourth grade. So I was surprised, and alarmed, when Sister Rose led me to the janitor's closet just outside the boy's bathroom. She opened the closet door, and told me to get inside. Then she closed the door and locked it after me, trapping me inside.

The little closet stank of ammonia and floor wax. There was only a sliver of light coming in from the crack under the door. I groped around under the sink and found a bucket and overturned it, and had a seat with my back to the wall.

At first I was relieved to be sitting in the closet, rather than having to explain myself to the old nun. But the longer I sat there the more frightened and worried I became. It was hot and uncomfortable. The stench of chemicals permeated the air. I was unable to understand what was going on. That was the scariest part. I began sweating from the sticky heat, making the waiting even more of a torment. I felt embarrassed and ashamed, and I prayed they wouldn't tell my parents. I got up and tried the handle of the door, but it wouldn't budge.

I knew it must have been Paul and his mother who had told on me, and I was angry with them. It was only much later that I came to understand the position they must've been in.

Several times I heard footsteps in the hall. I would tense up as they got closer, thinking someone was coming to get me, but then they would go by and die away down the hall.

One time I heard Mrs. Verne's voice close by. "Where is he? What have you done with him?"

I didn't hear the response, but then Mrs. Verne said, "You can't keep him in there!"

Then I heard our teacher, Mrs. Richards' voice say, "Go back to your library, Mrs. Verne."

I got up and tried the closet door again. Still locked. It had given me a ray of hope to hear Mrs. Verne's voice, but now I began to see that there was nothing she could do. I must have been locked in the closet for an hour or more.

Finally, I heard people approaching. I heard the bathroom door open, and there was the sound of footsteps as several people passed by my closet and entered the bathroom. A key turned in the lock and the closet door opened, the light blinding me momentarily. The principal motioned for me to get up and go into the bathroom. The bathroom was large, the ceiling and walls painted a pale green. The floor, and the stalls to my right, were gray marble. To my left was a row of sinks. Along the back wall, where a large window let in the light, was a row of urinals. I fixed my sights on the back wall. That's where the teachers had gathered, though at first I couldn't make them out individually because of the glare of the light from the window at their backs.

My eyes adjusted quickly. There were six or seven teachers assembled, all of them parties I had wronged. Mrs. Richards was there, looking like she wanted to kill me, and Mrs. Bream, Sister Mary Margaret, Mr. Snyder, and the rest. Certain teachers, such as Mrs. Ferguson, had apparently decided not to attend. Mr. Blount wasn't there either, maybe because he was only the janitor, or maybe because the principal would have been too embarrassed to show him my rendering of their illicit union.

It's too bad about Mr. Blount, that she didn't show him the drawing, I mean, because he would have got a kick out of it.

I breathed a sigh of relief when I saw that Mrs. Verne wasn't there. Maybe her presence would have lessened the severity of my punishment, but it would have just been too embarrassing to have her there.

I knew I was in for it. I was trembling in fear. But as I stood looking at the teachers I couldn't help thinking of my drawings. I couldn't help connecting each of them to the face it represented. And I wanted to burst out laughing. Raunchy Richards, with her spaghetti hairdo. Buttbreath Bream, with her deadly ass-attack. In particular, I couldn't stop looking at Mr. Snyder, the gym teacher, who stood there seething, twisting a rolled-up copy of *The Sexbook* in his hands. Snotty Snaggletooth Snyder. He seemed the angriest of them all, maybe because I had insulted not only him, but also his precious whistle. TWEET!

None of the teachers said anything. Sister Rose, the principal, stood beside me, holding a wooden paddle. "Do you know what you're being punished for?" she asked.

I nodded that I understood.

The old nun told me to drop my pants, and to bend over and place my hands on one of the sinks. "Underwear too," she said. And then she laid into my ass with her paddle.

It was a big paddle and it hurt like hell. But I was no sissy. I knew what they wanted. They wanted me to cry, and I wasn't going to give them the satisfaction. The nun gave me about twenty licks, and I bore up under it. Tensing myself for the next blow, I was surprised when she stopped suddenly. "I can't go on," she said, staggering back. I turned around and looked at her. She was supporting herself against one of the stalls, her face wringing wet with sweat. She never should have tried it. She was old and weak.

For a while there was only silence. No one made any suggestions. But I knew that my punishment wasn't over. I stood there in the same position, pants down and hands on the sink, feeling like an idiot, for what was probably only a matter of moments, but which seemed like an eternity.

Finally, Mr. Snyder said, "I'll take over for you sister."

"No, Mr. Snyder," the principal said firmly. But this had given her an idea. Addressing Sister Mary Margaret, she said, "Sister, please go over to the rectory and tell Father Hood that we need him here at once."

My heart sank. As much as I hated Mr. Snyder, I would much rather have received the whipping from him. But apparently the principal felt that he didn't have the moral authority to do it. It was only then that the real gravity of my offense began to dawn on me. This was a first, as far as I knew, calling in the priest to administer school discipline. As a rule Father Hood just ran the church, and didn't get involved in the everyday affairs of the school.

They let me pull up my pants while we waited, and I was grateful for that. I prayed that Father Hood would be out visiting the sick that day.

This time the wait went by all too fast. After a few minutes Father Hood came into the bathroom. He did not seem pleased. He took off his black jacket and hung it over one of the toilet stalls, then he rolled up the sleeves of his black shirt.

Sister Mary Margaret had followed the priest into the bathroom. Seeing the two of them enter together, I couldn't help but think of my drawing, and it was all I could do to keep from cracking up laughing. Sister Mary Suckoff. The name kept going through my mind. With Father Hoodlum here, she'd better not stand too close to that urinal! I felt a smirk forming on my lips. Luckily, no one seemed to have noticed. I knew it was going to be bad enough as it was.

As I mentioned before, Father Hood was a tall man. He was broad shouldered and sturdy besides, like one of those priests from the old movies who boxes on the side. He told me to drop my pants and bend over the sink, as I had done before. This time I was glancing back, terrified, waiting for the blow to descend. "Don't look at me," the priest said. The blows of the priest were ten times as hard as those of the nun. I did my best to hold back the tears, but it was no use. Soon they were streaming from my eyes and I was screaming for him to stop. That was all that was needed, though he gave me a couple more licks for good measure, maybe to pay me back for inconveniencing him.

It was a severe beating, and my ass was bruised and sore. The teachers filed out of the bathroom, and gave me a bit of privacy to pull up my pants and wash the tears from my face. As it turned out, they didn't tell my parents after all. And they knew I wouldn't tell either. We all understood the value of secrecy. I pushed the episode to the back of my mind and struggled not to let it bother me. Though I knew Paul had most likely told on me, I never confronted him. But our friendship was at an end. Somehow I never felt comfortable around him again. And like I said, Johnny transferred to our school later that year anyway, and I had a new friend.

8

"Don't be such a dumbass," Johnny said. It had been his idea about the beer and the cigarettes.

"You're crazy," I said. "She doesn't even smoke."

"How do you know? You don't even know her."

He was right about that. But I had a certain idea of Sheila in my mind. I didn't want her to be like we were. I wanted her to be innocent and virginal. Well, I'm pretty sure she was virginal at least. Like plenty of other Catholic school boys, I had a romanticized notion of girls. In fact, though I scoffed at her, my view was probably not that far from Mrs. Bream's. Johnny, who had a little sister, may have had a more realistic view of girls, but I wasn't ready to accept it.

I rode my bike to Sheila's house that Saturday. Johnny wanted to go, but I thought this was something I should do alone. It was the middle of October but it was still warm out and I just wore a light jacket. After peddling a ways I took the jacket off and tied it around my waist because I was sweating. It was an old tan jacket with a ripped lining.

Sheila lived a long way from me. The subdivisions where we lived were on the opposite edges of the range of the grade school. It was the farthest I'd ever ridden my bike before. I rode out along the highway in the right lane with the cars streaking by me on the outside of their lane so they wouldn't hit me. They didn't like it and sometimes one of them would honk his horn at me or yell at me to get out of the road.

I rode past the school and the mall, and then another mall. I had ridden to the first mall before, but then after that I still had a ways to go. I got tired and had to stop and rest a couple of times. One time when I stopped I bought a candy bar and ate it for energy. I drank a coke too. I thought about what Johnny had said, and I thought about buying some cigarettes. My views about girls were wishful thinking, but they were hard to give up. So instead I bought some more candy to share with Sheila. They probably wouldn't have sold me any cigarettes anyway.

Sheila lived all the way at the back of her subdivision. I had only been there one other time. It was a nice subdivision, with bigger houses than the subdivision I lived in. It was shaded by trees. And her house was bigger than the one I lived in. I decided that my jacket didn't look so good, so I left it draped over my bike.

I rang the doorbell. Sheila answered and I came in and said hi to her mother. Her mother was in the kitchen doing something, and she acted kind of suspicious. She was polite, but I got the idea that she wasn't exactly thrilled to see me. I had a reputation for being a bad kid.

Sheila's little sister was there too. She was sitting in the family room watching TV. The family room opened into the kitchen where we were standing. "That's Julie," Sheila said. Julie was prettier than Sheila, but still too young. She hadn't developed yet. She was really pretty though. Sheila was maybe mid-level popular, but based on her looks, Julie had to be at about the top of the ladder in her grade.

"We're going down in the basement," Sheila told her mother. We had to walk through the family room to get to the basement.

"I'm going down there too," Julie said, getting up to follow us.

"No, Julie. You're not coming," Sheila said.

Sheila led me downstairs to the basement. It was a finished basement, with a couch and some chairs. There was a stereo but no TV. I sat down on the couch. Sheila put on some music and sat beside me on the couch.

Julie came down. She snuck down the stairs, trying not to make a sound, and peeked around the corner of the wall. I saw her first, and didn't say anything, but when Sheila saw her, she immediately yelled, "Get out of here, Julie!" Julie laughed and ran back up the stairs.

We were just getting comfortable again. Then, after a few minutes, the sister snuck back down again. We heard the stairs creak, and could tell she was standing at the bottom of the stairs, out of sight. "We know you're there, Julie! We can hear you!" Sheila called out.

Her cover blown, Julie came out in the open. She plopped down in a chair next to the couch. "I know you from school," she said.

"Oh yeah? I've seen you around too." I knew she was Sheila's sister, that was about it.

"You're the one who's always picking on kids," Julie said.

That embarrassed me. Even though Sheila knew all about that side of me, I kind of wanted to hide it from her, as crazy as that sounds. "Uh, well, not always. Only when they deserve it," I said.

"Julie, quit bothering my guest," Sheila said, annoyed.

"It's OK, she's not bothering me," I said. Really she was, but I wasn't going to let on.

"You want a coke or something?" Sheila asked.

"Yeah, that sounds good."

"Come help me get the cokes, Julie," Sheila said, yanking Julie out of the chair and dragging her little sister along with her up the stairs. After a while Sheila came back downstairs with cokes and potato chips and pretzels. Julie stayed upstairs.

We drank our cokes and ate a few potato chips. I was sitting next to Sheila on the couch. We were holding hands. Sheila was cheerful and seemed glad that I had come by. But I couldn't get a chance to kiss her. While I was working up the nerve, Julie snuck into the laundry room and then crawled along the floor and got behind the couch. Just as I leaned in toward Sheila to kiss her, Julie popped up from behind the couch and stuck her head between us, giggling.

I thought it was kind of funny, and anyway it broke up the tension of the moment. I was nervous about trying to make out with Sheila. Sheila laughed a little, but I could tell she was pissed off.

Julie came around the couch and plopped down in the chair again. "I remember when I was in third grade and you were the milk monitor in the cafeteria," she said.

"Really?" I just vaguely remembered. It must have been two or three years earlier.

"You were just supposed to make sure that everybody poured their milk in the bucket to give to the farmer for the pigs," Julie said. "But instead you were making all the little kids drink all of theirs."

"So what? Helps them grow up big and strong."

"So, my friend Kristen had dumped her beans in her milk carton. And she told you that. And you *still* made her drink it!"

I laughed at that. I had a real good laugh. "And she actually drank the beans?" I asked.

"Yes. Because you told her to."

I laughed some more. It made me uneasy to have her pointing out my bad behavior. But I felt something else too. Pride, maybe. Because Julie had cut right to the heart of the matter. It was thrilling to me that I had such power over people.

"I don't even remember that," I said. "But it sounds like something I would do." It had an absurd artistry about it that was kind of my trademark, though I don't think everybody got that.

"Why are you so mean to people?"

"I'm not mean to everybody. Your friend Kristen was an idiot for drinking the beans. She should have just told me to go to hell."

Sheila was smiling all through this, but I could tell she thought it was a stupid story. I could also tell that there was a rivalry between her and Julie, and so maybe she thought that her sister was trying to horn in her date. She said, "Alright Julie, you've asked your question. Now go back upstairs."

Julie made no move to get up.

I had decided that I didn't mind Julie's attention that much after all, but Sheila was fed up with her sister's bullshit. And anyway, after the one good story, Julie just reverted back to little girl behavior, teasing us about being lovebirds, that sort of thing. Sitting in a tree and kissing. It got old pretty fast.

There was no way to get rid of the sister. She kept bothering us and simply wouldn't go away. I couldn't kiss Sheila, much less feel her up. We couldn't get anything going on.

Soon enough, it was time for me to go. We went out on the porch to say goodbye. I put my hands on Sheila's waist and tried one last time to kiss her, but her sister threw open the curtains and banged on the window. She still wouldn't leave us alone. I got on my bike and rode back down the highway past the two malls and the school.

The next day, Sunday, we had a football game and I told Johnny all about my date with Sheila as we stood over on the sidelines. I told him that we had kissed a little bit but didn't have a chance to do anything else because of the sister.

"Why didn't you throw her ass out?"

"I tried."

"Next time, try harder."

But all in all I thought it had gone pretty well. I even told Chip about it, and we even gave him a day off from the usual abuse. Johnny said he thought it sounded like it had gone well too, and we were both pretty excited about it. Johnny was confident that I would get another chance with Sheila later on.

But he was wrong. Monday morning Sheila sent another note. This time she was dumping me. Once again it wasn't from her personally. It was from one of the girls who had set us up in the first place. It just said, Sheila said she doesn't like you anymore.

I sat there reading it over and over, not daring to look across the room at Sheila. I couldn't figure out what I'd done wrong. It was her idea in the first place, I thought. Maybe her mother and her sister were telling her what a bad kid I was. Maybe the popular girls who set the whole thing up were teasing her. Those were the kinds of thoughts that were going through my head. I knew there was a lot about me to rub people the wrong way, but I didn't consider that it might have been because I was acting wishy-washy, not living up to my reputation as a bad kid. As Johnny had been trying to suggest, that was probably what had attracted her to me in the first place.

But Johnny didn't say anything about that now. He was wondering what the note was, and this time I showed it to him. "That fucking bitch," he said. "You can't let her get away with that shit."

I took the note back from Johnny and read it again, and then finally I looked at Sheila. She was ignoring me and not giving any clues. At first I had been dejected, but now I grew angry. It was a real blow to my pride. I wadded up the note in a tight ball and threw it across the room. It hit Sheila in the back of the head.

"Good shot!" Johnny said.

It was a damn good shot. I had had lots of practice. Sheila didn't turn around and didn't pick up the note, but one of the girls sitting near her snatched it up off the floor.

The rest of the day, Sheila tried to avoid me. She knew I was mad and she didn't want to talk to me. Johnny kept telling me I couldn't let her get away with it. I was depressed and wanted to let the matter drop, but he said if I didn't say something to her he would. Finally at the end of the day we saw her out by the water fountain. Johnny was right there beside me and he nudged me over toward her, saying, "Ask her what her fucking problem is?" I went up to her and said, "What's your problem, bitch?"

"I don't have a problem," Sheila said.

"Why'd you break up with me?"

"I don't know. I just don't like you anymore."

"Fuck you, bitch. That's no reason. I don't like you either. You started this whole thing, let me remind you."

She started to walk away from me but I got in her way. I put my arm against the wall and trapped her up against the water fountain. "I'm not through talking to you, bitch!"

I scared her. She started to cry.

"Boo hoo hoo. Go ahead and cry. What do I care, you fucking bitch." I stepped out of her way and let her walk away down the hall.

"You old milk cow! Look at those big ol' milkers! You slut! You whore! You stupid cow!" I yelled.

Johnny got a kick out of that. "Mooooooooo!" he yelled after her down the hall.

Part Two

I'm sure I hurt Sheila's feelings, and I felt sorry about that, but hell, she hurt mine too. She hurt me more than I wanted to let on. And though I wasn't one to regret what I'd done, the incident turned me off to girls for a while. But it was at about this time that I discovered liquor too, and that took my mind off girls.

The Saturday after Sheila dumped me, we were sitting down in Johnny's basement. Johnny had moved his bedroom down into the unfinished basement so he wouldn't have to live in the same room as his big brother. The corner of the basement that served as his bedroom was separated from the rest of the basement by some curtains he had tacked up. We were playing records on Johnny's stereo, Grand Funk and Black Oak Arkansas. Johnny's stereo, which was made of cheap, red plastic, sat on a big wooden spool that was supposed to hold electrical wire. We were trying to figure out what to do that day. We couldn't think of anything, and Johnny only owned about three albums.

Then I remembered that my Aunt Sally and Uncle Dave were having a party for my relatives that day. It wasn't anything I would have usually gone to, and it didn't seem like a very good idea, but I felt like I might as well mention it.

"They got any liquor there?" Johnny asked, suddenly becoming excited.

"Yeah, sure." I had tasted liquor before, but I had never really been drunk.

"Come on, then. What are we waiting for? Let's go over to your aunt's house and snag some liquor."

I had a large extended family, so the place was filled up with my aunts and uncles and cousins. All my uncles were already getting drunk, and most of my aunts were drinking too, so everybody was in a good mood. They were sitting and standing around the kitchen table eating and drinking and smoking. The air was filled with cigarette smoke.

The layout of the house made it difficult to steal liquor. The family room was sunken slightly below the level of the kitchen. There was a counter separating the two rooms, and that's where they kept the liquor. There were several quart bottles and fifths sitting out on the counter. Besides the people around the kitchen table, others were sitting on the couches and chairs in the family room and watching a football game on TV. Anybody in either room could see you if you went to pour a drink.

We hung around in the kitchen waiting for our chance. Everybody knew what we were up to and they were watching us to make sure we didn't drink. Especially my parents. I hadn't shown any tendency to drink before, but they weren't taking any chances. They knew I was usually up to no good. There were a few of my uncles who thought it was funny and they would have fixed me a drink, but they were afraid of getting in trouble with my parents.

It looked like I would have to be the one to actually steal the liquor, since it was my aunt's house. I leaned up against the counter and tried to edge closer to the stockpile of bottles without being too obvious. I had a big glass of coke in my hand and I tried to act like I was just drinking that and carrying on a conversation with Johnny. My mother was sitting at the table. She was watching us, but she was getting a little bit drunk herself. Plus, she was caught up in a conversation. She was telling one of her younger sisters that she was not living her life properly. The sister, that is, my Aunt Jane. "Well, you'd think if somebody had been involved with a man like that once then they'd learn," she said, sarcastically. My mother pretty much always spoke her mind, and in fact she was responsible for getting me out of a lot of the jams I got myself into with my crazy behavior. People just didn't want to mess with her.

Actually, my mother didn't care all that much if we drank anyway. The one we really had to look out for was my father. He never drank and he didn't approve of drinking, especially when it was his son doing it. Unlike most of the other adults there, he was sober and alert. He was standing near the counter, but at one point he turned and walked down the two or three steps into the family room. As soon as his back was turned I lunged for the bourbon. I picked up the bottle and tried to dump some into my coke.

"What are you doing there? You're too young to drink," my Uncle Dave said. He was the one who lived there, so I guess it was his job to watch the liquor. "Just drink your coke. Go get yourself a ham sandwich," he said.

I acted like I didn't know what he was talking about and I was just reading the label on the bottle. "Hmm, bottled in bond. One-hundred proof." I sat the bottle down, which seemed to satisfy Uncle Dave. Then the moment he turned his back I snatched the bottle back up and sloshed a bunch of liquor into my glass.

"I'll take that," my dad said. He was coming back up the steps from the family room. There was no point in protesting. I gave the drink to him. "You're getting a little bit too big for your britches, mister," my dad said. "And I don't want to see you with any alcohol either, Johnny. I don't intend to have to explain to your parents why you're coming home from this party falling-down drunk."

"Ah, they don't care. They let me drink all the time," Johnny said.

"I doubt that," my dad said.

"It's true," I said. "I was fixing that drink for him. He can drink anytime he wants."

"Well then, I suggest he go on home and start drinking," my dad said. While we watched, my dad went over to the sink and dumped the drink.

We hung around near the counter and waited for another chance to get at the liquor, but my dad wasn't letting us get too close. While we were waiting, we at least managed to steal a pack of Kools with four or five cigarettes left in it. That wasn't as good as liquor, but it was something. Once we had the Kools we went out to the side of the house to smoke them. People were playing croquet and horseshoes in the back yard, and in the front yard you never could tell who might pull up.

The Kools had seemed like a good find, but they were too strong. They didn't make us cough too much but they kind of choked us or gagged us. We were used to Salems or Belairs, which are milder. Still, we weren't going to waste them. We only smoked once in a while, so the Kools made us kind of high.

After we finished our cigarettes we went around to the back yard and hung around with some of my cousins, who were mostly younger than us and not too interesting. We played a game of croquet. Johnny had some firecrackers that his brother had brought back from Tennessee, and we lit some off in the back yard, scaring the shit out of one of my cousins just as he was getting ready to shoot.

When we got tired of that, or maybe when we ran out of firecrackers, we went back into the house. We wanted to see if they had stored any liquor down in the basement. It was a long shot. There was an old refrigerator down there, but all it had in it were soft drinks. We were sick of the soft drinks. There was a chest freezer, but it was stocked with deer steaks, wrapped in brown paper. Some of the little kids had followed us down, so we got the little boys to wrestle each other on the rug.

After a while, my dad came down the stairs. "What are you boys doing?"

"We're teaching these kids to wrestle," I said.

"Ha! I'll bet!" he said, like we couldn't possibly do anything like that. "Well, just so you're not drinking," he said. After he had determined that there was no liquor in the basement, he went back upstairs.

Anything I did was foolishness, in the eyes of my father. Maybe I had kind of half-hoped my dad would approve of the wrestling, or at least be interested, since, after all, it was a sport. But he never took anything I did seriously. Maybe if I'd been a good football player it would have been a different story. But after I showed him that I wasn't going to be one, I think he kind of gave up on me.

Johnny had a similar problem. His dad was an ex-army colonel who worked for a defense contractor. Maybe that's why we thought we had to be so tough. Who knows which of our fathers was the hardest to live up to. Johnny had an older brother too, one who was big and strong, and who he looked up to even though he didn't get along with him. His brother was always beating him up over something or other, so maybe Johnny had it harder than me. My brothers were younger than me, so I was the one beating them up.

We held a whole wrestling tournament. One of the boys was much stronger and tougher than the others, so we liked him best. We showed him how to do headlocks and full nelsons and scissor holds. Then one of the smaller kids got his head slammed on the floor and ran upstairs crying. My Uncle Dave came downstairs and told us not to do it anymore, not to hold wrestling matches. "Why are you teaching these kids to do that? Don't you know any better than that?" he said. "Your father could beat me up, but do you think that makes him a better man?"

"Uh, no," I said, though I wasn't at all convinced.

After that it wasn't much fun hanging around in the basement, so we went back upstairs and hung out in the dining room. The dining room was where they had all the food laid out. We picked at some of the food. The dining room was connected to the kitchen by a doorway. We stood in the dining room looking through the doorway to the forbidden stockpile. We figured if we weren't in the kitchen they might let down their guard and maybe one of us could dart in real quick and grab a bottle.

My Uncle Ron came in and got a paper plate and started putting food on it. He got a couple of ham sandwiches, and some baked beans and coleslaw and a deviled egg. He took a forkful of beans and put it in his mouth. Then he made a disgusted face and spat the beans out into a napkin. "Pitiful," he said, as both me and Johnny laughed. He wadded up the napkin and tossed it onto the table.

It was worth a shot. "Hey Uncle Ron," I said. "Why don't you do us a favor and make us a couple of drinks."

He thought about it, and said, "You can't have a drink, but I'll get you a beer if you won't tell your mother about it."

"Aw, come on, Uncle Ron," Johnny said.

"I don't know how I got to be related to you, boy. But anyway you can't have any hard liquor. You boys don't have any business drinking that stuff. Count yourself lucky I'm getting you a beer. I'm only doing it because it's a party, and I guess everybody's gotta start sometime," Uncle Ron said. "Don't you tell Edith about this."

Edith was my mother, his sister-in-law.

"OK, two beers," I said.

"I'll get you one beer to share."

"One? Come on, man!" Johnny said.

Uncle Ron left his plate on the table and went into the kitchen. He brought us back two beers, and said, "Take these outside and drink them, and if your mother catches you, don't mention me."

We laughed because we had no intention of getting caught. We kept joking around with him. "What should we tell her?" I asked.

"Tell her you bought it off some black guy on a street corner downtown."

"OK," we said, chuckling.

"That always worked for me," Uncle Ron said.

We went out on the side of the house and chugged our beers. At least it was something to do for a few minutes, and it gave me a little bit of a buzz. But you can't get much of a buzz off one beer even if you aren't used to drinking.

All my relatives got pretty drunk by late in the afternoon. So by then they weren't paying attention to the liquor anymore. Except to keep drinking it, that is. When my dad was out of the room I filled up a coke can with bourbon and we stashed it outside in the bushes on the side of the house.

11

The party was winding down and a lot of the people were leaving. Me and Johnny were ready to get away so we could drink the liquor we had stolen. We took along a couple of cokes to mix our drinks with. I got my dad's old jacket out of the trunk of his car to hide the coke and liquor in.

We were in the neighborhood of our school and our church. Since we were so close to church my dad suggested that we go to mass that evening instead of waiting until the morning. This was good because it gave us a reason to stay out, and my parents wouldn't suspect us of drinking if we were going to church.

We cut through the woods on the edge of the subdivision. It was the middle of October, and the leaves were getting ready to turn. The creek was high. We walked on a path that ran beside the creek. The open can of bourbon in my pocket was spilling out onto my dad's jacket. I knew he wasn't going to appreciate that.

There was a big tree on the creek bank with a root that hung out over the creek and curved around back into the bank. We sat down on the root and dangled our feet out over the flooded creek and watched the water rush by. We opened a can of coke and took a few sips, then we poured some of the liquor in and took turns drinking it. It had a real bite, but I liked the taste. It was good mixed with the coke. I started feeling the liquor almost immediately. It felt good. I got a buzz, and with it came a feeling of happiness and well being. I felt strong and confident. I felt like nothing in the world could touch me.

We were already late for church. "Fuck church," Johnny said. "Let's just stay out here and drink the rest of this liquor."

But I didn't mind the idea. Church didn't sound that bad in the state of mind I was in, a wide open state. What the hell, I thought, why not? "My parents will ask me about the mass," I said. My dad made me go to church every week, and I would have felt guilty for not going. And besides that, maybe I thought it would be different that night. I would have liked to have had some kind of meaning in my life, like football.

"What the hell can they ask about? It's just a damn mass," Johnny said. His parents didn't care whether he went to church or not.

"They'll ask who the priest was."

"So what? Tell them it was somebody you didn't know. Tell them it was some old guy you'd never seen before."

"They know I know who the priests are. And anyway they'll ask what the sermon was about."

"Just make something up. Tell them it was about love and brotherhood."

"Come on man. Let's just stop in there for a minute. Then we can leave."

Johnny was in a good mood too, so he didn't really care whether or not we went to church. We were just bumming around and didn't have anything else to do.

We didn't drink all the liquor, just about half of it. We stashed the rest in the weeds near the tree by the creek, the coke can with the liquor in it and the other full can of coke.

The liquor really started kicking in while we were walking the rest of the way to church. It was the first time I had ever really been drunk. I felt giddy and excited. The thing with Sheila meant nothing anymore. To hell with her, I thought. I felt energetic and strong. It was cool and breezy in the woods. I had a sense of power. I felt immortal, and I wanted the moment to last forever. The woods were beautiful, green and alive. We walked down beside the creek and then climbed up an embankment onto a road that crossed the creek.

We were late to church. The church was about half-full, and the mass had already started. It was a guitar mass. The priest was young and had long brown hair and a beard, and he wore sandals with his priest gown. He was up near the altar fooling around while a whacked-out guy with horn-rimmed glasses and a hairpiece played a song on the guitar. Kumbaya.

We went up in the choir loft at the back of the church. The stairway was roped off but we ducked under the rope. They never had a choir, but sometimes an old lady played the organ. But she didn't play it at the same mass where somebody was playing the guitar, so nobody was up there. We didn't like to sit in the main part of the church because then we would have to sit still and listen to the mass. Up in the choir loft nobody could hear you unless you were real loud.

It was an old junked-up choir loft, used for storage. There were stacks of old missals in the pews, and tangles of music stands and broken-down fans in the corners. The rest of the church had been renovated but they hadn't got around to the choir loft yet. We briefly fooled around with the organ. There wasn't really that much to do up there, but it helped that we were drunk. We didn't pay any attention to the mass, but after a while we sat down facing the front of the church. We sat in the front row and looked down over the rail. We would have liked to spit on some of the people down below us in the main part of the church. There were a lot of people there who made us sick.

The priest periodically looked up at us. He was the only one who could see us. He was kind of a hippie, and not a real disciplinarian, and probably he figured it was better for us to come to church and goof around than to go somewhere else and get in trouble.

While we were sitting there Johnny lit a firecracker wick to fool me into thinking it was a regular firecracker. He lit it right up on top of the ledge that overlooked the main part of the church. It scared the shit out of me. I thought it was going to explode, and I bolted for the stairs. Instead it just fizzled out. Johnny thought it was hilarious.

We had about had enough of the place. We knew to get out of there early so we wouldn't run into anybody's parents or any teachers on the way out. By that time I had started coming down from the liquor, and I wanted to drink more to pick me back up.

We went back to the woods and got our liquor, then walked a few blocks to the golf course in the middle of the subdivision. We got onto the golf course by cutting through somebody's back yard, and we walked straight out onto the fairway. Some of the people who had back yards that backed up to the fairway were grilling out and having cocktails. We went into one of the little shacks that had been set up along the fairway and sat down there to mix our drink. The sun was going down behind the trees.

It started drizzling.

This time I got totally trashed. So did Johnny. We ran around whooping in the rain. We were laughing and joking around in the drizzling rain. It just kept raining. By this time, nobody else was outside. The people living nearby had all gone indoors. The rain was cool and fresh. It ran down over my hair and into my eyes and mouth.

A big guy came walking out onto the fairway the same way we had come. He came towards us down the fairway. We had seen him around before, and we had noticed him in church. He looked older than us, too old to be in grade school. He looked like he was in high school at least. But he had long hair and he looked like a cool guy. We tried to settle down and act cool, and not run around whooping it up like little kids anymore. We went back in the shelter and tried to act like we knew how to hold our liquor.

"Hey man, how's it going," I said when he got up to us.

The guy's name was Harold. He had his own pack of cigarettes. Marlboro. He gave us each one. We lit up and smoked them. They beat the Kools.

"You want some of this drink?" Johnny asked.

Harold drank some of our bourbon and coke. "I had some earlier today too. I'm still pretty fucking wasted," he said.

We passed the can around and each had a drink.

"You go to that school, don't you?" Harold asked.

"Yeah," I said.

"Unfortunately," Johnny said.

"It doesn't seem that bad."

"It is," I said.

"I hope it's better than the place I'm coming from."

"So you're gonna be going to our school?" I asked.

"Looks that way."

"That's cool," I said. "So you're a Catholic?"

"Hell, no. I'm just going because I got thrown out of public school."

We were impressed. "What did you get thrown out for?" I asked.

Harold sighed and shook his head disgustedly. "I don't know. Numerous things. It was a bunch of bullshit. Those motherfuckers."

"What were you doing going to church if you're not Catholic?" Johnny asked. Johnny was Catholic and he didn't even go that much himself.

"I just went to see what it was like."

"How did you like it?" I asked.

"It was OK. I liked the guitar playing. The rest I didn't get."

It was getting dark. The rain had let up. We finished off the drink, then went out and ran around on the golf course. I was wasted. I ran up the hill onto a green and grabbed the flag and bent it and then let it go. It sprung back up.

Harold came up onto the green. "These greens are bullshit," he said. "My dad used to be a greens keeper." He grabbed the flag, pulled it out of the ground, and started using it to carve up the green. He dug up clods of dirt with the base end of the flag and wrote FUCK YOU in big letters on the green. "Look how weak this shit is!"

Me and Johnny thought that was great. We wanted to try it too. We took turns writing. We wrote SUCK ME on the green. After FUCK YOU that was the best we could think of. We were drunk as shit.

The greens keeper came riding down the road on his golf cart and turned onto the fairway. He was yelling and pointing at us. We couldn't hear what he was yelling, but we could pretty much guess. He was a skinny old man in a baseball cap. He was shaking his fist at us as he drove.

"Oh shit!" me and Johnny both said. I dropped the flag. We were ready to take off running.

When the man got closer he stopped yelling and concentrated on his driving.

"Come on Harold! Let's get out of here!" I said.

"He can't catch us," Harold said calmly. Harold picked up the flag. When the man got close enough he threw it like a spear. It hit the golf cart and the man.

Then we took off running. We ran through a back yard and hopped a fence, then ran up the driveway. It was better to split up. When we hit the street Harold ran a different way than we did.

The next morning I felt like shit, but not bad enough not to want to do it again. At least I had got church out of the way, so I had time to lie in bed and recover. After that me and Johnny started getting drunk whenever we could get our hands on any liquor.

That was how we met Harold. He was older and stronger and more experienced than we were, and we looked up to him. He was going to have a big influence over us. Not for the good, of course.

Harold got thrown out of public school because they didn't feel like fooling with him anymore. He had been held back two or three times. He missed a lot of school, and when he did come he just caused trouble. So once he turned sixteen they told him to get lost the same day. Harold was still in eighth grade, the same as us, though he was in a different class. He was kind of dense, but we still thought he was a cool guy. He was already driving in grade school, which me and Johnny both thought was hilarious. On his first day, the Monday after we met him, we saw him drive up to the school. We were watching from the classroom window, and were able to tell everybody that we already knew him. Nobody could believe he was a student. He parked his old station wagon in the lot where the teachers parked.

Harold was always cutting his classes, either not going at all or just walking out in the middle of them. He established this pattern in his very first week, and amazingly enough he never seemed to get in trouble for it. Apparently they had already given up on him in advance, and were doing him the favor of letting him slide until he could graduate and go to high school. They knew they wouldn't have to put up with him for too much longer.

We always saw Harold at our lunch period, though he was supposed to be in class. He liked to eat, so he took more than one lunch period. He told everybody to bring him whatever they didn't want. He said he would eat anything.

One day, me and Johnny decided to test him. We took a ham sandwich away from Chip and opened the sandwich up and spat some hockers inside. The sandwich had lettuce and tomato and mayonnaise and hockers. And we got some orange jello with carrot shavings in it and put that in there too, then mashed the bread back down on it. It didn't look very appetizing. It hadn't looked good in the first place, but now it looked worse.

Harold looked at the sandwich suspiciously. He was hesitant. "Thanks," he said, like he knew something was up. He didn't eat it right away. If he had tried to stay too long in one place, one of the teachers might have said something to him, maybe even ordered him back to class. Instead, he walked around the cafeteria and once in a while took a look at the sandwich. A couple of times we thought he was going to throw it down.

We saw him eating it though. He ate it standing in the hall. We had snuck around and watched him to make sure. His hunger got the best of him. That, and the fact that it was a source of pride to him to eat everything.

I could believe the hockers, since they would have just been a little bit slimy. They could have been some kind of dressing or condiment. But who's not going to notice that there's jello with carrot shavings in their sandwich?

Johnny ran right up to him. "Did you eat that sandwich? How was that sandwich?"

"It was OK," Harold said. He knew when we started laughing that we had done something to it. But if he had tasted anything unusual about the sandwich he didn't let on. "It wasn't that great, actually," he said.

"You didn't taste that jello we put on there?" I asked.

"I thought there was something kind of funny about that," Harold admitted. "But, you know, some people make funny sandwiches."

One day Harold told me and Johnny to come over to his house after school and smoke some reefer. We had never smoked any before. We had plans to ride home with him in his car that day, but somehow the teachers got wind of it and they wouldn't let us do it. We were supposed to ride the bus. The teachers said that was the rule. They said we would have to get permission from our parents to ride with Harold, and we knew that wasn't going to happen. We couldn't just walk off either and meet him out by the road. That was another rule, they said. They kept a lookout to make sure we didn't try anything funny. They thought Harold was a bad influence.

Since we couldn't leave with Harold, we said we'd meet him at his house. We asked the bus driver in advance if we could get off at Harold's stop, but she said we couldn't. She said it was a rule. That was the first time we'd ever heard of that rule. They seemed to be coming up with a lot of new rules lately.

But we were clever enough not to protest too much. Then when she stopped the bus to let off a few kids we jumped right off before she could shut the door. "Hey! You can't get off here! Get back on here!" she yelled at us. She came rolling along beside us on the road. She still had the door open and she leaned over to yell out it. "Get back on here! I'm not telling you again! If you don't get back on here this minute you're kicked off the bus for good!"

That would have been fine with us, since then we could have just got a ride home with Harold every day. But we knew she was bluffing anyway. She finally got sick of yelling at us and closed the door and drove on down the road.

Harold's house wasn't in the subdivision. His house was in the middle of the woods. It was an old farmhouse on the edge of the subdivision, and his family had been living there since before the subdivision was built. They didn't all live there now, just Harold and his mother. His father lived in an apartment with Harold's sister.

We walked on a path through the woods to get to it. The fall foliage was at its peak, and we were surrounded by red and yellow and orange trees. There was a scattering of leaves on the ground, and the air was damp and cool. There was the smell of rotted wood in the air.

We came into a clearing in front of an old, white, wooden farmhouse. We had seen the house a million times, but had only lately found out that Harold lived there. We had been inside a couple of times since then. There were old barns off to the side and in the back, though nobody was using them for anything now, and a couple of them were falling down.

Johnny rang the doorbell and I banged on the door. Nobody answered. But it looked like somebody was home, especially since the upstairs windows were open. We kept ringing the doorbell. We kept banging. We kicked the door and yelled for Harold to open up. We thought maybe he had just gone to sleep. That sounded like something he would do. Also, it was a big house and it was possible that he was in the back of it and couldn't hear us.

We went around and knocked at the back door. We banged on it good. There was no doorbell back there. We looked in the kitchen window, but we didn't see anybody. The house was wide open. The curtains were blowing out the windows. I guess they thought they still lived in the country.

We threw rocks at Harold's bedroom window. Not to break the window, but to make a noise. Some of them went in the open window, hopefully to hit Harold and wake him up. We yelled some more. We were determined to get some of that reefer.

Harold wasn't there. Nobody was there. The back door was unlocked so we went in.

It was a big house, with nice furniture, but everything was old and smelled kind of musty. We didn't fool around too much downstairs in case his mother came home and walked in on us. Instead, we went upstairs and went into Harold's room. He had a huge room, but there wasn't much in it. He had a bed and a desk, some metal shelves with his clothes and his stuff piled on them, an old couch, and a couple of chairs. It was mostly empty space, spread out along a bare wood floor, much longer than it was wide, and sloping down toward his bed by the windows.

And he had a pool table! That was the best thing. We played pool for a while. I wasn't any good and Johnny beat me every time. It was a bumper pool table.

When we got bored we fucked around with all the stuff in his room. We fucked around with his stereo. He had a great stereo, a Pioneer receiver with a turntable and a tape deck, and with gigantic speakers. They had to be big to fill up all that space. We jammed the volume all the way up on a Deep Purple album, shaking the house. We played some more pool and waited for Harold to get home.

After an hour we were getting sick of waiting. I was also getting pretty damn sick of losing to Johnny. "I wish we knew where he keeps his reefer," I said.

"He keeps it under the pool table," Johnny said.

"Yeah, sure."

"Look for yourself."

I did. I got down on the floor on my back and checked up under the table. There was a little ledge made out of plywood over in the corner, and I scooted over there and reached up on it. Sure enough, there was a plastic baggie with some reefer in it. It was just a small bag, with a few joints worth of reefer in it. I got out from under the table. "How did you know that?" I asked.

"He told me," Johnny said.

"Why would he tell you?"

"I don't know. We were just talking about it and he told me. He didn't think I was gonna come over here and get it."

We looked the reefer over. We smelled it and handled it. Then we set it out on the pool table. We put another record on but we were sick of listening to records by then. It didn't look like Harold would ever show up, and we were getting really impatient. The whole afternoon was going by.

"That jerkoff! Where the fuck is he?" Johnny said.

"It would serve him right if we ripped off his reefer. He's an idiot for telling you where it was anyway."

"We should steal everything in this whole house," Johnny said. "We should steal his stereo. We should steal the fucking TV!"

"Yeah, that would teach him a lesson."

"We should trash this whole house!" Johnny said.

We didn't really want to rob or trash the house. For one thing it would have been too much trouble. I just wanted to play a trick on Harold to freak him out. "Let's steal some of his posters off the wall," I said. I thought it would be obvious then that we were just fucking with him, and he wouldn't get too mad.

"What good will that do us?" Johnny said. "Let's at least get some of his fucking reefer."

"Oh man, he's bound to notice that."

"No, he won't. He doesn't notice anything."

I knew this was crazy. So did Johnny. Harold was kind of oblivious, but he wasn't that far gone. But we really wanted to smoke some of that reefer. And we figured that Harold deserved to have his reefer stolen, since he had told us to come over and smoke some and then made us wait for an hour.

At first we only took half, but we didn't know if that would be enough for a joint. So then we took half of what was left.

We didn't try to smoke it right there, where Harold or his mother could have walked in. We put the reefer in a cellophane from an empty cigarette pack. We couldn't find any rolling papers. They must have been hidden in a better place. But we figured we'd worry about that later.

"He probably won't care," I said, trying to rationalize it.

"He won't even notice," Johnny said.

"Probably he'll just think he smoked it all."

"You think we got enough?" Johnny asked.

"I don't know. We'd better get some more just in case." I unrolled the bag again and took another pinch out.

"What else should we get?" Johnny asked.

"Let's see if he notices these posters missing from his wall," I said. I was still thinking in terms of a practical joke.

We pulled a couple of posters down off the wall, and even got the thumbtacks that went with them. The posters we stole were those two posters you get free with Pink Floyd's *The Dark Side of the Moon* album. That was our favorite album. We had already stolen a few sets of the posters from other sources.

We went out the front door and left it standing wide open. We figured that would teach Harold to go off and leave his house unguarded like that.

14

We wanted to get as far away from Harold's house as possible, so we didn't hang out in the woods to smoke the joint. We dropped the posters off at Johnny's house so we wouldn't have to carry them, and then we walked through the subdivision to the spring-house.

The springhouse was just what it sounds like. There was a spring coming out at the base of the building, out of an old pipe made of bricks. The house was perched up over the spring. It had a lower level where the water gathered in a stone cistern before it flowed out in a creek. On the upper level was a seating area with wooden benches, and around this was a walkway and a railing. The building backed up against a hill, and was surrounded by trees with their bright fall foliage.

We still didn't have any rolling papers, because we hadn't felt like buying a whole pack just to get one, and anyway we would have had to walk all the way to the store. Instead we tore a couple of sheets of paper out of a phone book. We figured that phone book paper was similar to rolling paper. It was thin paper, after all, and for nothing you got a whole bunch of it, enough for thousands of joints. It didn't have any glue on it, but we figured that didn't matter.

We sat in the top half of the springhouse. Johnny tore off a square of the phone book paper and rolled up a joint. He didn't know what he was doing, and it just fell apart. My first attempt wasn't any better. We each tried to roll one a couple more times. It was my third rolling job that finally got smoked.

It was a disaster. There was too much reefer in the joint, enough for several joints. Half of the reefer fell out onto the floor of the springhouse. The joint didn't draw well because it wasn't sealed. As big as it was, we didn't get that many tokes off it. It kept unraveling, and the cherry kept falling off. We hadn't taken the seeds out, so it crackled and popped all over the place.

We didn't know how to smoke pot anyway. We knew how to inhale from smoking cigarettes, but we didn't know you were supposed to hold the smoke in. We smoked the joint about three quarters of the way, and then it finally just fell apart. There was enough left for another joint at least, but we didn't know that. We didn't know that the roach was worth anything, so we just threw it down.

Then we sat back on the benches and relaxed. Johnny said he was high. I felt a little bit high. Maybe I had held the smoke in my lungs long enough for it to have a slight effect. I didn't know how it was supposed to feel anyway. Me and Johnny both thought we were high.

But we didn't have much time to think about whether we were high or not. We saw Harold coming from a long way off, through the apartments on the other side of the tennis courts. There was another guy with him, and when they got closer we saw who it was. It was Jim Boyle, one of Harold's friends from public school. He was an even more worthless character than Harold, a real wild-looking guy, with long, frizzy blond hair. I don't know if he had been held back or not, but he looked like he deserved it.

"Maybe they won't see us," Johnny said. For the moment we were hidden by the trees. But they were clearly headed in our direction.

"Oh shit! Here they come!" I said. I started kicking the roach apart so they wouldn't be able to find it. Johnny was trying to play it cool, sitting on the bench. We kicked at the reefer that had fallen out of the joint and mixed it in with the dirt on the floor. I wadded up the burnt paper left over from the roach and tossed it over the side of the springhouse into the creek.

But they had smelled it. And now they were coming across the walkway into the springhouse. I was standing and Johnny was sitting. "What's that smell?" Jim Boyle said. "Yeehaaa! Alright! Party down!"

"I thought you guys were coming over today," Harold said.

"Ah, we forgot all about that," I said.

"Nah, maybe tomorrow," Johnny said.

"What have you guys been up to?" I asked Harold.

"Nothing. I went and picked up Jim at his school. We've just been driving around."

"You dudes got any reefer, man? Fire up a doobie!" Jim said.

"Nah, we don't have any," Johnny said.

"I wish we did," I added.

"We know you got some, man. We smelled it," Jim said. "Come on, man, be cool. We're ready to get high!"

Harold wasn't saying much. Of course, he was never real talkative. But you could tell he was mad. He was still smiling, but it wasn't a friendly smile. He was glaring at me. I could tell they blamed me. They figured it must have been my idea. Or maybe I just looked the most guilty.

They were both standing close up on me. Too close. "Somebody's been in my house and stole my reefer," Harold said. "Weren't you two supposed to come over today?" he asked again.

"Uh, yeah, but we just didn't get around to it," I said, nervously.

They backed me out of the seating area and toward the railing. They were smiling and laughing, so I thought they were just kidding. I hoped they were just kidding anyway. I didn't think they would try to do anything to me. I could take care of myself and fight back or at least get away from them. And Johnny wouldn't just stand there and let me get my ass kicked.

They backed me up against the railing. I still wasn't too worried because I thought they were just going to try and scare me. Then they grabbed me. They were still smiling and laughing, so I didn't try to struggle. They each had me by an arm. They bent me back over the railing.

I was getting more worried. "Hey guys, what are you doing?"

"I know you stole my reefer," Harold said.

I was bent back over the railing and my feet were just barely touching the ground. I was starting to get pretty damn nervous. "No, man. I don't know what you're talking about." Then they had me all the way back, with my feet all the way off the ground. "I don't even smoke pot!" I said.

They tipped me back and grabbed my legs and turned me upside down over the railing. Then they each grabbed one of my legs and lowered me and dangled me off the springhouse, over the rocks. They were laughing all the time, like it was just a big joke. I tried to act like I wasn't worried, but it was pretty scary being dangled over the edge like that. When I tilted my head back I saw the rocks down below me, a couple of stories down. The rocks of the creek were jagged and pointy. Even falling on your feet from that height onto those rocks wouldn't have done you any good. It would have killed me to drop me on my head.

They kept jerking me in a way that made me think they were going to drop me. When they did that my heart jumped up in my throat.

"Where's the reefer? Did you smoke it all?" Harold asked.

"I don't know what you're talking about!" I said.

"You better confess," Harold said, giving me a jerk downward.

"Confess!!!" Jim Boyle yelled, shaking me up and down wildly.

"Just say you did it, and we'll let you up," Harold said.

There was no way in hell I was going to confess while I was dangling over those rocks. I figured they would drop me if I did.

"We're not gonna let you up until you admit you did it," Jim said.

"I didn't do it! I swear to God!" Now they were scaring the shit out of me.

They shook me and threatened me a couple times more. Then Harold said, "I'm getting tired of this. I'm gonna smoke a cigarette. You think you can hold onto him by yourself?" He acted like he was letting go of my leg.

"I don't know. I guess we'll find out," Jim said.

"No! Don't let me go!" I screamed.

Then I heard Johnny come over to the railing. "He thinks you're gonna drop him if he says he did it."

"We'll only drop him if he doesn't say it," Harold said.

"He didn't do it. I did it," Johnny said.

"We didn't ask you," Harold said. "But if you did it, he did it too."

But that got them to thinking, at least. "If we let you up, then you'll admit it?" Harold asked.

"Yes! Pull me up!"

"Then that means you did it!" Jim Boyle screamed. They gave me a little jerk again, to fake dropping me.

"No! I didn't do it!"

They finally let me up. I was ready to run or fight if I needed to. "Alright, I did it," I said.

"You son of a bitch! I knew it!" Harold said. He was laughing about it still, so I guess he must've still seen some humor in the situation. I didn't ask him whether he had noticed that his posters were missing.

I deserved it, I guess. And I should have learned a lesson, but I was stubborn. I decided to be more like Harold and Jim Boyle, rather than less like them. I admired them. Their strength was a strength I could aspire to, unlike my father's, which seemed out of reach. Though the worst of it hadn't happened to Johnny, I think he learned more from the incident than I did. It was the first in a series of incidents that was going to turn him against me. Anyway, all in all, I thought it was a pretty damn funny thing to do. We would have to remember to dangle Chip out the window at school, I decided.

But our main problem was still the same, boredom. We couldn't hang out with Harold all the time since he had his own friends and his own things going on, and to him we were still just little kids. So after school and on the weekends there was nothing to do. There was nothing in the subdivision, just houses and trees and winding streets. Hell, not even that many trees, since it was kind of a new subdivision. There were no stores or anything to interest anybody. We were always bored out of our minds. There was football practice a couple of times a week, but outside of that we had a hell of a time finding anything to do. Homework, of course, was out of the question.

Sometimes we rode our bikes out of the subdivision and up to a little town that had been there since before the subdivision was built. The highway bypassed the old main street and ran parallel to it so that there was no need for cars to go up that way into the town. There were still a few shops left on the main street, though most had closed up long ago. Still, it was better than the subdivision.

We rode around looking for something to do, anything to relieve the boredom. There was a barber shop and a funeral parlor. Sometimes nobody was around and we went into the funeral parlor and looked at the dead people. One time we had some balloons and we blew one of them up and gave it an old man with a flag draped over his coffin. There was a post office. There was a hardware store and a feed store. At the feed store we found a rusty pair of scissors and cut the wires to the brake lights on the trucks in the parking lot. There were a couple of churches. They left them wide open and sometimes we would go in them and steal anything worth stealing and tear things up. The Rotary Club wisely kept their place locked up. There was a little grocery store that wasn't too interesting. And there was an old-time drug store where we went to get cokes and steal butane lighters.

People lived along the old road too. In particular, there was an old lady who lived in one of the houses. She must have been in her eighties. She always had her door open for a breeze, with just the screen door pulled to. She sat by the open window, looking out. We saw her every time we passed by. One day we had nothing better to do so we thought we'd mess with her.

There was a little gravel parking lot in front of her house before you got to the street. I rode my bike into the parking lot and pretended to crash into a metal trash can that was sitting out. I knocked the trash can down with my bike. Then I kicked the trash can a couple times to make a racket as I pretended to fall off my bike. "Owwww!" I started howling. "Owwww!!! I'm hurt!"

I grabbed my foot and rolled around in the parking lot, writhing like I was in pain. "I hurt my foot! I can't walk!"

The old lady saw this through the window. She got up and came to the door. She opened the screen door and stood in the doorway, then stepped out onto the porch, still holding the door.

She said, "Oh, poor little boy. Have you hurt yourself?"

"Arrrgh! I'm hurt! Oh, I'm dying!" I spoke in a funny voice, like I was retarded.

Johnny jumped off his bike and got into the act. "My friend wrecked his bike! My friend is hurt!" He spoke like a retard too.

"My goodness!" the old lady said.

I rolled around and held my foot. "Arrgh! My foot! It must be amputated!"

"Call the fire department!" Johnny said.

"Why, I don't think the fire department is the right place to call," the old lady said. She tried to explain what the fire department did.

"No! Please! Call the fire department!" Johnny yelled.

"My foot must be amputated!" I yelled. "Call the fire department!"

"Where do you boys live?" the old lady asked. "I'll call your mother and tell her you're hurt."

"We have no home!" I said.

"Who's your mother?"

"We have no mommy!" Johnny said.

"We are orphans!" I said. "Help us!"

"Are you our mommy?" Johnny asked.

"No, I'm not your mommy."

"Where's your mommy?" I asked.

"My mommy? My mommy's dead!" the old lady said.

"Oh! You're an orphan too!" I said.

"Yes, you're just like us!" Johnny added.

"No, I'm not." The old lady tried to explain the difference between a child who has lost their parents and an adult who has lost theirs. Or something like that. She wasn't real clear on the issue.

After a while we got tired of pulling her leg. I got up off the ground and picked up my bike. "Oh, I'm OK now." We both got on our bikes and rode away, leaving the old lady standing there.

We did the same thing the next day. This time Johnny did the crash. After the second time we did it, the old lady moved the trash cans around the side of the house. She must have thought they were an obstruction. So when we came back the third day we just had to fall down, and couldn't clank the trash cans around. That made it less dramatic. We had to yell louder in order to make the same racket.

But by the third time the old lady had caught on. She wouldn't come outside. She just stood in the door and yelled at us. "You go away! Leave me alone, you brats!"

In a way I felt bad about the old lady, but Johnny didn't seem to worry about it. He had a casual nonchalance that I was really coming to envy. And anyway, we hadn't hurt her. She had given us something to do for a couple of days, and something to talk about and laugh about, and that was more important to us than anything she might have been feeling.

The next day the old lady's son came to visit. We rode our bikes up and crashed in the parking lot and went into our act, rolling around on the pavement and howling in pain. We both did it this time. We howled and limped around dragging our legs, screaming for the old lady to call the fire department.

Instead of the old lady, a man came out. He was fairly old too, but not old enough to make fun of. "What's going on here?" he said. He wasn't fooled by our retarded act. He saw right through it. We didn't bother to carry it very far when we saw him.

The old lady came out behind him. "They come here every day and bother me!" she said.

It made the man really mad. He went after Johnny because Johnny had crashed the closest to the house, right up by the door. He grabbed Johnny off the ground by the arm and shook him. "Where do you live?" he demanded. "Who are your parents? Do they know what you're up to?"

"Ow! Let go!" Johnny said. He started struggling to get away from the man. I felt like I should help Johnny, but I hesitated, I hung back. I was scared of the old guy, he was so mad. After shaking Johnny a couple more times, the man released him. Johnny grabbed his bike off the ground. I already had mine up. We got on our bikes quickly and took off.

"What's wrong with you kids, teasing a poor old lady? Show some respect. You'll be old one day too," the man said as we peddled out of the lot. "How would you like it if I teased *your* mother?" he called after us. "Get out of here! And don't let me see you around here again!"

We gave him the finger when we were far enough down the road to where we knew he couldn't run after us and catch us.

16

"You could've helped me, you dick," Johnny said as soon as we had got safely away.

I felt pretty guilty. "What was I supposed to do? Why didn't you fight back?"

Johnny felt he had lost face in some way, even though I was the only one around to see. He blamed me, since it had been my idea. I guess he figured I wasn't such a good friend anymore if I was going to get him into shit like that.

That night was a Friday night. It was already dark when we met up after dinner and went back up into the little town. This time we left out bikes at home and walked.

"Let's go up to the pizza place and see if there's any chicks there," Johnny said as we walked. We had just discovered the pizza place as a place to hang out. In general, kids a little older than us hung out there, kids in high school, some of whom even had cars.

"Nah, I don't want to," I said.

"Come on, man. Don't be scared just because of that one bitch. Not all girls are like that. It's just those stuck-up Catholic bitches."

"I'm not scared," I said, though that wasn't exactly true. The thing with Sheila had shaken my confidence, and a month later I still hadn't gotten over it. I knew I was going to have to deal with girls sooner or later, but I preferred later. "I just don't feel like it right now," I said.

"Well, whatever," Johnny said. He shook his head in disgust. "It's not like you're coming up with any great ideas."

But then I did come up with a good idea, or at least a good way to take our minds off of girls. There was a fruit store on the main street, close to where the old lady lived. It was a big place and sold all kinds of produce and flowers, and even small plants and bushes on the lot behind the store. The store was a small building with garage doors that opened onto a concrete patio with a roof over it and a chain link fence around it.

Under cover of dark we climbed over the fence. Once inside, we went nuts, busting up all the fruit, especially the pumpkins. We threw a bunch of tomatoes up against the wall of the store and against the garage doors. We dumped out all the bushel baskets of apples and peaches and stomped them and kicked them around, and we threw the pumpkins on the concrete floor and busted them open. We lifted the pumpkins over our heads and smashed them down. We heaved them across the patio. In the end, the concrete was slick with pumpkin slime.

We ate as much fruit as we wanted, mostly apples and peaches. We ate it with our hands and got the juice all over ourselves. We were throwing fruit and pieces of pumpkin all over the place while we were eating, laughing and throwing it at each other. Soon the building had tomatoes and peaches busted all over it. The garage doors were stained red with tomato juice. Finally, we found a hose and washed the juice and slime off our hands and faces.

Using a broom handle, we tried to pry up one of the garage doors. But it didn't work, the handle just cracked, so we couldn't get into the building. There was no window to bust out, so we couldn't get in that way. We pissed on some of the fruit that we hadn't destroyed. Then we turned on all the water faucets and left them running. One of the garage doors opened a crack at the bottom, so we stuck one of the hoses inside the store and turned it on.

Then we knocked over the coke machine. We had to rock it back and forth to get it going and get it to fall. It made a lot of noise when it fell, so we got the hell out of there. When we got over the fence we picked up a bushel basket of rotten peaches that had been thrown out and took that with us. Each of us held a handle of the basket to carry it, climbing straight up into the woods on a path that went up a hill.

There was a spot in the woods where there was a clearing in the trees that overlooked the main street. There were tall trees behind us and brush in front of us about waist high, so we couldn't be seen. The trees were nearly bare and the brush was thinning out, but we were still pretty well hidden. The cars veered off the highway and came up the road onto the hill where we were waiting. Right when the cars came off the main highway they were really flying. That's when we got them. Nailed them right in the windshield. It took some skill to hit them, but when you did, the peaches really splattered.

If somebody backed up to find out who did it, we would throw at their car again. One time a guy got out of his car and we threw peaches at him and then ran off. I don't know if he came after us or not, but probably he thought better of running into the dark woods where he'd never been before. After a while, we figured he was gone, so we came back and threw some more peaches.

The time wore on like that. Long stretches of monotony punctu-
ated by brief interludes of excitement. Or what passed for excitement. I could tell that Johnny, in particular, was getting tired of
the childish pranks. And maybe all our aimlessness and clowning
was really just a search for an identity and a way to grow up. We
were good at being kids. Adulthood, who knew? We wandered
the streets because we wanted to find some direction. But as the
semester wore on our quest became more serious.

We had left the rest of the peaches sitting there in their basket.
When we came back a couple of nights later the ones that were
left at the bottom of the basket were really nasty. Most of them
weren't even fit for throwing, but we did our best. We had nothing
else to do anyway. It was too soon to go back to the fruit store for
more, since the guy who owned the place was sure to be hanging
around waiting for us with his shotgun.

After a while we got tired of messing with the peaches. We
went back toward the creek to wash the sticky peach juice off
our hands, walking back through the woods on an overgrown dirt
driveway.

That's what we were doing at the Hippie Shack. We called it
the Hippie Shack because there were some hippies living there.
One of them was my cousin, who was several years older than me
and out of high school. I kept meaning to go by and see him, but I
never got around to it. I never knew if he'd be there or not, and I
think he intimidated me because he was so cool, an actual hippie.
Johnny was impressed too, and I promised him that we'd go there
and smoke some pot with my cousin the hippie one of these days.

But we weren't headed straight back to the Hippie Shack, we were going around it. The house had a long gravel drive leading back to it, and another dirt drive going around it on the side. The Hippie Shack was an old wooden farmhouse, and around the back of the house were a lot of smaller farm buildings, barns and little houses where maybe workers had lived, or even slaves. Once we got back there we saw that there was a bus parked in a clearing in front of these buildings. It was quiet in the bus, but there were lights on inside, so you could tell somebody was in there. There was a car parked in the clearing too, near the bus.

Hari Krishna guys were living in the bus. The hippies who lived at the Hippie Shack had let them camp out there. We didn't want to get too close, so we just looked across the clearing. It was an old school bus, painted weird colors. It was dark so we couldn't see it too well. And we couldn't see inside at all. The inside was lit up but they had curtains over the windows.

We couldn't tell they were Hari Krishnas just by looking, but Johnny already knew that's what they were. It turned out he had seen one of them the day before when he was riding his older brother's motorcycle in the woods. He just hadn't said anything to me. Maybe he thought I wouldn't want to go back there if he said anything. He said he had seen one of the Krishna guys sitting cross-legged by the creek, meditating.

"I was making a bunch of noise, and he didn't even look up," Johnny said. "I was doing donuts in the dirt and everything."

Johnny was watching the guy and not paying attention to what he was doing, he said. He wrecked the bike and the guy didn't even look up then. "He was so deep in meditation, he didn't even flinch. Can you believe that?" Johnny said.

"Wow," I said. But I wasn't that impressed. I figured the guy could have been faking. What I really couldn't believe was that Johnny's brother had let him ride his motorcycle!

We stood on the edge of the clearing and thought about the incident as we looked at the bus. We really wanted to get a closer look at that bus. Also, we thought they might turn us on to some reefer. Maybe we could even ask them to sell us a couple of joints. We were too scared to knock on their door right then, and anyway it was a school night and we couldn't be out much later, but we decided to come back the next day after school and at least check out the bus.

When we got there the next day we were shy at first, so we acted like we were just strolling by and happened upon them. There were a few people hanging around outside the bus. They had a tape playing on the car stereo and a couple of them were dancing around. We stood a little ways off and watched them until one of them noticed us and walked over to where we were standing. He was dressed like a hippie, in jeans and a T-shirt, and had long brown hair. He was the same guy Johnny had seen, only then he had had on some kind of robe.

"Hey, how you guys doing?" the guy said. He said his name was Kenny.

"We were just looking at your bus. It's pretty cool looking," I said.

"Come on over and get a closer look."

We went over to where the other people in the group were hanging around outside the bus. They had a couple of lawn chairs to sit on. We didn't speak to them at first, but just looked at the bus, walking all around it. The bus was painted mostly blue, and had a bunch of dancing animal gods and crazy shit like that on it.

It was a real professional job. Artistic. We were impressed. Kenny told us a little bit about the gods painted on the bus.

There were five or six people there, all men except for one girl. The tape they were listening to just had their usual chant on it, but we had never heard it before, so it was new to us. It was pretty catchy. It was a tape of a special group that they had all been waiting to hear, and somebody had just brought the tape around that day. They were discussing it. Sometimes they sang along to it, and other times they danced. Kenny introduced us to a couple of them who weren't getting into the music too much. They were all real friendly.

Several of them came and went. One car would leave, and after a while another one would drive up.

Some of them were wilder looking than others. Most of the men just had long hair and wore jeans and T-shirts. But there were a couple of them who had shaved heads and wore Indian robes. But it didn't look like that was mandatory, and so we figured they had just got carried away.

One guy there was much older than the rest of them and had on the whole Indian getup, with stripes of mud on his forehead and everything, so I figured he was the boss. He was kind of creepy and reminded me of a vampire or a lizard. But he didn't say anything, and his movements were slow like he was on drugs, so we didn't pay much attention to him. He smelled like he had pulled a spice rack over on himself.

The one girl in the group was kind of pretty, and didn't wear a bra, I noticed immediately. She had long, sandy blond hair. She danced and whirled all about the clearing, and her big boobs bounced around under her thin top. I was way too interested in her to care much about the old guy.

We also really liked their bus. It was like a hippie bus, and we were impressed by anything having to do with hippies. They let us look inside it. They had taken out all the seats and put down rugs. There were mats and pillows thrown all around. They had some paintings of gods and of their leader on the walls. There were curtains on the windows, but they were drawn back to let the light in.

We were glad to get back outside. It was better outside. "You guys really live in this bus?" Johnny asked.

"Yeah. We travel all over the country, turning people on to the truth of the Lord Krishna," Kenny said. "We stay in one place for a couple months, and then move on to another town when the spirit moves us."

It seemed like a pretty cool scene.

Kenny told us about their religion. He told us more about the gods painted on the bus, and also a little bit about their beliefs.

"What about Jesus and Christianity?" I asked. I was leery of other religions since my father was so religious and he and the school had really drilled Catholicism into me. I had my own problems with Catholicism and I was looking for answers, but I was conflicted. The nuns would've told us that the gods on their bus were demons.

"It's all one religion. We respect Jesus as an incarnation of the one true God," Kenny said. And so that reassured me a little bit.

We hung out for a while by the bus and listened to the music. "You can't get a real idea of what our religion is like until you come to one of our feasts," Kenny said. He invited us to come back on the weekend for a feast. "We're having a big feast on Sunday, and afterwards we'll have some entertainment. We'll have some really great music and dancing and chanting. But the main thing's the feast, where we give thanks to the Lord Krishna for the earth's bounty."

"What kind of stuff are you gonna serve?" Johnny asked.

"Oh, all kinds of stuff, plates and plates of food, everything except meat. Fruits and vegetables mainly. We're vegetarians. We don't eat meat. But we know how to fix all kinds of great dishes out of vegetables. They really have a better flavor than meat if you know what you're doing when you prepare them. And they're so much better for you. Meat will make you sick, in body, mind and soul."

We got ready to leave. "Try not to eat any meat for the next couple of days. You'll be prepared to enjoy our feast more fully," Kenny said. "And don't eat anything at all on the day of the feast."

He didn't mention anything about reefer at the feast, but I think by this time we were getting the point that they didn't get into that sort of stuff.

Kenny gave us a book and some incense, the one book to share and a pack of incense with several sticks in it to divide up between us. There were lots of colorful, glossy pictures in the book. There were pictures of blue-colored gods and goddesses, and of demons who would attack and torment you if you ate meat or performed other evil acts. We took turns looking at the book as we walked home. We were excited about the feast. "Did you see the knockers on that bitch?" Johnny said.

"Hell yeah!" I said.

"You think she's with one of those guys?"

"I don't know. Maybe she has sex with all of them," I said, jokingly.

But that seemed to set Johnny's mind to thinking. That seemed to excite him. Maybe he thought there'd be an orgy. Or a gang bang, anyway, since there was only one girl. "Oh man, this is gonna be great," Johnny said.

I had already grasped that it wasn't that kind of scene, so I wasn't nervous about that. I was more curious about their religion. "Yeah, I can't wait," I said.

18

We got there right on time on Sunday afternoon, actually a little early. I had rushed to get ready after I got back from church, but it had turned out not to be necessary. We figured there would be trays of food set up outside, since it was kind of cramped in the bus, but there wasn't anything. A couple of guys were standing around near the bus, together with the girl. We walked up to them and said hi. "Where's the feast?" Johnny said.

They seemed puzzled. "The feast? Oh yeah, the feast," the girl said. "Let me get Kenny. He's inside the bus."

Kenny came out. "Hi guys."

"Well, we're here," I said.

"Glad you could make it." He shook hands with us.

"Where's the feast?" I asked. "Did we get here early?"

"Oh, the feast. It's inside. Come on inside the bus," Kenny said.

We went in. We didn't see any food. They had a small kitchen in the bus but it didn't look like they were preparing anything there. "Have a seat," Kenny said. We propped up some pillows against the wall of the bus and plopped down.

Kenny went back outside for a minute and then came back in. The girl and the two guys who had been outside followed him in. "We already had the feast," Kenny now announced. "You're a little late and you missed it. Too bad, because it was great! But we're getting ready to do some chanting. You can stick around for that."

"Man, I'm really hungry," I said.

"I'm starving to death," Johnny said.

"We haven't eaten anything all day, like you said. We're gonna have to go get something to eat," I said.

"Well, maybe we can find something," Kenny said, reluctantly. He told the girl, "See if you can find anything left over from the feast."

The girl got to her feet grudgingly and poked around in the kitchen area, clanking some pots and pans, for what seemed like an inordinately long time. Finally, smiling sweetly, she handed us a soggy paper plate filled with disgusting slop. There were slices of brownish apple and banana that had been picked-over and chewed-on, and some raisin-and-carrot mush in a sauce. It looked nauseating. It looked like something she had drug out of the garbage.

They didn't give us any utensils. We kind of picked at it. For one thing we were starving. And for another I guess we didn't want to be impolite. Nobody there seemed to think anything was wrong with the feast. With the slop. They looked at us as if they were expecting us to enjoy it. I ate a slice of apple. It didn't taste too fresh. I didn't feel like messing with the raisin-and-carrot slop.

Kenny was sitting there the whole time watching us eat. "How is it?" he said. "Great, isn't it?"

"Yeah!" Johnny said.

"Oh, yeah!" I said.

We picked at the feast awhile longer until we were both sick of looking at it. I put the plate on the floor in front of us.

"You guys had enough?" Kenny asked.

We both said we had had plenty.

"Sure you don't want some more?"

"Nah," we both said. Not wanting to send the girl back to the garbage can, we both shook our heads, no. Now we couldn't say we hadn't had anything to eat.

"You can just hang onto that plate in case you want to nibble a little bit more," Kenny said.

They shut the curtains and suddenly it was dark in the bus. Then they lit several sticks of incense and the whole bus filled up with smoke. "We're gonna do some chanting," Kenny said. He acted like they were just going about their business. "Feel free to join in at any point," he said. "Of course you don't have to. There's no pressure."

They started chanting and they just kept on going. Though the words were always the same, they had several varieties of the chant, several tunes or tempos. They would start out slow and then get faster and faster, building up to a frenzy. Then they would start over with the slow chanting again and build again. Over and over.

One time I looked up and the old guy had come out of somewhere. I hadn't seen him come in, but he was sitting there now. He was chanting too. There was a back sleeping area that I think he slipped out of.

They had the bus sealed up to keep the incense in. The thick smoke was swirling all around. There was no other light except what sunlight got in around the edges of the thick curtains. Outside was a bright, sunny day.

I was weak from hunger and feeling light-headed. The chant kept going on and on. "Once you learn it, feel free to join in," Kenny repeated, then went back to his chanting. The sound was ringing in my ears. By this point I had the song memorized. It would have been hard not to have memorized it.

Hari Krishna, hari Krishna. Krishna Krishna, hari hari. Hari Rama, hari Rama. Rama Rama, hari hari. Over and over.

LORDS OF THE SCHOOLYARD

All the Krishna people looked at us, expecting us to join in. I always felt stupid singing, and I never would sing in church, except maybe to make fun of the words.

But after a while they made me feel stupid not to sing. At first I looked at Johnny, but after a while I looked at the other people. I forgot about his presence. At first me and Johnny looked at one another as if it were a joke. But then the song took me over. Pretty soon it was all that was in my brain. At one point I looked over at Johnny and he was chanting. I was still resisting. But then I looked over at Johnny again and he looked at me like I should start chanting too. Like I should get with it. So I started chanting.

At first I felt like an idiot. But then I started enjoying myself. It carried me along and I forgot what I was doing. I forgot myself and went on automatic pilot.

Soon enough, it was tripping me out. I was going into a sort of a trance. We just kept chanting and chanting. It was like I was under a spell and couldn't stop if I wanted to. The smoke was swirling all around in the dark and I was breathing it in. I kept looking at that old vampire dude. Sometimes he had his eyes closed and his head thrown back and he looked like he was really getting into it. Other times he was looking straight at me. He scared me.

It went on and on. I just kept chanting. Sometimes I looked at Johnny. He kept on chanting too. Everybody kept on chanting. The whacked-out vampire dude kept on chanting. It was dark and smoky and I was sick of breathing the smoke. Beads of sweat were breaking out on my forehead and I was shaky from hunger. I was sick of all their shit, nauseated. I wanted to get out of there, but it just kept going on. Finally it was over.

Things seemed oddly silent and we didn't talk much as we walked home. We didn't speak at all for a while as we walked down the drive toward the road.

Johnny finally broke the silence. "I feel good! I feel high!"

I felt high too. I also felt disoriented and confused.

My mind was still filled with the chant as we walked out onto the road. I was so hungry, I had to get a sandwich. We took a path through a patch of woods that was the quickest way to get to my house. I knew we could get sandwiches there.

There was some baloney and cheese in the refrigerator. I got that out, and some mayonnaise.

"Let's not eat any meat," Johnny said.

"Suit yourself. You can just have a cheese sandwich," I said. "I'm eating some of this baloney."

"We're not supposed to be eating any meat," Johnny said.

I felt kind of guilty but I said, "I don't care, I'm starving."

We ate a bunch of chips and fixed our sandwiches. Baloney and cheese and mayonnaise. Johnny broke down and ate the baloney too. We stuffed ourselves, two sandwiches each and a whole bag of chips between us, a couple cokes apiece, and two orange cupcakes each. Johnny went home and I sat around and watched TV the rest of the afternoon.

I didn't read much of the book but I looked at enough of it to get an idea of what they believed. Reincarnation and Karma had its appeal. You act like an animal, you'll come back as an animal. Seemed fair enough. And if you act right, you come back as a higher person, like a priest or a rich person. I sure as hell didn't want to come back as a priest, but I wouldn't have minded a couple million bucks.

It seemed like all you had to do was avoid eating meat, and killing people and animals. They didn't like that idea of killing animals especially, and it was easy to see their point if you didn't think about it too much. I was beginning to realize that that's the way it went with religion in general.

The best part was the pictures. The book had lots of pictures. There were pictures that showed how if you were greedy you would come back to earth as a pig. Or if you murdered somebody you'd come back as a wolf. There were other pictures that showed what you would come back as if you committed other sins. They had some good artists in their group.

One day the next week we were going up to the store, walking through the subdivision. Johnny started chanting that song as we walked. He shut up after a few verses but I couldn't get it out of my head once he started.

"I'd like to just get on that bus and travel around the country. That would be pretty cool. Just hanging out, chanting, having feasts," Johnny said.

"Yeah, that would be pretty cool," I admitted. We walked and thought about it. "I can't say much for that feast though."

"That stuff probably would have been pretty good if we had gotten there on time," Johnny said.

I had my doubts.

"That chanting freaked me out," I said.

"I liked it," Johnny said.

That song still kept running through my head. For the life of me, I couldn't get it out of my head. I had to admit it was a pretty good song. It may not seem like much the first couple of times you hear it, but when you chant it over and over a couple hundred times it starts to grow on you. "Yeah, I guess I kind of liked it too," I said.

But I was ambivalent about the whole thing. It seemed like the sort of thing that the nuns and the priests, and especially my father, had warned us to avoid. Not that I cared too much what they said, but they had managed to make me pretty superstitious. I didn't want to wind up in hell.

"It's weird to have two gods," I said uneasily.

"Who cares about that Jesus crap?" Johnny said. "Jesus can't do shit." Johnny seemed ready to jump on their bus and go with them.

It did make a lot more sense to me intellectually. And I was sick to death of hearing about Jesus. Everybody connected with that religion was a hypocrite, I had long ago decided. Krishna was something new, at least. And it was cool young people doing it, hippies apparently, although their leader was a bit of a weirdo. Still, I couldn't quite get past my superstition.

And now Johnny saw that I was afraid. He saw that I was all talk.

I wished I could have been more like Johnny, and not worried about things so much. That was one of the things I admired about him, he could just go with the flow. "What did you think of that one creepy-ass old guy?" I asked. He was the part of the scene that bothered me the most.

"Ah, he was alright. He wasn't doing anything." Johnny hadn't been as thoroughly indoctrinated into Catholicism as I had been. With some people, it just didn't take.

"He looked evil," I said.

"He didn't bother me," Johnny said. "You're letting your imagination run away with you."

Kenny had invited us to another feast the next Sunday. He promised a good feast this time, but I didn't know if I wanted to go through that again. I didn't know if I trusted him. Besides, it was too much like church for me. It made me anxious thinking about it.

Also, Kenny said drop by during the week if we wanted.

Johnny went on chanting that song from time to time. He wanted to go back, but I kept putting it off. Though I wanted to be open like Johnny, I was nervous about it. And when you get right down to it, I'm sure Johnny had his doubts too. He said he wanted to go back, but he was waiting for me to go along with it. On some level he still needed my approval.

It seemed to mean a lot to Johnny, and so I finally relented. When we finally went back it was Thursday afternoon. But we stopped at the edge of the clearing because there was a cop car parked near the bus. There were two cops sitting in it. I didn't see any Hari Krishna people around, though maybe they were in the bus. We didn't get too close and we didn't stick around. Neither of us liked cops very much.

We came back on Sunday to see if they were going to have another feast. I had taken the precaution of eating in advance this time. But when we got there the bus was gone and there was no trace of them. The spirit had moved them. And they didn't come back.

Since they were gone, their spell wore off us gradually. Their gods didn't have any influence over us at a distance.

And my influence over Johnny returned too. One day we got a shovel out of Johnny's garage and went back in the woods behind Johnny's house. We cleared an area in the brush, then dug a hole with the shovel and lit a fire in it with some newspapers and dried brush. We had a little bottle of lighter fluid, and we squirted some of that on there and watched the flames shoot higher.

We tore out some of the pages of the Krishna book and fed them into the fire. The book was hard to burn. Even with the lighter fluid it didn't burn well. The pages were made of heavy paper, and there were lots of glossy pictures in the middle. The book charred around the edges though, and after a while we figured that was good enough. Figuring we had exorcised the spirit of the evil Hari Krishna, we shoveled dirt over the book and the ashes.

Since our experiment with eastern religion didn't pan out, we were back to the point we started from, still looking for a way forward. Perhaps we were best suited for a life of crime. All indications seemed to point that way.

One day toward the end of November we cut school. It wasn't that hard to do. We just got Johnny's dad's secretary to call in for us and say we were sick. It was something we did from time to time, and nobody was going to catch on if we didn't do it too much.

Past the subdivision where we lived was farmland and woods. Early that morning, me and Johnny were wandering around down the back roads looking for something to do, when we came upon an old gravel driveway we had never noticed before. It was overgrown with weeds and brush, and ran winding back into the woods. We followed the drive back through the trees, crunching through the carpet of leaves that had covered the gravel, until we came to a clearing where there was a large, two-story farmhouse. It didn't look like anyone had been living there in a while, but the house was still in good condition. The white paint was peeling, but the windows were intact. Through the windows we could see that the place was empty. We busted out a pane of glass in one of the windows around the back, opened the window, and climbed in.

The air had a stale, musty smell. There was no furniture, and not much of anything left in the place. We ran around from room to room, downstairs, then upstairs, exploring. Nothing much to see. But there was a narrow, creaky little staircase that led up to a finished attic, and there was some junk up there. There were *National Geographics* and other old magazines in stacks and scattered about over the floorboards. We scattered them even more. There was a trunk with some old shirts in it. They were white dress shirts, in good condition, but they were huge, shirts for a giant. We pulled them, one by one, out of the trunk, but couldn't figure out what to do with them, so we put them back in. We figured somebody else might be able to use them some day.

I was the one who found the cash register. It was way back in the corner, wedged in against the sloping roof and partly concealed by magazines. What a find! I couldn't believe our luck. I knocked the magazines off and drug the machine out into the middle of the floor to get a better look. "Hey, check it out!" I yelled at Johnny, who was rooting around in some junk on the other side of the attic.

"God damn!" he said when he saw it.

It was a real find, alright. The cash register was an old-time one, an antique. It was shiny and gold-colored and ornate, with lots of fancy metal work. And since it had been buried in magazines, it wasn't even very dusty.

Unfortunately, none of the keys worked. When you pushed a numbered key, it didn't register on the display. The display was permanently stuck at $1.25. But at least when you pushed the sale button and turned the crank on the side, the cash drawer opened. So that was pretty cool, we thought. Even better, the cash drawer actually had some change left in it. Almost two dollars worth. Not much, but better than nothing. We quickly divided it up.

We played around with the cash register's one function for a while, opening and closing the cash drawer. But all the while, we were scheming.

"This has got to be worth a lot of money," Johnny said.

"Hell, yeah," I said. "I wonder where we could sell it."

"There's got to be somebody who would buy it."

"Definitely," I agreed. "Somebody could easily fix it up. It's much better than the junk you see in stores these days."

We couldn't just leave it in the farmhouse. It was much too valuable to take that risk. And neither of us could take it home, as there'd be too much explaining to do. So we knew we would have to sell it that day. We decided that the best course of action was to take it downtown. Surely, we figured, there had to be businesses there that bought and sold such things.

The damn thing was heavy as hell. Probably to keep people from stealing it. I had the privilege of carrying it first. I lugged it down the two flights of stairs, out the door, and down the gravel drive. Despite the cool weather, after a while I started sweating, and by the time I got to the road I was ready to let Johnny take a turn. It was a long way along the back roads to the highway where the bus stopped. The few people who drove past slowed down to gawk at us. They probably thought we ought to have our heads examined.

We had to use part of our earnings from the cash drawer to pay for the bus, but we figured we could make it back with plenty to spare. We'd been speculating along the road about how much it was worth. We figured close to a hundred, but no less than fifty. A lot, anyway.

The bus driver was a man named Charles, a middle-aged black man. We knew him since we rode the bus a lot, and he was a good guy. We were always joking around with him. Sometimes he even let us smoke cigarettes on the bus when no one else was on it. "How's it going, Charles?" I said, boarding the bus. Johnny came right after me up the steps, carrying the cash register.

"What in the world? What are you boys up to now?" Charles said, chuckling. "Don't tell me. I don't even want to know."

"We found this cash register out in the woods," Johnny said.

"A cash register in the woods! Now I've heard everything," Charles said. "Where are you boys taking that thing?"

"Downtown, to sell it," I said.

Charles had a good laugh over that.

But that didn't bother us. We figured Charles just didn't know much about selling stolen goods. We went to the back of the bus, to our favorite seats on the bench that ran along the back. Johnny set the cash register on the floor and we plopped down, one on each side of the bench. We swung our legs up onto the bench and looked out the back window, watching the scenery change from rural to suburban, becoming more and more urban as we went by the stores and the malls.

A cop pulled up behind the bus. Instead of passing, he just drove along behind us. We were feeling like real tough characters at this point, and so we made faces at the cop through the back window. He just laughed at us. That pissed me off, because he wasn't taking us seriously. We were real outlaws, I thought, not anyone to be messed with. You fucking pig, I thought. I felt a stronger message was necessary. So I gave him the finger.

The smile left the cops face, and the blue lights came on. "Oh shit!" I said. I hadn't thought that a cop would pull over a bus.

"You idiot!" Johnny said. "Now we're busted for sure!"

The bus pulled over to the shoulder and the cop got out of his car and walked around the side of the bus. "Quick, hide that cash register!" I said, and Johnny grabbed the machine and stuck it under a seat a few rows up. It wasn't hidden very well, however, and since there was nobody else sitting anywhere near it, it would have been clear to anybody that it belonged to us. We knew we were dead.

Charles the bus driver opened the door and the cop got on the bus. He was a husky blond-haired cop, a young guy in his twenties. He didn't say a word to Charles, just headed back down the aisle. He walked past the cash register without seeing it. He was so pissed off that all he could see was me.

"You little punk," the cop said when he got near me. "Who the hell do you think you are?" He got right up on me and stuck his finger in my face.

"Uh, I don't know," I stammered. I was terrified.

"Damn right, you little asshole. You don't know what you're doing. You go around giving people the finger like that and somebody's gonna kick your ass!"

"Sorry, sir."

"Don't you give that sign to somebody you don't know!" the cop said. "And especially not a policeman!"

"Yes sir. Sorry about that."

"You little dumbass!" he yelled in my face. "Do I make myself clear?!"

"Yes sir."

He backed off a little bit, sizing me up. "I'm gonna be seeing you again someday, aren't I?" I guess he had me pegged for a criminal type.

"No sir!"

"I know damn well I'll be seeing you again," the cop declared, then turned to leave.

Then he saw the cash register. He bent down to look at it. "What the hell is this?"

He turned back and looked at me again, but I was too petrified to answer. Luckily, Johnny had a story ready. He said, "That's an antique cash register, officer. My dad had it down in the base-ment of his drug store. He's got a new one now, so he said we could have that one to try and sell it."

The cop bought the line, or at least pretended to. The cash register didn't look like anything we could have stolen out of a store, that's for sure. He shook his head disgustedly and left the bus.

"Man, you're one stupid motherfucker," Johnny said once the cop was gone. "What the hell were you thinking?"

"I don't know." It seemed too involved to get into, and I fig-ured if I tried to explain I would end up looking even stupider. "Nothing happened to us anyway," I said.

We didn't say much for the rest of the trip. I could tell I had lowered myself in Johnny's eyes. I was just glad he had had the presence of mind to make up that story and bail us out. Once we got close to the city, we started passing by manufacturing busi-nesses. There were stock yards where they slaughtered hogs, and the river, and a big plant that dredged sand from the river. Then there were warehouses, and row houses, and tall office buildings. Traffic was heavy since it was a weekday, and the bus made its way along slowly, stopping at all the bus stops and filling up with more and more people.

I had no idea where we should get off. But Johnny did, and he reached up and pulled the cord at the right place. It was my turn to carry the cash register, so I grabbed it up. We tried to make it out the back door of the bus, but Charles wouldn't open it. "You boys come up to this door up front," he called back to us.

Charles was more traumatized over the cop incident than we were. He didn't like cops either. Before he would open the door, he asked me, "What did that policeman want?"

"Oh, nothing."

"I know it wasn't just nothing."

Johnny came to the rescue again, making up a story about how the cop was my dad, and he just didn't know I was going downtown.

"I don't know if I believe that story or not," Charles said. He opened the door for us, then said, "I don't know what you boys are up to, but I know you're up to something and I don't want any part of it. I've had it with you this time, and I don't want to see you on my bus again. If you see me coming, you just wait for the next bus, because you're not getting on this one again."

I didn't say anything. I just went ahead and got off. But Johnny stayed on the bus to talk to Charles. "Aw come on, Charles," he said. "It's no big deal. That cop didn't do anything."

Charles wouldn't give in, so Johnny finally got off the bus. "You really fucked us over now," he said.

21

The downtown had gone to seed. The main attraction was a big outdoor mall running down the middle of one of the main streets, which was closed off to traffic for several blocks. The street was paved with cobblestones, and trees were planted down the center. But the mall was run down, dilapidated. Half the shops were boarded up, and the rest of the space had been taken over by dollar stores and discount clothing stores and wig shops. There were a lot of black people hanging out and shopping, and many of them had big Afros and wore bell bottoms and platform shoes and looked real cool.

In the rush of excitement we forgot about the incident with the cop and the bus driver. At least I did. While I guarded the cash register, Johnny went into the Woolworth's and bought a pack of cigarettes with the change from the cash drawer. When he came out, we sat down and had a smoke and wondered what to do next. None of the shops on the mall looked like they dealt in used cash registers.

We figured we'd just ask someone where to go. Surely some of these city people would know. But it was hard to know who to ask. We didn't feel comfortable approaching the older people. Maybe they'd laugh at us, or report us. They seemed to be giving us strange looks. So we just hung out, close enough to the cash register to keep an eye on it, and checked out the windows of the wig shops, laughing at the long gold and silver wigs, and at the immense red-white-and-blue Afro. We couldn't figure out who in God's name would wear such a thing.

We watched the high school girls walk by. Most of them were way out of our league. There were a couple of good-looking ones hanging around near a hot dog stand. Johnny wanted me to go up and talk to them but I was afraid to, and soon enough they went away. Johnny was disgusted with me, but then he didn't dare to go up to them either.

There was a big clock that looked like a racetrack in the middle of the mall. It looked pretty cool, though it could have used a paint job. On the hour, some horses were supposed to come out of their stable at the top and race around the clock. We waited for the hour to come around, but when it did the horses didn't come out.

Finally a hippie wandered by, a white guy, since we were too intimidated by the black ones, and he seemed like our best shot. "Hey man, how's it going?" I said.

"Pretty good, pretty good," the hippie said, making to walk on past us.

"Hey man, you know where we can sell this cash register?" Johnny asked him.

The hippie stopped in his tracks. It was only then that he noticed the cash register. "Wow man, that's a pretty cool cash register. Where'd you get it?"

"We stole it," I said proudly.

"That's cool. Does it work?" the hippie asked.

"A little bit," I said. We showed him its one function. He didn't seem too impressed. It was the first time that it occurred to me that this might be a major drawback.

"So, you know where we can sell it?" Johnny asked again.

"Hmm, I've never thought about selling a cash register before. I guess you could try an office machine company. I think there's one over on Market Street. And if that doesn't work, there's always the pawn shop. But don't tell them you stole it."

"Aw, we're not that stupid," I said, and we all had a laugh.

The pawn shop was around the corner, but it didn't look like a place that would pay a lot of money. It was a dump. So we lugged the cash register several blocks down Market Street instead, looking for the office machine company.

But they didn't want it there. They didn't want it even though they had a cash register in their storefront window, along with adding machines and typewriters. The woman in the office was nice about it however, and seemed to take us seriously. "We don't buy them," she said, from her chair behind a gray metal desk. "We just sell them."

We tried to convince her. Johnny was the one carrying the cash register. He set it down in front of the lady's desk. "You must buy them from somewhere first," I said. "You don't make them here, do you?"

"No, we don't make them here. We buy them from the manufacturer."

"You could buy this from us and resell it," Johnny said. "Surely someone would buy such a nice cash register."

"I don't know about that. Usually business people want modern ones." The sales lady paused, then asked, "By the way, does it work?"

There was that question again. We showed her the cash register's one function. "Can't you fix it up?" Johnny asked.

"Well, I guess we could. But it really wouldn't be worth it for us. Thank you for thinking of us though."

We lugged the cash register back to the pawn shop. We were getting pretty damn tired of carrying the thing, and since now it looked like we weren't going to get so much money out of it after all, that made it all the worse.

"How am I supposed to know that thing isn't stolen?" the man behind the counter in the pawn shop said. He was huge and fat, with a big red nose and big fucked-up lips. A harelip, I guess. And he spoke with a lisp. We had placed the cash register on the floor in front of the glass counter.

That kind of pissed me off, just assuming right off the bat that the cash register was stolen. But Johnny wasn't bothered. "I guess you'll just have to take our word for it," he said.

"Even if I believed you, and I'm not saying I do, what am I supposed to tell the cops when they come around? That I just took your word for it? They'd laugh in my face. Do you have any proof that it belongs to you? A sales receipt or something? Without that, that cash register's not worth anything."

The idea of a sales receipt for a cash register seemed crazy. We admitted that we had no proof that we owned the thing. The fat man didn't seem surprised or disappointed. But we knew we were goners when he asked if it worked.

"So what am I supposed to do with it?" the fat man said. "I can't give you anything for it. I don't need the trouble. I've got enough trouble without the cops breathing down my neck about some worthless cash register. That thing's not worth a penny to me. I wouldn't take it if you gave it to me. I wouldn't have it if you paid me."

He had us convinced. The cash register wasn't worth anything and we'd gone to all that trouble for nothing. Dejected, and without any clear idea of what to do next, I picked up the cash register and we headed for the door.

"Wait a minute," the fat man called after us. "Where are you going with that? Nobody else is gonna give you anything for that, but since I feel sorry for you, I'll give you two dollars."

It didn't seem like a very good deal, especially since we were counting on a fortune, but what could we do? We didn't feel like lugging the cash register around anymore. Johnny and I looked back and forth between ourselves and silently agreed. "OK," I said.

But the fat man wasn't about to give up two whole dollars as easy as that. "Wait a minute," he said, and went in the back room. When he came back out he was carrying a piece of paper, which he sat on the counter in front of us. "One of you needs to fill out this form," he said. "It doesn't matter which one."

The form asked for a name and address. "What do you need that for?" I asked, suspiciously. "We're not gonna fill out any forms."

"Suit yourself," the fat man said. "But if you don't fill it out, I can't give you any money."

"Go on, fill it out," Johnny encouraged me. "We didn't steal anything."

I figured what the hell. How the hell were they going to find me? I filled it out, though of course I was clever enough to use a false name and address.

Then the fat man produced an ink pad from under the counter. He wanted me to put my thumb print on the form. There was a box on it for that purpose. I was reluctant, but Johnny encouraged me. I figured I had come this far, so what the hell. I stuck my thumb in the ink and printed my thumb print on the form.

The fat man snatched the form from the counter and held it before him triumphantly. There was something about his manner that made me suspect a trick, and I got scared. The cops would track me down and arrest me, I thought. That cop I gave the finger to could identify me, and Charles the bus driver knew who I was. All sorts of things like that flashed through my mind. I broke into a cold sweat. "Hey, give me that back!" I blurted out. "I don't care about the two dollars. You can just keep the cash register."

"You don't want the two dollars?" the fat man asked. He seemed surprised. He was still holding my form.

"No, I don't want the two dollars. I've changed my mind. I don't want to sell the cash register. Forget about it. You can just have it," I said nervously.

"Well, OK. I'll take it," the fat man said, smiling broadly. "If you insist."

"Hey, wait a minute!" Johnny broke in. "I didn't agree to that. Let me sign the form. I want that two dollars!"

"Your buddy signed the form," the fat man said. "That means it's his. And he just gave it to me."

I didn't care about the cash register anymore. "Give me that form," I said. "You don't need it now."

"Look, I'm tearing it up," the fat man said. He tore the form once down the middle.

"Now give it to me," I said.

"It's OK. I'll just throw it away."

"No, I want it. I'll throw it away myself."

"Look, here it goes," the fat man said. He stuck the form beneath the counter. "It's in the trash now," he said.

"Well, get it back out and give it to me."

"No," he said.

"You're a crook!" Johnny said.

The fat man smiled and chuckled. His teeth were yellow and rotten.

"You big fat-ass crook!" Johnny yelled at him.

The fat man stopped smiling. "Alright, I've had enough of this," he said. "Get out of here, you damn kids, before I call the cops. I know you stole that cash register. Now get out of here or I'll have you arrested."

There was nothing else to do but leave. I was out the door first. "Fuck you, fat ass!" Johnny yelled back as he stood in the doorway. Then we took off running down the street.

The pawn shop man didn't try to chase us. After running a couple of blocks, we ducked down an alley to catch our breath. "Why didn't you take the two dollars?" Johnny asked me.

"Man, I didn't want the cops to come and get me."

"The cops won't do shit," Johnny said. "They don't even give a damn."

"That's easy for you to say. That fat son of a bitch has my thumb print."

Johnny didn't say anything more for a while, and neither did I. We wandered around through the city streets. It was still pretty exciting to be downtown. At least I thought so. After a while I stopped worrying about the cops. We sat down on a bench and lit up a couple of cigarettes. I didn't give a damn about the two dollars. I had wanted a hundred. "Well, at least we don't have to lug that cash register around anymore," I said.

Johnny screwed up his face. Only then did I notice that he wasn't having as good a time as I was. "You idiot, you cost us two dollars," he said. "We could have at least gone to eat in Woolworth."

We finished our cigarettes in silence, then flicked them away. "So what the hell are we gonna do now? We don't even have the money for a coke or a plate of French fries," Johnny said, dejected.

22

We were left wandering around downtown with no money and nothing to do and no place to go. I had shown myself to be a pretty sorry excuse for a criminal. I had let Johnny down once again, and that made me depressed. We didn't even have enough money to get the bus, so we were trying to think of how to get some. That way at least we could get out of there and get home.

Eventually, we found ourselves in front of the convention center. The enormous building was wide open. The place had a lot of doors for people to exit through when the events were over, and all the doors were open onto the surrounding streets. We peeked in one of the doors, and since there didn't seem to be anybody around, we went on in.

The building was old and run down, and it was dark inside. There was a breeze coming through, but it was a stale, foul smelling breeze. Everything was locked up. The concession stands were closed, with metal screens pulled down over them. It smelled like piss and vomit, especially near the bathrooms. The trash hadn't been taken out and was overflowing the trash barrels. There were puddles of sticky crap on the concrete floor.

We had never been in the building except when there was some kind of event, like maybe a basketball game, going on, and now the place was strangely silent. We were quiet too, because we kept expecting to run into somebody.

We went into the auditorium. There had just been a concert the night before, and nobody had cleaned up yet, so there was garbage strewn all over the large room. We thought maybe we could find some change, maybe even some bills. We walked up the stairs into the stands and walked down the rows of wooden seats, looking under all the seats, most of which hadn't been flipped back up yet. There was a lot of regular trash, like plastic cups and hotdog wrappers, but there was no money to speak of. We found some nickels and pennies, maybe a couple of quarters. Somebody must have been there before us and got all the bills. Probably the janitor. And now he was out drinking beer with the money instead of sweeping up.

Instead, we found a bunch of roaches, some pretty big. By this point we knew these were worth saving. We found a plastic baggie to put them in, and a pack of rolling papers with a few papers left in it.

I even found a roach clip, a hemostat. "Ha! Look what I found!" We both saw it at about the same time, but I got there quicker. It was sitting right up on the arm of the seat, and I snatched it up. It still had a roach clamped in it.

"You owe me that for giving away my money," Johnny said.

"No way, man."

I'm sure we would have found more stuff too, if some guy hadn't come in and run us off. When we saw him he was down on the floor. "Hey, what are y'all doing up there?!" he yelled up at us. You could tell from the uniform that he was the janitor. He wanted to keep all the loot for himself. We had to run for it.

Once we got out of the convention center we looked around for a place to smoke our reefer. But there were people everywhere and we didn't know the area very good. Even when we went down an alley, a car or a truck would come down it and we'd have to act like we weren't doing anything.

Finally, we found an abandoned building down one of the alleys. The windows were boarded up, and weeds and weed trees were growing up out of the cracks in the pavement near the build-ing.

The back door of the building was ajar. We pushed it open with our shoulders and went in. There was a very small room just inside the door. There was another room further back, but it was pitch black. No light got back there at all. And in fact there wasn't much light in the first room either once we shut the door. We had stirred up the dust and you could see it swirling in the light that filtered in around the boards over the windows. There was a big hole in the middle of the floor with a cargo chute running down it. Workers could throw boxes down the chute and store them in the basement. We couldn't see to the bottom of the chute.

We had to stand right by the hole because there wasn't any place else to stand. Johnny had the baggie with the roaches in his pocket and he pulled it out. The rolling papers were strawberry-flavored double-wide, which were about the coolest we'd ever seen. We had practiced on tobacco since the last time we tried to smoke reefer, and though reefer was different, drier and rougher, the principle was the same. Johnny unraveled the roaches into the pink rolling paper and I rolled them up. We put the joint on the roach clip immediately since it was so cool that we had to try it out.

But we still didn't know how to smoke pot. We still hadn't caught on about how long you were supposed to keep the smoke in your lungs. This joint smoked a lot better than my previous attempt, however, so I was still getting a bit of a buzz. It got me dizzy and giddy. And the same for Johnny. We were joking around as we smoked, laughing and cutting up. There wasn't much of anyplace to stand, except around the hole in the floor. I laughed so hard that I wasn't watching what I was doing, and I stepped off the edge of the hole and fell down the chute, tumbling down head over heels. I rolled all the way down the chute and tumbled off onto the floor at the bottom and flopped out on my back.

Johnny was laughing his ass off. "Ha ha, you dumbass! Serves you right!"

I let him laugh. I didn't say anything.

"That was funny as shit. You should have seen the look on your face when you stepped off that ledge," Johnny went on.

I hadn't hurt myself, though at first it kind of shocked me. I felt like I should be hurt. I felt like I should be dead, or knocked out at least. It was dark down there, and I just laid there on my back. I closed my eyes. It was cool and quiet down there in the basement. My breathing was slow and steady. I felt calm and contented. I heard a truck go by in the alley. It rattled the building.

"Hey, you OK down there?" Johnny called down.

I didn't say anything. I pretended I had been knocked unconscious.

Johnny bent down and looked into the hole. I could see the outline of his form , but he couldn't see me down there in the blackness. "Hey! Hey Tommy! Quit fucking around!" he yelled. "Hey Tom! Say something!"

I lay there in the dark and felt high. Listening to Johnny, I felt like busting out laughing.

Johnny was getting worried. He was getting paranoid. Maybe he had smoked the pot better than me. "Oh shit! Oh fuck!" Johnny said, and I heard him shuffling around up above me. "Shit man, fuck! What the hell do I do now?"

I chuckled to myself. I bet Johnny is sorry now, I thought. He's not mad at me anymore.

Johnny opened the door wider so he could see better. He looked down into the hole but I still don't think he could see me very well. "Hey Tommy, are you OK?" he yelled down. I didn't answer him. I chuckled to myself some more. Besides the sympathy angle, I guess I wanted to punish him for being mad at me, and to rattle him since he always seemed so calm and cool. "Come on. Let's get out of here," he said.

Johnny finally found his way down to the basement. He found the staircase in the dark room at the front of the building and came down and found his way into the room where I was lying on my back. I probably looked pretty bad, all covered with dirt.

He shook me. I didn't respond. "Wake up!" he said. "Oh shit! Oh fuck! What do I do now!" He was flipping out.

I opened my eyes. "Ha!" I said. "I had you going!"

"What?!"

I stood up and started dusting myself up.

"You were knocked out!" Johnny said.

"No, I wasn't, you idiot."

"You fucking asshole!" he yelled. He gave me a shove. "I wish you would have killed yourself!"

We got out of the building. My clothes were filthy and I was scratched and bruised.

We were short on the bus fare, but I managed to bum a dime from a businessman, and that made up the difference. When the bus showed up it wasn't Charles driving. It was just a woman bus driver who didn't have any reason to ban us from her bus, at least not yet. We got on and went to the back and sat in our usual seats. They were the best seats on the bus, I thought, wondering why nobody else ever seemed to want them. We didn't talk much, just watched the scenery go by. The thing with the pawn shop man was bugging me. I felt I had really lost face with Johnny over that and the thing with the cop. Maybe on some level I had even fallen down the hole on purpose, just so Johnny would feel sorry for me.

The bus drove us out of the city, and soon we were back in more familiar territory.

"By the way, where's the rest of that joint," I asked.

"I threw all that stuff away when you fell down the hole," Johnny said.

"What about the roach clip?"

"I threw that away too."

Son of a bitch. I knew he was lying. Especially about the roach clip. But I figured I deserved it, so I was willing to let it go. Maybe he threw away the joint, I thought. I doubt it, but maybe. But I knew damn well he wouldn't have thrown away that roach clip.

Of course Johnny hadn't sworn off girls as I had. In fact I wasn't at all sure that I had done so myself, though I was still worried about that thing with Sheila. Sometimes we went to the pizza place or the mall and looked at girls, but for the most part neither of us could get up the nerve to talk to them.

When it didn't look like I was going to be much help in that department, Johnny turned to Harold for advice. Harold knew perfectly well what our problem was. You needed a car if you were going to get any pussy, he told us. You couldn't reasonably expect to get any without one. "What are you gonna do," he asked, "pick her up on the bus?"

Harold's old station wagon had been broken down for a month, rusting in the barn behind Harold's house. Harold tinkered with it once in a while, but he really didn't know what he was doing. Sometimes he got pissed off and hit it with a hammer. Me and Johnny helped him to hit it with the hammer. Then he finally got somebody who knew what they were doing to take a look at it. He paid the guy a few bucks and got him a case of beer to drink while he worked on the car.

The guy who knew what he was doing was able to get the car moving, but then it turned out the battery was about dead. Every time we wanted to go out cruising we had to get a jump from Harold's mom's car and keep the car running no matter what. If it stalled, we had to jump out and push it to the side of the road and wait until somebody came along to give us a jump. This got to be a real pain in the ass. There was no way to pick up any girls with the car in this state, even me and Johnny knew that. And the car was showing signs of not wanting to start at all anymore, even with a jump.

We decided to steal a battery. We got a jump and drove around looking for a good car. Harold drove and Johnny sat beside him in the front seat and I sat in the back.

Soon enough we saw a truck in a church parking lot. There were no other cars in the lot and the closest houses were across a field. The truck looked new, so we figured it would have a good battery. Harold parked and we got out and lifted the hood of the truck. The battery didn't look like a very new one, but it looked a lot better than ours. We figured if nothing else this battery would work for a while and we could drive around and look for a better one.

All we had brought along was a screwdriver. We didn't think about bringing a wrench. I guess we hadn't planned this out very well. We tried to pry the clamps up off the terminals with the screwdriver, but they were clamped on too tight. There was a lot of corrosion built up over the clamps and the terminals. We bashed at the clamps with the butt of the screwdriver to try to loosen them up, and scraped at the corrosion buildup. We were getting the clamps loose but it was taking awhile.

A big black guy came riding over the top of the hill on his lawn mower. He popped up all of a sudden. We had heard him off in the distance, over on the far side of the hill, but just hadn't paid any attention. Now he was heading straight for us, and I thought we were in trouble. I didn't think he would kick our ass, though he could have if he wanted to. He just looked too clean cut, in a neat new uniform, like a church sort of guy. But I thought for sure he was going to bitch us out and run us off at least.

Johnny and Harold weren't paying any attention. Harold had found a stone and the two of them were taking turns bashing at the clamps. "Hey," I said. "This must be that guy's truck."

"Don't fucking worry about him," Harold said.

The black guy didn't come all the way up to us. When he got about ten yards away he veered off. He hadn't been cutting grass, just raking leaves. He was towing a trailer with a big mound of them piled up in it. He drove to the other end of the parking lot and stopped by a dumpster, but he didn't unload the leaves. Instead he just stood there, glaring at us, watching us like a hawk. He didn't take his eyes off us, but he didn't make any move to come after us.

Maybe he didn't think it was worth it to fuck with us for a battery.

After a bit more bashing, the rock loosened up the clamps and we got the battery out of the guy's truck. Harold turned off his car and we switched the batteries. We put the old battery in the black guy's truck, but we didn't bother to hook it up. We figured, let that guy mess with it if he wanted.

24

Now all three of us sat up front in the big car. I got the window seat. We chipped in for some gas and went for a drive.

Harold said now we'd be able to get some pussy for sure. Maybe Harold really could set something up, I thought. In one way I hoped he could, but at the same time I dreaded it.

But it was too early for that yet. We had to kill some time while we waited. Harold knew a way to lock his horn in place so it went off continually. We drove crazy like that down old country roads with the horn blaring. When a car came the other way Harold would swerve over into their lane and act like he was going to hit them. When we came across somebody walking down the road we would yell at them, "Out of the road, motherfucker!"

Some of the curves in the road were blind, but Harold didn't care. It just made things a little bit more exciting. At one point we roared around a blind curve in the wrong lane and there was a tan LTD coming right for us. It seemed only inches away. There was a gray-haired man driving. I saw his face since he was right there in front of us. He had his mouth wide open in surprise. I could've sworn I saw his hair standing straight up too!

The guy cut his wheels and swerved off the road onto the dirt shoulder. Luckily there was a shoulder. Otherwise he would have gone into the ditch. We kept driving. The guy in the LTD put a blue light on top of his car and whipped around and came after us.

"Oh shit!" Johnny said.

Harold didn't seem worried. "Ah, it's just old man Anderson," he said. He slowed down and found a place to pull over.

Harold knew the cop since the cop hung out with Harold's dad at the feed store and drank beer. The cop came up to the window of the car. He didn't have his uniform on. "Hey, Mr. Anderson," Harold said.

"Harold!" the cop said. "I came out when I heard that horn. I should've known it was you!"

"Yeah, it's me," Harold said.

"What the hell is wrong with you, boy? Driving like a lunatic! If I was on duty I'd run your silly ass in."

Harold shrugged his shoulders.

"And what's this shit with the horn? Why were you laying on your goddamn horn like that? You got no sense in your head?"

"It's broke, sir. It got stuck. I was trying to get it loose. That's why I was driving all erratic like I was."

"Your registration is expired, and I know damn well you've got no insurance on this thing so I ain't even gonna ask," Anderson said.

"I'm getting some next week," Harold said.

"Get the hell home, Harold."

"Yes sir, Sergeant Anderson, sir," Harold said, and saluted.

"Don't give me that shit. I'll be by your house in a half an hour and that car better be parked in the driveway."

"I gotta give my friends a ride home, and they live all the way across town," Harold said.

"Alright, an hour. And I don't want to see you out on the street again until you've got this car registered and got your insurance."

"OK, boss," Harold said.

"Aren't you on probation now, too?" the cop asked.

"No sir. I'm done with that now."

The cop shook his head in dismay as he walked back to his car. He got in his car and drove around us. Harold waited until he had got well out of sight, then he turned the car around and drove in the other direction.

"We'll go down some roads where we can't get in any trouble," Harold said. We stopped and got a pint of liquor first. There was a bait shop that would sell it to Harold. We passed the whiskey around as we drove.

The roads we ended up on were even further out in the country. It took us awhile to get there. The roads out there were just one lane and they were part gravel, but mostly just dirt. They were bumpy and uneven. We had a good buzz going now off the liquor and we did the same thing, drove around like nuts. It raised a cloud of dirt when we drove. You could look back and see where we had been, a cloud snaking up along the path of the road. By this time it was sunset, and you could see the dirt cloud in the diminishing light, rising up over the bare trees of the woods. The cops would see where you were if you tried to do it in the day, Harold said. For the same reason we didn't do the horn thing anymore.

There were little wooden bridges here and there going over a creek, just big enough for one car. We flew up onto them and barely touched them, like going over a jump ramp.

When we came down off one of the bridges a curve came up too quick, and we slid around the curve and smashed into a fence post. Johnny's head cracked into mine.

It was completely dark now. We got out of the car and looked at the damage. The fence post was bent over. The back door on the passenger side was knocked in and wouldn't open. We all tried to pull it open, and kicked at it a few times. Harold got in the back seat and tried kicking it open from inside, but it was no use. It was better off closed anyway. Once we got it open it wouldn't have closed back. We sat on the hood of the car and finished off the rest of the pint. I had a headache now, but the liquor helped.

Johnny was annoyed. He said he thought we were supposed to be getting some pussy, rather than trying to kill ourselves off. But Harold said it was no problem. He said now it was time to start looking.

We drove back toward town. When we got back into our home area we stopped in at the Burger Chef. People our age and a little bit older hung out there. Harold knew some people in a car in the parking lot and he stayed out there to talk to them. Me and Johnny went inside the restaurant and stood in line to get some food.

Harold came in and got in line behind us. We were up to the counter by that time and were giving our order to the girl who worked there behind the counter. Her name was Heidi. That's what it said on her name tag. Harold knew her from public school. He butted in front of us and said, "I'd like a Heidi burger, fries and a shake."

Heidi had blond hair, and she was kind of plump and had big tits. She wasn't bad.

Heidi didn't say anything, but she blushed. She got our food off the warmer and gave it to us. Harold stayed up at the counter and talked to Heidi while we went into the dining room and ate our food and fooled around. We were nervous at the prospect of getting girls, and we kind of reverted back to childhood, laughing and cutting up and being silly.

I didn't like pickles on my burgers. They were all over the burgers at this place, a whole handful of them. I picked one off my burger and threw it up on the big plate glass window and it stuck there. Then I threw a few more. They all stuck up on the window. They had ketchup and mustard on them that served as glue. Johnny got his off his burger and threw them up there too. We flung them like Frisbees. They would hit the window and slide down the glass a bit before they stuck, leaving a trail of red-and-yellow slime. The pickles looked real scummy up there. They went well with the décor of the place, since it looked like they hadn't cleaned up the garbage for several days.

I didn't think Harold's approach was going to work, but it did. Harold said Heidi was going to call up a couple of her friends for me and Johnny. We got back in the car and drove around some more, then we went back to the restaurant and picked Heidi up when she got off work. There were no friends. I was disappointed, but at the same time mostly relieved. We parked in a dark parking lot by a baseball diamond. Harold and Heidi sat up front kissing and making out. We were sitting in the back seat, me and Johnny. The radio was on.

It was getting pretty boring. Johnny reached up to the front seat and ran his hand through Harold's hair. Harold left it in there for a while until he figured out that the girl's two hands were somewhere else. Then he smacked at Johnny's hand. "Get the fuck off me," he said, and went back to kissing Heidi.

We laughed our asses off. Johnny tried it again in a couple of minutes. Again it worked for a while. Then Harold turned around and climbed halfway over the seat and grabbed Johnny and punched him several times.

Harold and Heidi decided they'd like it better in the back of the station wagon, so me and Johnny got up front and Harold let down the back seat. He had a hard time doing it because the door was knocked in on the back seat from the wreck earlier. Then, while Heidi waited outside, Harold spread a blanket on the bed of the station wagon. Harold and Heidi pointed their heads in our direction but too far back for Johnny to run his fingers through Harold's hair. Johnny tried to grab his hair one time but he could only just brush it, and Harold swatted his hand right away.

Harold and Heidi kissed some more. Then Harold took Heidi's pant's off and got on top of her and put his dick in her. He started fucking her.

We were supposed to just listen to the radio while this was going on, I guess, and we tried to act like it was no big deal. There was light from a distant street light and we watched the action. It was the first time I had ever seen anything like that.

Heidi had to stop and get a coke at the Seven-Eleven. It had to be a coke in a bottle since it was for birth control. The reason it had to be a bottle was that she was going to shake it up and spray it up her pussy, and a can wouldn't work for that. Unfortunately, we didn't get to watch. She went into the bathroom at the Pizza Hut and sprayed it.

Heidi lived way out in the country. We had to get on the expressway to get to Heidi's house. On the way back on the expressway Harold let the front seat back all the way. The seat in Harold's car went back an unusually long way. He stuck his foot up on the steering wheel and steered with his foot. Then he lit up a cigarette and relaxed. He controlled the gas pedal with a baseball bat he carried in the car. It didn't work that well for the brake, however. When he wanted to put on the brake he had to get his foot down and jump forward in the seat.

25

Johnny was obsessed with getting a girl. And as I had become less sure of myself, Johnny had gained confidence. I knew he was bound to find a girl on his own sooner or later, with or without my help.

Sure enough, one day after school, toward the middle of December, Johnny called me on the phone. He said, "Come over and bring some smokes."

"What for?" I asked.

"Hurry up. It's an emergency. This girl I met at the pizza place is next door babysitting and she called me and said to come over with some smokes. I told her I was doing the dishes but it doesn't take that long, so hurry up."

I was reading a book and didn't want to be bothered. "Why don't you just go buy some?"

"I can't do that," Johnny said in an anguished voice. "She might see me leave the house."

I didn't have any cigarettes of my own so I had to steal a pack of Larks from my mother. With the pack in the pocket of my jacket, I walked the few blocks to Johnny's house. "What is this shit?" he said when I showed him the Larks.

"That's what my mother smokes."

"They'll have to do," he said with a sigh as he took the cigs from me. "Come on."

"You want me to go over there too?"

"Yeah, what's wrong? Come on."

I got the feeling that the thing about the cigarettes was mainly an excuse to get me to come along. Johnny still felt he needed my help in talking to girls.

We walked next door and went around to the side door. A girl came to the door. She had funny buck teeth that made her look real cute, like a little chipmunk. "This is Brenda," Johnny said.

I already knew her. Her brother was on my baseball team in fourth grade. Her dad was the coach, and she used to hang around at the practices and help her dad with the equipment. Back then she was a kind of a tomboy, but not anymore. She was a year or two older than me, and went to public school.

"Hi Brenda," I said. "You remember me?"

"Yeah, you're Tommy Donaldson. I haven't seen you in ages. How's your mom and dad?"

"Oh, they're fine. What's Brett up to? Is he still playing base-ball?"

"Yeah, he is."

"Is your dad still coach?"

"No. He still goes to watch the practices, though," Brenda said.

This conversation annoyed Johnny. I guess I could see why.

"I've got some cigs," Johnny said, pulling out the pack of Larks.

We went into the house and Brenda showed us into the family room. There were a bunch of toys scattered all over the place, a real mess. There was also a Christmas tree in the corner by the sliding door. It had a bunch of glass balls and assorted ornaments on it but the lights were turned off. I thought about plugging them in, but nobody else seemed to care, so I didn't bother.

"Come on in and have a seat," Brenda said. "I put the kids to bed." It was the middle of the afternoon. Brenda was on the phone with somebody. She picked the receiver up off the counter and said, "Gotta go now."

Then she turned to us and said, "I usually have a pack of cigarettes with me, but I'm all out today."

Brenda brushed aside a load of plastic junk and sat down on the couch, and Johnny sat in a chair near her. I rolled a yellow dump truck onto the floor and sat at the other end of the couch. Johnny was closer to her than I was. Right away he opened the Larks. "These suck," he said. "Dumbass here brought them over."

"Yeah, they're mine," I confessed.

"They're not even his!" Johnny said. "He stole them from his mom! If I had known he was gonna bring over this shit, I never would've called him."

What's his problem? I wondered.

Johnny passed cigarettes around and we lit up. Johnny lit Brenda's cigarette. The Larks tasted like shit. They had charcoal in the filters to protect you from cancer. Or something. We all took a few draws. We were sitting back and relaxing. The people who lived there had ashtrays out for company.

"They're not that bad," Brenda said.

"Better than nothing," I said.

A little girl came out of the back and stood in the middle of the rug. She stood there awhile, looking at us. The way we were sitting, I was the only one who saw her.

"I smell smoke," the girl, who was about five, finally said.

Brenda rolled her eyes, annoyed. She turned her head and looked at the girl. "Yeah, we're smoking. So what? Go back to bed."

"Who's that?" the girl said, pointing at me.

"Nobody. Rumpelstiltskin, OK? Now mind your own business. Go back to bed."

"I'm not tired. Can I get up now?"

"No! Get back in bed. Go to sleep. And don't wake up your brother."

"But I'm not tired," the girl whined.

"Yes, you are! Now go in there and close your eyes and go to sleep," Brenda said.

We sat around for a while and talked to Brenda about public school. The public school was right in our subdivision, right down the street. It was a lot better than going to Catholic school. Everybody knew that. Brenda said it sucked, but she had to admit it sounded better than Mother Goose. For one thing, it wasn't just suburb kids. There were different kinds of people going there. There were people from the working class, and even black people. Nobody cared what you did and you could get away with anything. You could do whatever you wanted. They didn't care if you did your work or not.

"I'm thinking about going there myself," Johnny said. He told Brenda that. I didn't take him seriously. He said his parents were sick of paying all that money for him to get yelled at by nuns.

Of course I would have liked to go there myself, but I knew my parents wouldn't go for it.

After a while we smoked more cigarettes. Then it was time to go. "I guess I gotta clean this shithole up now," Brenda said. "Thanks for coming over. Thanks for the cigarettes, Tom."

We went out onto the porch. "Say hello to Brett for me," I said as we walked away.

26

The next day after school Johnny went up to the pizza place to meet Brenda again. He didn't invite me along this time, since now he was worried that Brenda might like me better than him. But he still felt he needed some back-up, so he took Chip. They stayed there all afternoon, hanging out with Brenda and her friends. It was a Friday, and that evening they came over to my house.

Johnny was happy and excited because he thought now he had a girlfriend. Even Chip thought he might have a girl. Fat chance, I thought, about Chip anyway, but still I was bummed out about the whole situation. We stole two half-pints from my parents' liquor cabinet, one of bourbon, one of vodka. My parents didn't usually have any liquor to speak of, but there had been a party at my dad's office and he had brought home the extra liquor because no one else wanted it. Of course it wasn't in half-pint bottles. We supplied the half-pint bottles ourselves and filled them up off the fifths of bourbon and vodka my dad had brought home.

Johnny carried one of the half-pints in his pocket and Chip carried the other as we started out walking through the subdivision. Johnny said he knew where there was a party. He said it was at the apartment complex, in their party room, so we decided to go over there and check it out.

I was talking about something with Chip, so we didn't notice it when Johnny lagged back. All of a sudden one of the half-pint bottles flew over our heads. It flew down the middle of the street and shattered when it hit the pavement. I turned around. Johnny was screwing up his face from drinking the liquor. Even so, he was chuckling.

"Asshole!" I said. "That was for all three of us."

Johnny kept chuckling.

I realized that Johnny was anxious over the thing with Brenda, but that made me even more annoyed. "Well, you don't get any more," I said.

Johnny didn't seem to care. We kept walking and soon we were at the edge of the subdivision. There were woods to one side of the road. I got the bottle of vodka from Chip, took a swig, and handed it back.

"Let me carry that other bottle," Johnny said. He wasn't walking so good. He was already beginning to weave.

"No way," I said.

"Come on, man. I won't drink any." He was slurring his words. "Don't you trust me?"

"No," I said.

I should have carried it myself. As soon as I wasn't looking, Johnny jumped on Chip and took the bottle away from him. He ran off a few yards and guzzled the vodka down before I could get to him. I was amazed at how fast he guzzled it. He threw that one down the street too, even farther than the first one. Johnny had a good arm.

This time I wasn't even mad. It didn't seem worth the effort. We were almost at the apartment complex. "Maybe we can get a drink at this party," I said.

"I don't think we need any more to drink," Johnny said. He was really fucked up now. He was lurching from side to side. I did my best to ignore him.

Johnny was lagging back again. I didn't pay any attention to him, since there was no more liquor left for him to steal. Then all at once Chip sprinted away, and I felt something warm on the back of my pants leg. I turned around. Johnny had his dick out and was pissing on me. "Oh, shit! You motherfucker!"

Johnny took off running. I ran after him. He was running down the street with his dick out. "I'll kill you!" I yelled as I chased him down the street.

Johnny could usually outrun me, but this time he was so drunk that I ran him down easily. As he cut off the road into the woods to evade me, I gave him a shove from behind and he fell face down into a pile of rotting leaves. He rolled over onto his back and started giggling hysterically. He still had his dick out.

I stood over him. "I should kick your ass for that!"

"Ah, leave him alone. He's drunk," Chip said.

"Shut up, Chip," I said. I reared back my leg to give Johnny a good kick, in the ass or wherever.

But before I could do it Johnny started playing with his dick and pretending to be masturbating. "Oh Brenda! Oh Brenda! Oh Brenda!" he said. He was laughing the whole time.

What an idiot, I thought. I forgot about kicking his ass. I said, "You stay here and jerk off, idiot. We're going to the party without you."

Chip wanted to stay and make sure Johnny was alright, but I grabbed him and made him come along. Me and Chip walked on down the road. But we hadn't got twenty yards when Johnny jumped up and came running after us. "Wait for me!" he yelled after us. At least he had his dick back in his pants.

The night was turning into a real bummer. Now I had to go to the party with piss all over my jeans.

When we got to the party place we stood back from the building and looked the place over. We saw several people go in, but they were all much older than us, in their twenties and thirties at least. "Looks like a great party, Johnny," I said sarcastically. "Where did you hear about it?"

"From my parents," Johnny said.

"Good source," Chip said, sarcastically.

"But they're not gonna be here," Johnny said. "So don't worry."

We went into the lobby of the building. It had a marble floor and a high ceiling, and there were potted trees set around the room. Music was playing upstairs. Light rock, like Tony Orlando and Dawn, or maybe The Captain and Tennille. Since the party was upstairs, there was no one in the lobby except for us. We stood around wondering whether or not to go upstairs.

I decided I was going to try and bum a drink. By this point I didn't care what Johnny and Chip did. I started up the stairs. Chip didn't know whether to follow me or not. He was lagging back at the bottom of the stairs before finally trotting up after me. When I got halfway up I heard a crashing and clattering. I turned around and saw that Johnny had pulled over one of the potted trees. He had busted the tree's pot and exposed its ball of roots and dirt, and he was dragging the tree around by its branches. He was slinging it around, strewing dirt and leaves all over the lobby. Then, all at once, he spun the tree around in an arc and launched it right at us. We ducked to avoid it. The tree crashed into the metal railing of the staircase, sending dirt and branches flying in our faces.

Amazingly, no one upstairs seemed to have heard it. But it still seemed like time to get the hell out of there. Johnny ran away from us down a hall toward the indoor pool. We followed him. The pool was all lit up and steaming. Before we could stop him, Johnny took off his pants and shirt and shoes and jumped into the pool in his underwear.

Johnny knew how to swim, but he wasn't swimming. It was more like flopping around like a wounded fish.

There was a deck on the second floor, overlooking the pool. Ten or fifteen people from the party were out on the deck. Some of them saw Johnny and started laughing at him for flopping around like that. When he got out of the pool, they laughed even harder. He was standing right there below the deck. One of the men yelled, "Hey, look at that kid down there in his underwear!"

Johnny gave him the finger. "Hey, fuck you!" he yelled. "I'll kick your ass!"

"Shut up, kid! Get lost!" the man yelled back.

Me and Chip were standing by the exit, yelling at Johnny to get out of there.

Johnny pulled down his underwear and whipped out his dick. He jiggled it at the man. "Suck on this!" he said.

Then Johnny took off his underwear. He wadded up the wringing wet underwear and threw it at the man on the deck. The man dodged the underwear and it hit the lady next to him right in the face. SPLAT!!!

We yelled at Johnny to come on, and the three of us took off running through the apartment complex. Johnny struggled to get into his clothes as he ran. We darted down a path into the woods. Luckily, nobody seemed to be following us. We walked through the woods and came out along a four-lane road. A dirt path ran alongside the road, shielded by trees and set far enough from the road that we could walk on it without attracting attention. By this point Johnny had got his clothes back on. His hair was still wet and he was shivering in the chilly night air, but at least that seemed to have sobered him up a bit. Chip gave him a cap to wear.

"That was pretty embarrassing," Chip said as we walked.

"I thought it was kind of funny," I said. "I hope his parents were there after all."

"Hey! What the hell is he doing now?!" Chip said.

Johnny had sobered up just enough to cause more trouble. He came out of the woods with a big log in his arms. He lifted it over his head and ran toward the road.

"Oh shit!" I said.

"Johnny, put that down!" Chip yelled.

Too late. Johnny heaved the log at a Cadillac that was speeding by. The log bounced back off, but it shattered the rear passenger window. The Cadillac screeched to a halt several yards down the road.

We ran back into the woods. It wasn't long before we heard police sirens coming from the road. We didn't stop to rest until we were deep into the woods. Once I caught my breath I told Johnny, "You have got to be the stupidest motherfucker I have ever met in my life."

Johnny smiled. He seemed about ready to laugh or say something stupid. Then he staggered to one side and stepped off the path into a sink hole. "Ouch! Shit!" he said. He was lying on his back in a patch of brambles that had broken his fall.

The cops didn't seem to be coming into the woods after us, but Chip was getting nervous and wanted to get away. I thought it was riskier to be walking around on the street. "If the cops catch you, you'd better not say anything about me and Johnny," I said. Chip left and walked home.

Johnny was too drunk to get out of sink hole without help. Especially since every time he moved around the brambles poked into him. "Help me up out of here," he said.

"No way."

"I'm freezing my fucking ass off!" Johnny said, shivering.

"It's your own damn fault," I said, but I threw him my jacket to bundle up in.

"Let's go back to the party," Johnny said. Then he passed out. Except for that one swig I hadn't had anything to drink all night. I sat down on a log, shivering as the night got colder, and waited there while Johnny slept it off.

The next day at noon I was wandering around in the neighborhood and found myself by the pizza place. Johnny was still in bed with a hangover. And probably, I thought, pneumonia. I saw Brenda leaning up against a car in the parking lot, talking to some of her friends. I decided to go up to her. Though it made me nervous, there was something that drove me to do it.

Brenda didn't have a bad body, I noticed as I approached. I tried to cut through the rows of cars in a way where I could get a good look at her ass.

"Hi Brenda," I called as I came walking up.

She had already seen me coming. "Oh, Hi Tommy. What are you doing over there?"

"I was just walking by and I saw you here so I thought I'd come over and say hi."

"What's up with you?" Brenda said.

"I was with Johnny last night," I said. I had just intended to make small talk, but then for some reason it all came pouring out. I told Brenda all about what Johnny had done the night before. I told her about Johnny uprooting the plant, throwing the underwear in the woman's face, and throwing the log at the car. I especially made sure to tell her about the jerking off part. "He said, Oh Brenda! Oh Brenda! Oh Brenda!!!" I said. "Can you believe that? That's hilarious, isn't it?"

She didn't know what to say. She looked like she'd never heard anything so horrible before. Her friends, two girls who no doubt knew Johnny, were looking shocked and uncomfortable too. Finally, Brenda said, "Yeah, that's pretty funny."

None of us were laughing, and I started feeling kind of uncomfortable myself. "Well, I just stopped by to say hi. I guess I'll see you later," I said. I turned around and walked back across the parking lot.

That night Johnny banged on my front door. I saw him out my bedroom window and went down and answered the door. We stood out on the porch. "Did you tell Brenda I was jacking off and yelling her name?" Johnny asked.

"Yeah," I said.

"You dick! Why'd you tell her that?!"

I didn't really know myself. Maybe, as I told myself at the time, to get him back for his rampage of the night before. Or maybe it was because I sensed him slipping away, and didn't want to lose him as a friend. I hadn't set out to go to the pizza place that day, but I'm sure it was no accident that I ended up there. I shrugged my shoulders. "I don't know. It's true, isn't it?"

"So what? Now she won't even talk to me."

"And you think that's my fault?"

"Yes! You've got to call her and tell her you made that up."

"Why would I make something like that up? That wouldn't make any sense."

"I don't know. Because you're an asshole. Tell her that," Johnny said.

"Yeah, right."

"Just make something up."

"I don't want to call her," I said. The idea made me anxious. I felt I had made enough of a fool out of myself that day.

"You've got to," Johnny said.

"I don't have her number."

"I've got it right here." Johnny pulled a scrap of paper out of his pants pocket.

There was no way out of it. I felt bad about what I'd done to Johnny and would have undone it if I could have. We went inside and went up the stairs to my room and closed the door. I got on the phone and dialed Brenda's number. "Hello," I said. "Is Brenda there?" I was desperately hoping she wouldn't be there.

But she was. "Oh hi, Brenda. It's me, Tom. You know, Johnny's friend."

She seemed happy to hear from me. Maybe she likes me better than Johnny, I thought. I was beginning to realize that maybe that was what this was really all about for me. "Yeah, I'm doing OK," I said. "Hey Brenda, you know when I told you about Johnny jacking off and screaming your name?"

"Yeah?" she said. She sounded disappointed. I got the feeling she was hoping we were going to talk about something else.

"I just made that up," I said.

"Why?" Brenda asked. She sounded genuinely confused.

"Oh, I don't know. I just thought it would be funny. It was just a joke. That's the way I am. I always make stuff like that up. Johnny really didn't do anything like that."

"What about throwing that underwear in that woman's face?" Brenda asked.

"Oh, that part's true," I said. "I didn't make that up. Just the part about jacking off. That's the only thing I made up."

Brenda still seemed puzzled. She didn't seem at all convinced. "Did Johnny tell you to call me?" she asked.

"No. I just wanted to tell you this so you didn't get the wrong idea. I just like to joke around like that."

"Oh. OK," Brenda said.

"OK. See you later, Brenda." I hung up the phone, knowing that I hadn't done Johnny any good. And knowing, too, that after this I would be too embarrassed to ever try to get anywhere with Brenda myself.

"Did she believe you?" Johnny asked hopefully.

"Yeah. She seemed to," I lied.

Part Three

28

I didn't think that much about the episode with Brenda. I blocked it out of my mind. If Johnny said anything more about it, I don't remember it. But I'm sure it meant more to him than it did to me. I thought things were back to normal, and for what little remained of the semester, I guess they were. So I was shocked when Johnny announced over the Christmas break that he was going to public school. I can't say I felt betrayed. Maybe a little. Well, more than that, but we had talked so much about wanting to do it that I couldn't blame him, that was for sure. Johnny was excited to be going somewhere where there were girls worth having, rather than the usual stuck-up bitches he was always complaining about. I pretended to share his enthusiasm.

Still, when school started back I felt kind of lonely. Now I didn't hang out with Johnny much anymore. Even though he only lived a few blocks away, he had other things going on connected with his new school and seemed to want to make a clean break. I had thought the past few months had cemented our friendship, but maybe Johnny felt differently. I'm sure he had many reasons for transferring, but I can see now that one of them was to get away from me. While he had thought before that I might help him get a girlfriend, I believe now he thought that I was holding him back.

School was the same old shit. I never could get into it. It was just so damn boring. I never did my work. I couldn't be bothered. I had always felt this way, but now it was even worse. Now I was even less cooperative. What was the point? I had other friends at Mother Goose, I guess, but nobody I could really relate to.

Though I went through the motions, I couldn't even get into picking on Chip anymore. I just didn't fit in there. Though I didn't want to admit it to myself, losing Johnny to public school was a major blow. I missed him.

One day we were supposed to be doing math problems in class. I did two of them, but then I got bored with the whole thing. Mrs. Bream had gone out of the room for a minute while we did the problems. I was fooling around and talking to the people around me. The kid sitting in front of me was a fat, stupid kid. I snapped him in the ear with a plastic ruler. Then Mrs. Bream came back and was walking around the room helping people. She came up behind me and looked over my shoulder at my paper.

"You've made a good start, Tommy. Keep working. You'll get the hang of it," Mrs. Bream said, encouragingly. She acted like she didn't even know who I was. She acted like I was some kind of a retard.

"I already know how to do these problems. There's no reason for me to do any more," I said.

"Do the rest of them. Show me that you can do all ten of them," Mrs. Bream said.

She didn't get it. She was a slow learner. "Listen, I know how to do these problems, and you *know* that I know how to do these problems."

She tried to tell me something about how I needed more practice, but I wasn't buying it. She could kiss my ass.

Actually, I didn't mind math problems that much, and as Mrs. Bream knew, I was pretty good at them. But Johnny had been as bad an influence on me as I had been on him. We had always said that schoolwork was bullshit, and I still felt that way.

But Mrs. Bream wasn't quite ready to give up on me yet. She kept bothering me. One time I surprised her and did the assignment. Then when we were handing our papers in, the stack came around and I wadded my paper up and mashed it down in the middle of the pile of papers. I crushed the pile up some too to make it look fucked up. Then I threw the pile up on her desk. Mrs. Bream went through the papers, straightening them out. She picked my paper up and looked like she was real disgusted. I laughed. Everybody else laughed about it too.

After that I tried to make my papers look as shitty and unreadable as possible. One time I wadded the paper up a dozen times and rolled it around and crunched and crinkled it in my hands. I rubbed it on the wooden desk. And I drew stupid pictures all over the paper.

Mrs. Bream made a point of ignoring it. She just graded it and gave it back to me. She had even put a star on it. I felt like I was being drawn into her scheme. When she handed it back to me she said, "It's so sad that some poor children can't afford decent paper."

Then everybody laughed at me. That really burned me up.

I was tired of doing homework anyway. The next time I soaked my paper in the mop bucket and threw it up on her desk. She didn't ask me for any assignments for a while after that.

In class I fucked with everybody and sassed the teacher. I caused trouble and created disturbances. I sat in the back of the room and threw spitballs or launched paperclips with a rubber band. Mrs. Bream tried various things to shut me up and make me settle down. First she made me sit in the front row. But there was still too much trouble I could get into even there. Then she made me have my desk right up by hers so she could keep an eye on me. I couldn't see what anybody else was doing, but I could still mess with things on her desk and even get into her desk drawer if she left it unlocked.

So Mrs. Bream made me put my desk facing into the corner. What next, I wondered, a dunce cap? This was cruel and unusual punishment. There was nothing to look at except the plaster wall. When I tried to look over my shoulder Mrs. Bream yelled at me to turn back around.

January and most of February passed like that. Sometimes Mrs. Bream would let me sit with the rest of the class on a trial basis, but after a day or two I always did something to get sent back to the corner. "Since you insist on acting like a child," Mrs. Bream said, "I am forced to treat you like one." It was a long, boring winter. It almost made me want to do my work.

29

They couldn't watch me all the time. Though I didn't get much pleasure out of it anymore, I was constantly causing trouble. Maybe I felt that with Johnny gone I had to cause enough trouble for two. Or maybe I just wanted to fuck up so I could get thrown out of school. I had too much history here, and I was never going to live it down. Whatever it was, from this point on my trouble-making began to take on a more desperate character.

One day toward the end of February, a guy named Joe Wood-head had a smoke bomb out on the playground. Joe was a big oaf, an uncoordinated kid. He wasn't one of the ones I picked on. There was no reason to pick on him, and anyway he was a lot bigger than me.

He must have saved the smoke bomb from the Fourth of July. That was the only time you could get them in the stores.

There were no teachers around. Joe lit the smoke bomb in the middle of the parking lot and it smoked for a while and then went out. It was a round, red cherry bomb. The smoke blew away in the breeze, red smoke.

It wasn't very exciting. I had seen it a million times. Nobody cared. Everybody had seen it a million times. Once it had stopped smoking, Joe stomped on the smoke bomb. It cracked open and a bit more smoke filtered out and blew away in the breeze.

Joe had another one, a yellow M-80 type. "This oughta be a good one," he said. He was getting ready to light it up. But what was the point? He was just going to waste another one.

"Let me have that. I'll do something funny with it," I said.

"What are you gonna do with it?" Joe asked.

"I'm not saying. You'll see. It'll be something good."

Joe figured he could trust me, so he handed over the smoke bomb. He knew I had a good imagination when it came to mischief.

I went into the building ahead of the class, right before the recess period was over. We weren't supposed to go in early, but this policy wasn't strictly enforced, and nobody saw me. The front door was where the teachers generally hung out, and where they lined the kids up at the end of recess to let them back into the school. While they were busy doing that, I snuck in the back door.

The halls were deserted. I could have lit the smoke bomb in the bathroom, but that was too far away from our classroom and I figured nobody would have cared. And I didn't want to just throw it into the classroom because then nobody would come into the room. The teacher's desk drawer was a possibility, but I didn't want to light her papers on fire and burn down the school. Besides that, I reasoned, the drawer was too small. What I wanted was someplace that would contain the smoke, and maybe just let a little bit of it out, so the whole class would be back in the classroom, maybe even sitting at their desks, before anything happened.

There was a closet at the front of the room. I thought it was large enough to contain the smoke for a few minutes before it started coming out through the crack at the bottom. After I lit the smoke bomb I planned to sneak out the back door and around the school, go in through the front door, and come into the classroom last and act like I had no idea what was going on. I was going to act like I was as surprised as everybody else. More surprised, even. I lit the smoke bomb up and threw it into the closet.

The smoke started pouring out within about one second. Not just at the bottom, but all around the sides and at the top, streaming out. Billowing clouds of acrid, yellow smoke. It surprised the hell out of me. I panicked and started fanning at the smoke. I still thought I would have a few seconds to run away.

But people started coming in early. I heard them coming down the hall. The best thing to do still would have been to get the hell out of there. But the smoke was coming out so fast that it freaked me out. I went over and opened some of the windows.

I was still fanning at the smoke. People came into the classroom and took their seats and watched, laughing at me and my antics. I realized I must have looked real suspicious, so I sat down at my desk and tried to act cool, like I didn't know anything about it. But since my desk was right up there by the closet it looked like I had something to do with it anyway. Everybody just naturally assumed it was me who had done it.

The room was quickly filling up with smoke. The teacher came in. "What's going on in here?!" Mrs. Bream said. Smoke was curling all around my head. She saw me through the smoke. "Tommy! What have you done now?! Oh my God!"

"I didn't do it!" I said. I jumped up and started fanning at the smoke again.

She didn't believe me for an instant. "Get down to the principal's office right now!"

"But I didn't do it!" I repeated. "I don't know who did it. I was just trying to clear the smoke away."

"Now! Go to the principal's office now!" Mrs. Bream yelled. "And the rest of you, don't just sit there laughing. Evacuate the room immediately!"

I told the principal, Sister Rose, that I didn't do it. I told her Mrs. Bream had gone crazy when she saw the smoke and had just started looking for somebody to blame. "I think she's got it in for me, Sister," I said.

The principal had to go and see about the disaster in the classroom. I sat in her office and waited. When she came back, maybe
ten minutes later, she had Mrs. Bream with her. They stood over
me where I sat. "Tommy told me he doesn't know anything about
this incident," the nun said.

"He did it, Sister. I assure you," Mrs. Bream said.

"I don't know what she's talking about," I said.

"He says he didn't do it," the principal said.

"He did it. Believe me, Sister."

"Well, I know I can believe you, Mrs. Bream."

Just like that. "What kind of evidence is that? You have no
proof," I said. "She's lying," I told the principal.

"Now Tommy, you know Mrs. Bream wouldn't just make this
up," the old nun said.

They had made up their minds. I didn't bother protesting
anymore. It didn't matter what I said.

"What was that, tear gas? All the children are coughing and
choking!" Mrs. Bream said, in a tone of alarm.

"How should I know what it was?"

"You'd better tell us what that was!" Mrs. Bream said.

They acted like it was a terrorist gas attack or something.
The secretary came in too, another old lady. The three old ladies
grilled me, without success. Then they brought Father Hood over
from the church to try and scare me. As I think I mentioned earlier, they didn't bother him except in especially bad cases. It was
the first time I knew of that he'd been involved in school discipline since the *Sexbook* incident.

"It was a noxious yellow cloud, father. I think it may have
been chlorine gas," Mrs. Bream said.

I rolled my eyes. I was no longer afraid of the priest. He had
done his worst to me, and it had hardened me.

"You'd better tell us what that was, mister. You'll be severely dealt with if anyone is damaged," the priest said.

"You'd better pray that no one is harmed by that gas!" Mrs. Bream broke in. She was getting hysterical, I thought.

"If anyone is hospitalized it will be very important to the doctors to know what kind of gas they have been exposed to," Father Hood went on.

I shrugged my shoulders.

"It will go easier on you if you tell," the priest said.

I couldn't believe they didn't know what a goddamn smoke bomb was. "I don't know what it was. It could have been nerve gas for all I know," I said. "But it smelled like just a regular smoke bomb to me."

"Ah ha!" the priest exclaimed.

"Not that I'm saying I did it."

"That was no regular smoke bomb, Father. That was a cloud of noxious yellow gas," Mrs. Bream insisted.

The janitor came into the outer office and the secretary went out and talked to him. He had found the smoke bomb. The secretary came back in and said, "Mr. Blount has recovered the device." They all went out into the outer office and examined the smoke bomb. Then they came back in.

"You're really lucky, mister," Father Hood said.

"You're lucky that's all that was was a smoke bomb," Mrs. Bream said. She seemed kind of disappointed that it hadn't been mustard gas.

They couldn't have class with all that smoke in the classroom, so all the kids got to hang out in the cafeteria and fool around for the rest of the day. I was a big hero that day.

They cleared the smoke from the classroom in a few hours, but there were still lingering fumes. They tried to have class there the next day, but people were puking when they breathed the fumes. Some kids got bad headaches and had to be sent home. A girl named Cynthia Hotchkiss passed out face down on her desk, and later when the teacher woke her up she was found to have drooled on herself.

I don't think it helped that Mr. Blount washed the place down with ammonia.

So it was back to the cafeteria. They had to have the class there for a week while they aired the room out. They wouldn't let me go back to class at all. Back to the cafeteria, I mean.

Instead, they put me to work. They gave me a brush and a can of shellac and I had to shellac all the carrels in the library.

I kept right on denying that I had lit the smoke bomb. I never did admit it. But nobody believed me. I thought, hey, I could have just discovered it and been fanning the smoke, right? I could have been doing a good deed. I felt there was still some question as to who had done it, and it offended me that everybody just assumed that I was guilty without proof. I would have appreciated at least being given the benefit of the doubt.

After I finished the carrels I had to shellac some new bookshelves too. That suited me just fine. The job took several days, but I was in no hurry. There were plenty of books for me to read to pass the time. I only had to work when the librarian was there to watch me, and she only worked part time. So basically I just hung out in the library for a week. It was a different librarian by this point, by the way, not Mrs. Verne.

When I was done they still didn't want me to go back to class, so I had to sit in the principal's office. Sister Rose, Principle Pale Butt herself, as I had called her in the fourth grade, sat right in there with me. I had to look at her all day. I couldn't stand to look at her face. It was like an old prune. I hated her guts.

The teachers brought me work, and with the principal watching me, I had no choice but to do it. Sister Rose was eighty years old now. She was stooped and shriveled. She had gone downhill since she gave me the beating in fourth grade. Now she was senile, and getting ready to retire. The secretary did most of her work for her, but somehow the old nun was still capable of watching me to make sure I did my work. She could tell when I was fooling around. She sat there at her desk and read prayer books and took notes from them.

One time the old nun looked up and caught me daydreaming, looking out the window. "I know it's not that interesting," she said. "But we all have to do things we don't like in order to grow in the ways of the Lord. You want to grow up to become a good Christian gentleman, don't you?"

"Yes, Sister," I said automatically.

"God put us here on this earth to work and to suffer, to do good works in His name. He gives each of us work to do in life. He gives to each according to his ability. It's a sacred trust, the work God gives us each to do. By doing our work to the best of our ability we bring glory to God and we grow in the fulfillment of God's plan. You know that God has a plan for you, don't you, Tommy?"

"Yes, Sister," I said, this time rolling my eyes.

"God has a plan for each of us. Each of us is special in His sight. We must work hard in order not to disappoint Him. He who sees all, and sees into our hearts. He knows when we are doing our best. He wouldn't ask more than He knew we were able to achieve."

"Yes, Sister."

"I know it's hard, and that it would be easier to run and play, or to watch TV, but you have to keep trying. God doesn't want everything to be easy for us. We must earn His love and trust," the nun went on.

She must think I'm in third grade or something, I thought.

"Just look at Jesus and all He had to go through. Whenever I think I have it tough, I just look at what Jesus went through for us, what He went through voluntarily, because He is God and didn't have to do it. And I say, you know what? I don't have it so hard. In fact I've got it pretty easy. And that gives me the strength to go on. It makes me want to show God that I'm worthy of His love and of the sacrifice He made for me."

She could go on all day like this. She hadn't been studying that prayer book for nothing.

"And if you just accept this, and say you're going to do it to the best of your ability, Jesus will help you. He doesn't make it so hard after all, you'll see. And He'll reward you with a good life. Not an easy life, but a good Christian life."

What could I say to that? I didn't know what the hell to say. I usually just did my work in order to avoid lectures like this.

"You'd like to grow up to be a good Christian gentleman, wouldn't you?" Sister Rose asked me again.

"I'd rather grow up to worship Satan," I said.

She actually took me seriously. She shivered in fright.

"Oh, my God!!!" the old nun said. She clasped her hands together and raised her eyes to heaven. "Forgive him, Jesus! He's a mere child! He knows not what he says!"

She got up and made a move for me. "Come and kneel with me and we will ask Jesus for His forgiveness!" She grabbed at me with her claws as I jumped out of my desk to get away from her. She was trying to get me to kneel before a shrine she had set up in the corner. It was a shrine to the Virgin Mary, but we were still going to pray to Jesus, apparently.

I backed away from her. "I was just kidding, Sister," I said nervously, trying to avoid a full-on exorcism.

The old nun didn't understand how anyone could joke about things like that.

31

While I was in the principal's office I couldn't even read a book. I had to keep working. The only time I had a break was when Sister Rose left the room. Sometimes I was able to get away with writing a story or a poem. Besides causing trouble, that was basically the only thing I liked to do. Luckily, that counted as work for the old nun, just as long as she saw me scribbling away.

I had to sit there in the principal's office for a few weeks. So I guess I have to credit this ordeal with helping me to develop my talent for writing. I had always taken pride in my talent, but at the same time I didn't take it too seriously. It was just a funny thing I did so people would like me. But having to sit on my own and entertain myself, I began to see the value of it in and of itself.

One of the things I wrote while I was there was a play. It wasn't anything that was assigned. Nobody else wrote one, just me. I did it to kill time, but also I did it because I was interested in doing it. I had never written a play before, and it was a challenge.

I wanted to put it on. Sister Rose thought that was a good idea too. I don't think she ever read the play, but I told her the idea and she liked it. Plus, she liked the idea of me doing something that wasn't destructive and anti-social. That was the main thing. She thought it would be good therapy for me and teach me to work well with others. And I guess after all she was right. It was a good opportunity for me to change my ways, if only I had understood that better.

It was Mrs. Bream's job to read the play to make sure it was doctrinally correct. But she saw no problems with it. I had made sure to give it a real traditional Christian message. I knew I would win points for that.

The play was about a bum who everybody spits on and pushes around and throws garbage on, but in the end he turns out to be Jesus. So it was also a funny play, since it's funny to throw garbage on people, Jesus or whoever. But I don't think the adults picked up on that.

They let me out of the principal's office so I could produce the play. I had to be back in class to find other people to do the play with me and to rehearse and things like that. Of course, I had thought of that beforehand. That was part of my reason for doing it. Mrs. Bream let me sit in a regular place in the class instead of up by her desk. I moved my stuff into a desk in the back row.

I had already decided who should play the major parts. I just had to convince them to do it. Some wanted to do it and some didn't. It was mainly based on who my friends were, or, since I really didn't have many friends, on who I wanted to be my friends. I chose the most popular kids for the best roles. For the most part they got to be the rich people who threw trash on Jesus and insulted him. Parts as extras went to the less popular kids. Real social outcasts didn't get to do anything. Harold, predictably, thought the whole thing was bullshit. And of course I didn't ask Sheila to take part, and she certainly didn't volunteer.

The people who didn't want to be actors got to work on costumes or sets, or whatever they wanted to do. Jo Anne, who may have still owned the last remaining copy of *The Sexbook*, got to be the script girl, responsible for mimeographing. My old buddy Paul Verne volunteered to do the lighting because his dad was an electrician and had stored a bunch of lighting equipment in their basement when he moved out.

But then Mrs. Bream butted in. She determined that I shouldn't be allowed to choose who got to be in the play. She decided that we should vote on who got the roles, so it could be a project for the whole class. So now we had to have an election. No big deal, since all of my choices won anyway. They were the most popular kids, after all.

Then we voted on the lead character, the part I had designed for myself. I was sure I would win, totally confident. Me and the other candidates stood up at the front of the room and people raised their hands for the person they wanted. And *nobody* voted for me! Not a single person. I was shocked and crestfallen. It was embarrassing. And it didn't help at all that it was Chip who beat me out for the lead! Little Chip, that wimp. No, that didn't help at all. And in fact I got the feeling that they had voted for Chip just to embarrass me. Even the kids that I gave the best roles in the play voted against me. A lot of people didn't like me to begin with, and people were pissed off and maybe jealous that I was controlling the whole thing.

Or maybe, after all, it was the part about me being Jesus that bugged them. I had intended it as a joke, of course, but still it sounds like some pretty heavy symbolic shit there. I didn't think of that at the time.

"Sorry I won," Chip said, annoyingly. But I think he *was* sincerely sorry. I didn't even have any desire to take it out on him, especially since I think he ran for the part as a joke himself.

Still, that sucked, that they wouldn't give me the lead in my own play. But at least I had put a narrator in the play, to introduce the play. They elected me to that, as a consolation prize. It wasn't a very good part, but it was better than nothing. It allowed me to retain a little bit of pride.

"At least now we get to work together," Chip said. "It'll be fun!"

Come to think of it, I *did* want to kill him. But most of all I wanted to kill Mrs. Bream.

32

But I took it like a man. I swallowed my pride and got on with
the play. It wasn't like I was always hell-bent on trying to cause
trouble. Sometimes I tried to get along. I wanted to be liked, or
at least there was a part of me that did. I wanted to be accepted,
just on my own terms, and I realized that the play offered me an
opportunity to do that. But it's hard to fit in, even if you want to,
and especially if you've spent your whole life rebelling. Things
were going along OK, but I had lingering resentments. There
were times when I thought all the people around me were idiots
and all the things we were doing were ridiculous, even the play.
And then I *definitely* didn't want to fit in. I was bound to do something to fuck things up sooner or later.

There were other activities going on at the time. One of the
things we were doing was making angels for some kind of charity
project. Care packages or something. You know, here's something
from your Guardian Angel. We were doing the project in the
cafeteria. This was for art class.

The angels were made out of cardboard. They had blank
heads where you could draw a face, and then the outlines of hair
and a dress that you could fill in. They had cardboard wings
tacked onto the back. They were going to have children's names
on them, the names of poor children from other countries. And if
you wanted to give one of these children a gift, like a teddy bear,
or a savings bond, or a Summer Sausage, you pulled an angel off
the bulletin board and stuck it on your gift.

We were supposed to color and decorate the angels with
crayons and magic markers. We had glitter and stars to put on

them too, and you could get pretty elaborate if you wanted to. Some of the angels had already been done by children in the lower grades. They weren't all supposed to be perfect. Some people thought it was cute to get an angel that was scribbled on by a first grader.

I had no artistic ability and absolutely no interest in the project. In fact, since the *Sexbook* scandal, I had developed an antagonism against all forms of art. I resented having to take part in the project, but since it was required I fooled around with one of the angels, not really working very hard. The best I could think of was to make it look crappy, but anything I did was going to look crappy anyway, so that wasn't much of a challenge. Maybe I'll scribble all over one and people will think a retard or a first grader did it, I thought.

Then I had an inspiration. I threw down the angel I had been working on and got another one. I colored the dress and hair black. Then I drew a face with a big nose with a wart on the end of the nose, and a mouth with half the teeth blacked out. Basically the same as in *The Sexbook*, only this time the G-rated version. I put big, round, black glasses on the angel's eyes, and gave her a bushy black mustache.

I showed it around. Everybody laughed. They got the joke immediately. The joke was that the angel looked just like the art teacher, Sister Mary Catherine. You might remember her from the time when Chip yanked off her veil and tried to throw it into the dumpster. Mary Catherine wore round black glasses with coke-bottle lenses, and she had a small mustache. She had a big nose too, though there wasn't a wart on it. I just made the part about the wart up, same with the missing teeth. Inspired by my success, I made several more angels like that and tacked them up on the bulletin board.

When the nun saw them she went nuts, just completely bonkers. She started screaming and snatching them off the bulletin board. "Who did this!?" she screamed hysterically. "Who has done this!? Who?!"

"Oh shit," I said under my breath. After the *Sexbook* thing, you'd think I would have known better. I guess I was just a slow learner. When the nun wasn't looking I took the angel I was working on and folded it and stuck it in my pocket.

Mary Catherine frantically searched the big bulletin board for the bad angels. I had scattered them all around. When she thought she had found them all, she crunched them up and threw them in the trash can. Then she stormed around the cafeteria, looking at everybody's work. I had started work on another angel, and was trying to make it look as little like a nun as possible.

Just when Mary Catherine had settled down a girl came up and showed her another angel she had missed. And the nun went nuts again! She snatched it out of the girl's hand and crunched it up and threw it in the trash can. She said, "I will find out who did this if it's the last thing I do!"

I believed her. She went around making more deliberate inquiries now, talking to all her informants. Now she was containing her rage, plotting her sweet revenge. Then she said, "Tommy Donaldson, come here this moment!"

I went up to where she was standing. I stood there in front of the whole class. The nun pulled one of the wadded angels out of the trash can and waved it in my face. "Why?! Why have you done this?!"

"Uh, I don't know."

"You have made them into monsters!" the nun proclaimed. She reared back her arm and swung it at me.

I blocked it.

"You'd better stand there and take your punishment!"

Fat chance, I thought. I backed away from her.

"You stand there and take your punishment, or you're going straight back to the principal's office!"

The last thing I wanted was to go back there. I stood there in front of her. She reared back her right arm and let me have it in the face. It really stung. Then she reared back her other arm and let me have it on the other cheek. There were tears running out of my eyes. I wiped them away with the back of my hand.

I was mad as hell. In addition to the humiliation of standing up there getting smacked in front of everybody, there was the issue of somebody ratting me out. If there was one thing that would set me off, that was it.

It wasn't too hard to find out who had told on me. Turned out it was Sheila who did it. Sheila still had it in for me. And it was some of those same girls who had fixed us up in the first place who were the ones who told me.

I wasn't going to let her get away with it. Why should she get away with it just because she was a girl? Why should girls get away with that sort of shit just because they're weaker? If anything, that's all the more reason not to rat people out. That's how I reasoned, but maybe it had something to do with the fact that I still bore a grudge against Sheila. I wanted to think I would have acted the same with anyone, but that was probably not the case.

I waited for her outside at the lunch break. I hid in the bushes and then rushed out and confronted her. I said, "Why did you tell on me, you bitch?"

Sheila kept walking. "I don't have to tell you."

"The hell you don't, you fucking bitch."

Sheila kept walking across the parking lot. She was walking faster now. "I don't want to talk to you. Leave me alone."

I grabbed her by the arm and spun her around. "You think you can get away with that shit? What did you think, I wasn't gonna find out?" I shook her by the arm.

"Get off of me! You ruined it for everybody! That's not right, what you did. You have no right to do that to her. The Sister never did anything to you. She's a nice person."

What she said surprised me. Maybe she no longer found my behavior attractive. Maybe she was growing up.

"That nice fucking bitch almost took my head off!" I said.

Sheila screamed and tried to get away from me. She got her arm away but I held onto the sleeve of her coat. "Fuck you bitch. You don't tell on me." I slung her around by her coat. The coat started to rip.

"You're ripping my coat! Get off me!"

"That's what you get. I'm gonna do worse than rip your coat."

She was pulling against the coat and I wouldn't let her go. I felt the coat rip some more. "You better never tell on me for anything again, you bitch. I'm warning you."

"I'll do whatever I want. You can't tell me what to do."

"I don't care if you're a fucking girl or not. You're risking your fucking life. I'll kick your ass anyway. I don't give a shit." I raised my fist real fast and faked a swing at her.

Sheila put up her hands to block it, and then grabbed my arm.

"Ha! I oughta hit you, you fucking bitch!" She still had hold of my arm. My fist was clenched and I pressed down on her arms. I pressed my fist toward her face. I was up in her face, grinning at her.

She was pushing back on my arm. She was trying to push it away.

"I oughta beat the hell out of you," I said. "The only reason I don't is because you're a girl."

All of a sudden she let go of my arm, she just relaxed her grip. I was still pushing, and my arm shot forward and I popped her right in the nose.

I let go of her. "Fuck! I didn't mean to do that! Why'd you let go of my arm, you stupid bitch?"

Sheila looked startled for a moment. Then her nose started bleeding. She grabbed her nose and then looked at the blood on her hand. When she saw the blood she burst out crying. She staggered away and ran away crying, holding her nose.

I walked after her. "Look, I'm sorry. I didn't mean to do that."

She was really bawling. Blood was pouring out of her nose.

I had a handkerchief, so I pulled it out of my pocket and said, "Here, use this."

Sheila snatched it away from me and held it to her nose.

All this was going on in the middle of the parking lot. Everybody was standing around, watching. They were at a distance, but they could see what was going on. Now the teachers came running up. One of them was Mrs. Bream. "Now you've done it! You're really in for it now!"

"I didn't do it on purpose!"

They led Sheila away to get her nose fixed up at the nurse's office.

At first I was sorry. But when I thought about it I wasn't sorry anymore. I flat out refused to be. I thought Sheila deserved it, and that's what I told everybody. That's what I told the principal and Mrs. Bream. I told them that if you ratted people out you deserved to be punched in the nose. You deserved worse. They said you weren't supposed to mistreat girls like that, whatever they did. I didn't accept that, and I told them so. I gave them my reasons too.

Girls confused me. I was afraid of them. So naturally I was mad at girls and wanted to punish them. And who better to start with than Sheila.

I didn't go into any of that, of course, since I didn't really understand it myself. Instead I reacted defensively, swearing up and down that I had been right. I was unrepentant. I told them that I hadn't punched Sheila on purpose, but that I should have done it on purpose. I said that under similar circumstances with anybody else, I would do the exact same thing.

This message didn't go over so well. Mrs. Bream believed that I had punched Sheila on purpose. The principal was more willing to give me the benefit of the doubt, but she was disturbed by my attitude. They suspended me from school for a week. I didn't know why they thought it was a punishment to miss school, though I guess I did resent it that they wouldn't let me see my play. I guess after all that was my punishment. They went ahead and had the play without me and it was a big success. Mrs. Bream read my part.

All in all I was glad I had done it. I was just pissed off that they hadn't thrown me out for good. I told my parents I didn't like Catholic school and didn't want to go back. My dad refused to listen to any such nonsense. He just told me to shut up and do as I was told. My mother listened, but I didn't have much luck getting through to her either. She felt that Mother Goose was a better school than the public school, and that it made you work harder. She was right about that, but to me that was all the more reason to get out.

My parents were smart enough to see that I might be having some real problems. But aside from ordering me back to school, they didn't know quite what to do with me. They could only turn to religion, which to me was a big part of the problem in the first place. Their solution was to send me to a nun who was supposed to counsel me. She was at a different church on the other side of town. Religious school, and then when that didn't work out, religious counseling. My dad drove me there two nights a week, Tuesdays and Thursdays. We played the radio, as always, but I didn't really care to listen anymore.

The room where I met with the nun was just a tiny space connected to her bedroom. There wasn't much room for anything but two chairs. There was a lamp, and a little table with magazines on it. There was a crucifix on the wall. The nun asked a lot of questions while I sat in my chair for an hour.

"Do you think it's right to pick on weaker children?" the nun asked at one of our sessions. She was old, but not old enough to be senile. She wore regular clothes instead of the nun's habit, maybe to put her patients at ease.

"No, I guess not," I said.

"Why do you do it then?"

"I don't know. Because it's funny. Because they're idiots."

"Not all people are blessed by God to the same degree. Do you think Jesus would like to see you act that way?"

Was this a trick question? "How should I know?"

"But what do you think?"

"Probably not," I had to admit.

She looked at the note pad that she had in her lap as I sat there in my chair and fidgeted. She changed the subject. "Why don't you like to do your homework?"

That was easy enough. "It's boring."

"Do you understand why your parents and teachers are so concerned about having you do your homework?"

"I have no idea."

"Do you think it's because they want to be mean to you?"

"Probably."

"You don't really believe that do you?" the nun asked.

"I guess not," I said.

"Do you have any idea at all then?"

"I guess because they want me to grow up to be a success and get a good job."

"What do you think you'll do now to change your actions?"

"I don't know."

"Any ideas?"

"I guess I'll try to do my homework, and try not to pick on weaker kids." I don't know what else she expected me to say. I was sort of half serious, I guess, and not only because of the brainwashing hour. It would have been nice to get along.

That was the way our sessions usually went. I spent half the time bullshitting the nun, and the other half of the time feeling that I really did want to change, to grow up. But overall I was stubborn. I believed that I was right, and even if I wasn't quite convinced anymore, I wasn't going to back down. I wasn't one to admit that I had been wrong. I was prepared to go down with the ship.

There was a small clock on the wall. I had been watching it all along. "Looks like my hour is up," I said.

The nun ignored me. "Sometimes in moments of strength we make resolutions that we fail to carry out when temptation arises. Let's ask Jesus to give us the strength to carry through our resolutions."

I never could figure out whether this old lady was trying to help me, or to brainwash me, or whether she thought my problem was that I was stupid. "Can't we ask the Virgin Mary?" I said.

The counseling nun seemed puzzled. She didn't get that I was being sarcastic. "Uh, yeah. We can ask her for strength if you'd like that better."

"No, Jesus will be fine," I said.

34

When I came back from my suspension, they let me attend classes with the rest of the students. But I still hated it. I was sick of that place. I don't need to tell you that I didn't listen to the counseling nun. I tried to get along for a while but it was the same thing all over again, and once again I was bound to do something crazy sooner or later. I felt I was sticking to my guns, and then again, in a way, I simply couldn't help myself.

In March we had to do science projects for class. Towards the end of the month everybody brought theirs in. The projects were models of the solar system. Some people set theirs on a table in the back of the room, and others set theirs on the window ledge. It was a big marble ledge with plenty of room to set stuff. I didn't set mine anyplace because I hadn't bothered to do one.

We were all milling around the classroom, looking at the science projects, while Mrs. Bream was busy. It was a warm spring day and the windows were open. Mr. Blount, the janitor, was out on the lawn with his riding mower, cutting the grass for the first time of the season. He was starting real early this year. The grass was just beginning to sprout, and didn't really need cutting. Maybe it was an easier job than what he would've been doing otherwise. Anyway, we could hear him off across the lawn. Our classroom was on the second floor.

"Look at this piece of shit," I said. I was talking to some kids standing in a group by the window. We were looking at what had to be the worst science project of all time. It belonged to George Hurlbutt, who was almost retarded. He had hung a bunch of Styrofoam balls in a shoe box to represent the planets and the sun.

Pretty standard, but George had fucked the whole thing up. He had tried to color the balls with crayon and that hadn't worked. He had pinned the names of the planets on them, and had misspelled a couple of names. He couldn't even get the order of the planets right!

"Look at this quality workmanship," I said. I jerked one of the balls off its string and tossed it over in the corner.

Everybody laughed.

Then I threw the whole thing out the window. "Whoops!" I said. "I knew we shouldn't have set these things on the window sill. That was just an accident waiting to happen."

Everybody laughed, but not too loud, because they didn't want to be caught. They got out of the area and went back to their desks. I wasn't that worried about it. It could have fallen out on its own. A strong breeze could have sucked that project right out the window. But after a while I got bored and went back to my desk too.

The teacher hadn't graded the projects yet. It was a big competition, to see who had made the best project. Now she was going around grading them. Finally, at the end, when she had seen them all, she announced the winner. Of course I didn't win, and George didn't win. No surprise there. One of the girls won, probably Jo Anne. Mrs. Bream gave her some holy cards as a prize.

I thought Mrs. Bream would ask George where his project was, and then they'd start looking around for it. But she didn't say anything to George. She didn't say anything to me either. Probably she didn't want to embarrass the people who hadn't done their projects. So after a while I got tired of waiting and went over to the window again.

I had given George's project a good toss and it had sailed well out onto the lawn. It was still in the same place. But now Mr.

Blount was getting close to it with his lawn mower. He was only a couple of rows away. When he passed below the windows you had to yell to be heard over the mower.

Mr. Blount had to have seen the project by now. I wondered why he didn't get out and move it out of the grass. I figured he was just lazy and would move it out of the way when he came to it. I showed some of my friends. "You think he'll hit it?" Nobody thought he would. He passed right by it, within a foot of it. When he got down to the end of the row, he swung his mower around and headed back our way.

I yelled across the classroom. "Hey George, come over here for a minute."

George got up out of his desk and came over. "What?"

"I was just looking at these science projects and I didn't notice yours anywhere."

"Uh, I put it right here. Where is it? What happened to it?" George said, too stupid to suspect me. He started looking around for the thing. He checked the other projects on the ledge. He went back and looked at the projects on the table in the back of the room. He didn't think to look out the window.

Mr. Blount was getting closer. The noise from the mower was growing louder and I had to raise my voice to be heard over the noise. I called George back. "Isn't that your science project lying down there in the grass?"

He looked out the window. "Huh? Yeah! Hey!"

Mr. Blount was heading straight for it.

"Hey! Hey! Nooooo!!!" George screamed out the window.

Even above the lawn mower Mr. Blount heard him. He looked up at us in the window. Then he looked back down and just kept going. He acted like he didn't see the science project. He ran right over it, and pulverized shreds of it shot out from under the mower. The noise of the mower died away as he passed.

Once again I remembered why I liked Mr. Blount.

George ran up to the front of the room and stammered some nonsense to the teacher. When she understood what he was talking about she let him go, and he ran out of the room. We saw him come out of the building and stand over the pile of chewed up paper and Styrofoam that used to be his science project. He stood over it and tore at his hair in despair. When he came back he had an armload of scraps. He stood up at Mrs. Bream's desk and showed them to her. He was almost crying. I laughed my ass off. What a retard, I thought.

"It's alright, George, I know you did the work," Mrs. Bream told him. And she gave him an A for the damn thing, which was way better than he deserved. He didn't even deserve a D.

"Why don't you give him some holy cards too?" I suggested.

George would have never figured out that I had done it. But it came out that I was the one who had told him about it. Knowing me pretty well, Mrs. Bream asked me if I had thrown the project out the window.

"No. It probably just fell."

She didn't believe me. She never believed anything I said anymore. She told me to go to the principal's office.

It pissed me off, since once again there was no evidence against me. I couldn't get away with anything. I had really had it with this place. On my way out I slammed the door shut.

It didn't have the effect I wanted. I wanted that bitch to run into the hall and yell at me. I stood there in the hall and waited. It pissed me off that she was ignoring me. Maybe I didn't make myself clear, I thought. I opened the door again. It swung outward. Then I kicked it shut as hard as I could. It made a hell of a noise, and busted the window out of the door. Glass flew all over the classroom. "Oh shit!!!"

The principal and Mrs. Bream stood over me where I sat in a chair in the principal's office. Throwing the project out the window was no big deal, but now I was in real trouble. My violent behavior was getting out of hand, Mrs. Bream said, endangering the other children.

What a bunch of bullshit, I thought. The only person the glass hit was Joe Woodhead, who was bending over his desk, so he just got it on the back and the back of his head. It didn't cut him. It just bounced off him. "A little bit of glass couldn't hurt Joe Woodhead's big wooden head," I said.

Neither Mrs. Bream nor Sister Rose appreciated my humor. Mrs. Bream didn't want me back in her classroom. She simply couldn't deal with me anymore, she said.

"Well, it seemed to work when Tommy was sitting in the office with me," the principal said. "He seemed to respond well to that. Maybe we can try that for a couple more weeks. I didn't mind having him here. He was quiet and we both did our work."

The hell, I thought. I couldn't bear to sit with that old nun again. I just blew up. I jumped up and yelled in her face. "You goddamn motherfucking senile old bitch! You gotta be crazy if you think I'm sitting in this fucking office with you again! I'm sick of looking at your fucking ugly-ass old face! You make me want to puke, you senile old bag!"

Sister Rose was on her last legs and it about gave her a heart attack. She staggered over to her desk and clung to it. Mrs. Bream helped the old nun into the chair. "Get out of here," Mrs. Bream said to me. "I'll deal with you later."

I went out into the hall. I walked down the hall and went into the bathroom and took a piss. When I was finished, I stood looking out the bathroom window. Though I knew Sister Rose was becoming senile, I hadn't really thought about her being so easily shocked. To me she was still a larger-than-life figure, something like the personification of evil. Well, maybe not that bad, but pretty bad. Anyway, that oughta do it, I thought. Surely they'll kick me out now.

They called my parents to come and get me. My parents weren't too thrilled about it, especially my dad, since he had to get out of work. My mother, I'm sure, had something better to do too. They wanted them both down there for a conference.

It was the principal and Mrs. Bream and my parents and me in the principal's office. Mrs. Bream took the lead, once again calling for my head and denouncing me in the most vigorous terms. She was laying it on pretty thick, making it sound like I was the Antichrist or something. She said I was a threat to the health and welfare of the entire student body. She said I had no respect for my elders either. And she wasn't about to forget the terrorist gas attack.

My dad didn't know what to say. His face had gone pale. I think this was the first time that I began to see the limitations of his power. He knew how to use threats and intimidation, maybe even violence, but when subtlety was called for, he was at a loss.

But my mother defended me. "He's just a little boy, lady," she said crossly. "And you're supposed to be an adult."

I was sitting right there, and that kind of embarrassed me to be called a little boy like that, but still I had to admire how my mother had put a cork in Mrs. Bream. When I think back on it, my mother had no doubt helped me to get away with a lot.

In the lull that followed, the principal took the opportunity to speak. She seemed to have rallied from her earlier setback. I hadn't sent her to her grave after all. "Tommy doesn't seem to want to sit in here with me anymore, but I'm sure we can work something out," she said. "He seemed to be doing so well, too, with the play and everything. He seemed to have really found his niche. Maybe if he just stayed home for a couple of days we could use that time to think things through."

How much more did it take to get thrown out? "Look, I've had it with this place. I don't want to go here anymore," I said. "I'm sick of getting blamed for everything. Is that so hard to understand?"

So that was that. I didn't back down this time and finally we all agreed that it would be better for me to make a new start somewhere else. Mrs. Bream, of course, backed me up on this. At least I could count on her for that. And my dad didn't put up too much of a struggle this time. He seemed to have accepted defeat. Sister Rose seemed kind of disappointed, but even she eventually gave in. I guess it didn't look like I was growing up to be much of a Christian gentleman anyway.

Part Four

36

Somewhere else meant public school. And of course that was fine by me. I was hoping to take a couple of weeks off, rest up from the traumatic experience of Catholic school, but they said to come in right away. At least they didn't want me to come in first thing in the morning. I got to sleep an hour late.

I could walk to the public middle school, which was another thing I found appealing about it. It was right in the middle of my subdivision. Though I was a little bit nervous that first morning, I was excited and filled with anticipation. I hadn't said anything to Johnny, figuring I'd surprise him. I stole a cigarette from my mother and cut through some back yards and had a smoke by the creek before I went in. There was no big rush, so I took my time, enjoying my cig as I checked out the fresh sprigs of grass and the buds on the trees. The school was a big modern building and it stood out in the open by itself. It was multi-sided, and it didn't have many windows, maybe on the theory that that would cut down on distractions. Or maybe as a new form of torture. It had just been built the year before. I cut across a field of grass to get to it.

I had to go see the principal first. I filled out some forms in his office and then I talked to him for a while. His name was Mr. Snyder. Mr. Snyder asked me why I wanted to switch schools. I said I had done some things wrong at the Catholic school, but now they had me pegged for a troublemaker and they had it in for me. I got blamed for everything, I said, things that weren't even my fault. They expected me to act wrong and I couldn't get away with anything.

"I can understand how it might be too restrictive in a religious school," Mr. Snyder said.

"It sucked."

"Yes, well, people are given more freedom here, and there's room for all sorts of people to fit in." I could fit in too, he said, if I set my mind to it. "You'll be starting all over with a clean slate. Whatever mistakes you've made in the past are history. We won't be holding those mistakes against you."

"I'm glad to hear that," I said.

"Give the place a chance to work, and I'm sure you'll like it here," Mr. Snyder said. "You'll be starting all over with a clean slate," he said again. "*Tabula Rasa*."

"That's all I need," I said. "A clean slate and a second chance." I was mocking him, of course. The thing is, I could have made something out of it, if I had wanted to. Mr. Snyder was right that there was more room to develop there, if that's what you wanted to do. Unfortunately, there was also more freedom to cause trouble. I was more excited at the prospect of running wild.

"That's what you'll have then, a clean slate," Mr. Snyder said. "But you'll have to hold up your end of the bargain as well," he warned me.

"I'm turning over a new leaf," I said, just to change the metaphor.

"I'm pleased to hear that," Mr. Snyder said. "Good to have you with us, Tom," he said, standing to shake my hand. I had told him my name was Tom, rather than Tommy, since I was beginning to think that Tom sounded more adult. "If there's ever anything I can do for you, or even if you just want to talk, feel free to drop by my office at any time."

This was a modern school, at least more modern than the Catholic school. It was bigger, for one thing. It was a much bigger building, and there must have been five times as many students. You went to your classes by yourself. You got out and wandered the halls, and didn't have to stay with the same group of students all day. You had a choice of classes, and they didn't all have to be math or English or science. Some of them were crazy, off-the-wall things that didn't have anything to do with school, like home ec. or music appreciation. Some of the classes were a real joke. I signed up for all kinds of ridiculous crap.

And the class set-up was different too. Not all the classes were in little rooms. My first class of the day was called Core, and it was in a huge, sprawling auditorium that curved all over the place. There were several different classes in the same big room. They were separated by distance, or by portable walls, or by bookshelves. You moved around from one to the other every half-hour or so, and got most of your main academic subjects out of the way in one fell swoop. It was a real nuthouse.

I took my time getting there, and walked around the school for a while. The Core period was almost over by the time I arrived. I asked the first teacher I saw which group I was supposed to be in, and it turned out I was supposed to be in her group and she was expecting me.

I stood up in front of the class and the teacher introduced me. The teacher was a young woman who looked like she was just out of college. She told the class I'd been kicked out of the Catholic school.

Which was true, in a way. Still, I wondered who had told her that, since the principal said I was supposed to have a clean slate. "That's right," I said proudly. "How did you know?"

"Oh, I'm just joking," the teacher said. "Tom didn't really get kicked out of Catholic school. He's just transferring," she told the class.

"Yeah, I really did get kicked out," I said.

She thought I was joking too. "Oh, come on. Why are you transferring?"

"I'm serious," I said. "So you really didn't know? That's hilarious! I guess I just look like the kind of person who would get kicked out of school."

It embarrassed the young teacher. "Oh no, no! You look like a perfectly nice boy. That's not what I meant at all." She paused and then she said, "I'm sorry. I didn't know you had really been kicked out."

"That's OK. I don't care."

"No, I'm really, really sorry. I would never have said anything if I had known."

"It doesn't bother me." I was glad she had told people. In fact I wanted to encourage this perception. I knew I had to make a new reputation for myself at this place.

"Well, all that's in the past now. Welcome to the class, Tom. I'm sure you'll like it a lot better here."

"Yeah. Mr. Snyder said I had a clean slate."

"That's exactly right."

"I'm turning over a new leaf."

The teacher was still curious. She asked me quietly, not in front of the class, "May I ask what you got kicked out for?"

"Endangering the other students and cursing out a nun," I said proudly.

"What did you do to endanger the other students."

"Busted out windows over their heads."

"Oh, I see," the teacher said.

I sat with the rest of the class and listened as the teacher talked. After that she gave us some work to do, and then she sat at her desk and ignored us. It was a social studies class.

I looked around the big room. There were several groups of kids scattered around the sprawling room, each with a different teacher. I knew some of the kids from around the neighborhood. Or at least they looked familiar. I walked around in our area and pretended to look at some of the books on the bookshelves, then I went out in the hall for a drink of water. The room was open to the hall and the water fountain was right there.

When I came back in I spotted Johnny sitting in one of the groups, all the way across the room. He was talking to some other people in the group and he didn't notice me.

The bell rang and the Core period was over. Johnny was going out through a different exit than the one nearest me. I rushed out into the hall and ran around and hid behind the wall where I thought he was going to come out. Sure enough, he came out that way. I let him get a little past me, then I jumped out and grabbed him in a bear hug and lifted him up off the ground. "Hey Motherfucker!" I dropped him back down. "How you doing?! What's going on?!"

Johnny was sure surprised to see me there! I don't know if he was exactly glad to see me, but he was surprised, all right. "Oh shit! You scared the shit out of me! What the hell are you doing here?" Johnny said.

We shook hands and I said, "Ah, they finally kicked me out of Mother Goose."

"That's not surprising. I'm surprised it took them this long."

"Yeah, they were getting really sick of me. It was just a matter of time."

"What did you get kicked out for?" Johnny asked.

I told him the same thing I told the teacher, though I went into a little more detail to make myself sound more heroic. "I'm glad to get the hell out of there," I said. "So how is this place, better?"

"Oh yeah, much better. It's still not the greatest place in the world, but it's a big improvement, that's for sure."

We stood there looking at each other. The hall was beginning to clear out. "Well, I gotta get to class," Johnny said. "Where are you going now? What class you got now?"

"Art. But I don't know where the hell that is." I got my schedule out and looked at it. "You know where that is?"

"Oh, I've got art now too. With Miss Quarles?"

I checked my schedule. "Yeah," I said.

"We're in the same class. Come on. I'll show you where it is."

We seemed to have gotten on the same basic schedule. People who had Core at the same time ended up in some of the other classes together too.

37

The structure of art class was loose too. The teacher gave us fifteen minutes or more before she even bothered to come out of her office.

While we waited for the teacher, we sat around in the art room, which was a big, angular room with all kinds of supplies and equipment. We sat on plastic chairs at long tables. Johnny introduced me to a couple of his friends. One of them was Nick, who had long hair and seemed like a cool guy. Johnny and the other guys told me about the school. They told me what the good things about the school were, and what teachers to watch out for.

We exhausted the subject of my newness pretty quickly. Then we got onto another subject. "Did you see those shoes Freddie's wearing today?" Nick asked.

"Yeah, I saw them," Johnny replied.

"I can't believe he would dare wear that shit to school," Nick said.

"Yeah, he's got a lot of nerve," Johnny said.

"What a fag," another guy said. "What a fairy."

"Where the hell do you even get shoes like that?" Johnny wondered. "You must have to go downtown to a special fag store or something."

"I can't believe nobody's kicked his ass," Nick said.

"Neither can I," Johnny said.

"What the hell are you guys talking about?" I asked.

"See that guy over there?" Johnny said. There was an effeminate boy at one of the other tables, talking to some of the girls. He had red hair, and it was long, but styled with hair spray and piled up in curls and waves on top of his head. There was a big flip of hair on his forehead.

"Yeah," I said.

"He's wearing blue suede penny loafers."

Penny loafers were looked down upon, even regular brown ones. I looked at Freddie again, studying him closely. The rest of his clothes were preppie too. He had on a pink alligator shirt tucked into khakis. I couldn't see his shoes because his feet were under the table. "Why does he wear them?" I asked.

"Because he's a fag," Johnny said.

That didn't seem like much of an excuse. "Does he always wear them?"

"No, this is the first time."

"I can't even believe he's fucking doing it!" Nick said, irately. "All I've got to say is, he's got a hell of a lot of nerve."

"This I gotta see," I said.

"Well, go over there and ask him. I'm sure he'll show them to you," Johnny said.

"Yeah, it's not like he's trying to hide them," Nick said, disgustedly.

I went over and said hi to Freddie. Johnny and the other guys came over to get another look at the shoes too. They were blue suede penny loafers all right. Tassel loafers, if you want to get technical. Freddie got up and modeled the shoes for me. He struck a number of poses, like he was a fashion model. We all laughed at him.

"Those suck!" I said, laughing.

"Coming from you, that's a compliment, I'm sure," Freddie replied.

"Don't you notice that nobody else is wearing anything like that?"

"I can't account for the poor fashion sense of the masses."

What kind of place is this, I wondered, where kids can get away with wearing such shit. That wouldn't be tolerated where I come from, I thought. "You mind if I see one of those for a moment?" I said.

Freddie rolled his eyes. "I don't think so."

"Aw, come on. I've never seen anything like that before. I just want to get a closer look at it."

"I'm sure," Freddie said. "Now that you gentlemen have had your jollies, I trust you'll excuse me." He made a move to go back to his table.

People there didn't know me. I felt I had to establish myself, show who I was, what I was about. I had to make my reputation there. So I certainly couldn't have anybody like Freddie talking to me like that.

I shot down to the ground and grabbed Freddie by the leg. He let out a yelp. I wrenched his leg around and tried to pry the shoe from his foot, but it wouldn't come off easily. Freddie squealed and struggled and put up a good fight. He twisted his foot out of my grasp so I couldn't get hold of the shoe. I tried to pull him to the ground but he wouldn't come down. He was a pretty big kid, and surprisingly strong. Not weak like Chip, that's for sure. The stakes were higher here, where even the sissies were tougher. Freddie dragged me across the floor and tried to bash my head into the table. I wasn't letting go, but I just couldn't manage to get that shoe off. He kept wrenching it out of my grasp.

"Grab his ass! Help me get this fucking shoe!" I yelled.

Johnny grabbed Freddie in a bear hug. Freddie quit struggling so much, but he kept squealing. He tried to kick with his leg, but now I had control of it. I got hold of the shoe again, but the damn thing was really clamped on there. Finally I got my fingers inside it and wrenched it off his heel.

Then I had it. I jumped up and ran out of the classroom and ran down the hall. Freddie ran right after me, hot on my heels. I heard Johnny and Nick and a couple other guys yelling and whooping, bringing up to the rear. Though I scarcely knew where I was going, I managed to find a bathroom. I burst through the door to the bathroom and ran inside.

Freddie caught up with me just as I got into the bathroom. As I reached the first stall, he grabbed me and tried to pull me away, but I had hold of the door. I had one hand holding the shoe and the other holding onto the door. Freddie grabbed me around the waist and shoulders and pulled me back. I kicked at Freddie to knock him off of me, but he wouldn't let go. He tried to get hold of the shoe, making repeated grabs. I had to hand it to the guy, he had a lot of fight in him and he was stronger than he looked.

I still managed to keep the shoe away from him. Then he went for my head, pulling my hair and scratching at my face. "Jesus!" I said. Then Johnny and the other guys grabbed him from behind and pulled him off me.

I threw the shoe in the toilet. "Nooooo!" Freddie cried out in pain. But it was too late. I flushed the toilet. The shoe didn't go down, of course, but the flushing was, after all, more of a symbolic thing. I figured I had made my point.

Johnny let Freddie go. Freddie got his shoe out of the toilet. It was sopping wet. He took it over to the sink and ran more water over it. Pointlessly, since the water in the toilet hadn't been dirty in the first place.

Besides Johnny, Nick was there in the bathroom with us. A couple of other guys had followed too. They were all laughing. They told Freddie he had got what he deserved.

Freddie's hair was messed up and hanging down over his face. We laughed at that. "Nice hairstyle, Freddie," Nick said.

"You smeared your make up," somebody else said. He did seem to have some kind of make up on. It was only noticeable now that it was smeared. Which meant he had done a pretty good job! We laughed at him some more.

"Fuck you. Fuck you, assholes," Freddie said, nearly sobbing.

We left him in the bathroom and went back to class. Freddie didn't come back. We told the teacher he was cutting class to have a cigarette.

I was glad to have started things off on the right foot, pun intended. It put Johnny in a good mood too, and the other guys seemed to appreciate my sense of humor. Most people did, basically, at least until they found out how serious I was about it. We laughed and joked around about Freddie all through the art class.

After art class was over it was time for lunch. Me and Johnny had the same lunch period. We got in line and got our trays and silverware and then picked our food off the line. We went to a table and sat down and ate. The lunch wasn't very good, though it beat the hell out of what they served at Catholic school.

And it was cookie day. They were pretty damn good cookies. Chocolate chip cookies, big ones. They actually baked them right there. Johnny told me you only got a cookie once a week. Other times you got jello with carrot shavings in it like at Catholic school.

"If you walk around the lunchroom, sometimes you can steal a cookie off somebody's plate," Johnny said. Seemed like the same old Johnny, I was glad to see.

After we finished our food, we walked around the lunchroom looking for cookies, but everybody watched theirs pretty closely. Even the little kids were wise to that trick. They were sixth graders, I guess. The middle school we were in covered sixth through eighth grades.

I got sick of waiting for a cookie to be left unattended. I went up to a table of sixth graders and snatched a cookie off a kid's plate.

"Hey! Gimme that back," the kid said.

"No," I said.

"Come on," he whined.

"No. What are you gonna do about it?"

"That's not fair. Give me back my cookie!"

"Look, I'm not a bad guy. I'll tell you what. I'll split it with you. I'll give you half of it." I broke the cookie in half and gave half of it to the kid. "How's that. I told you I'm not a bad guy."

The kid didn't say anything. He was glad to get half his cookie back.

Johnny had to try it too. We went on the other side of the cafeteria and did the same thing to another kid. We did it a couple more times. "But I even gave you the big half!" I told another kid who continued to protest. We didn't want the cookies anymore, but it was a fun thing to do.

Coach Riley came into the cafeteria and walked in our direction. He was a husky man with salt-and-pepper hair. We tried to act like we weren't doing anything. He went up to Johnny. "Norris, what the hell are you doing?" he said. Norris was Johnny's last name.

"Uh, nothing coach."

"That's what I thought," the coach said. "I want to see both of you in the locker room right now."

We walked down a long hall and through a door into the locker room.

It was the first time I had been in there. The coach came in after us. "Stealing cookies!" he said. "From little kids! What the hell is wrong with you? Norris, you know better than that."

Coach Riley was the wrestling coach. Johnny was on the wrestling team. "I've told you about that shit before. You want to pick on somebody, save it for the mat!"

"Yes sir, coach," Johnny said. Though he wasn't any good at football, Johnny was a good wrestler. It was a form of fighting, after all.

"You think that's funny, stealing cookies from little kids?"

"No sir, coach," Johnny said.

"It was my idea, coach," I said. I hadn't meant to get Johnny in trouble with his coach. Though it didn't interest me, I knew he had come to care a great deal about wrestling since he started public school.

"Who the hell are you, boy? I don't remember seeing you around here before."

"It's my first day, coach."

"Your first day! Well, you sure are starting things off on the right foot!"

"Yeah, I've got a clean slate."

"What?"

"I'm turning over a new leaf."

"You making fun of me, boy?!"

"No sir, coach!" I glanced at Johnny. He was scowling. I could see he didn't appreciate my humor here either. He really had switched schools to get a fresh start.

"What's your name, boy?"

"Tommy Donaldson, coach."

"Well, Donaldson, what about you? You think it's funny stealing cookies from little kids?"

"No sir, coach. But it's funny when you steal a cookie and then let the kid have half of it back."

The coach actually chuckled a little at that. "Yeah, pretty funny, boy. I can see you're a real wise ass. I'll show you something funny," he said. "Line up for ping pong!" he bellowed.

LORDS OF THE SCHOOLYARD

The coach went into his office and got a big wooden paddle out of the closet. "Line up for ping pong!" he yelled again.

"What?" I said.

"Norris will show you. Get over here Norris. Assume the position."

Johnny had to bend over and the coach whacked him in the ass with the paddle. When the coach whacked him the coach yelled, "Ping!" Then Johnny ran across the room and smacked the wall and yelled, "Pong!" Then he ran back and turned around and bent over again.

"Got the picture, Donaldson?"

I lined up and bent over and the coach played ping pong on my ass too. He got us going at the same time. "Ping!" He whacked Johnny's ass and Johnny ran across the room. "Ping!" He whacked my ass and I ran across the room.

"Pong!" Johnny said and smacked the wall.

"Pong!" I said, and we both ran back for more.

The coach laughed his ass off through the whole thing. There were some other guys there for gym class and they laughed too. It hurt like hell when he hit my ass, but I couldn't help laughing about it myself. The coach wasn't kidding when he said he was going to show me something funny.

39

So it was just like old times, at least that's what I thought. Me and Johnny were a team once again. A machine of destruction. And at public school, where they didn't watch you so closely, we could cause more trouble than ever.

Art class was the best. One day we were in art class and I was sitting next to Johnny at one of the long tables. The teacher had given us squares of beige linoleum. We were supposed to gouge patterns on them with our linoleum knives. If you've never seen a linoleum knife, it's just a short scooped blade on the end of a stick. My knife was dull and rusted. I used it to carve out a flower, a daisy. When I was done it looked like a piece of garbage.

Johnny carved out a peace sign on his linoleum. He was more of an artist, and his looked slightly better than mine.

"What the hell are we supposed to do with this linoleum once we carve it anyway? You think we're supposed to frame it or something?" I asked.

"No one in their right mind would think of that," Johnny said. "We're supposed to ink them and stamp some things."

"That's not gonna turn out worth a shit!"

I got bored with the linoleum carving. Instead of getting another square to work on my technique, I got up and walked around the classroom, looking for something better to do. Johnny got up too. Like I mentioned, it was a large room, and the class was chaotic. The students, and Miss Quarles too, just ran around and did as they pleased. There were lots of art supplies and things to mess with scattered all around.

206

We wandered to the back of the room and looked at some of the art work tacked up on the bulletin boards. There were bulletin boards all over the damn place, on nearly all the walls. Each one was dedicated to a different thing. Some had drawings on them. Others had linoleum stamps.

"Look at this crazy shit," I said.

"Fuck this shit!" Johnny said. "This sucks!" He was a budding art critic. He ripped one of the art works down off the bulletin board and wadded it up and threw it in the trash. I laughed and pulled one down too. It hadn't been hard to get Johnny back into the old mischief again. It was fun being a kid.

We went around checking out the things that were tacked up all around the room. If we saw one by somebody we didn't like, we pulled it down and wadded it up and threw it in the trash. Johnny knew more people at the school than me, so naturally his list of enemies was longer. I didn't even know most of the people whose work we tore down.

We kept an eye on Miss Quarles. She was at the front of the room, helping a group of students with their linoleum. She had her back to us. Miss Quarles had big tits and long blond hair. She was a hippie chick and she wore mini-skirts and lots of beads. She was pretty cool for a teacher.

"I always wondered about art teachers," I said.

"What do you mean?" Johnny asked.

"I mean, where the hell do they get these ideas? God's eyes, leaves pressed between wax paper, that sort of thing. Miss Quarles is supposed to be an artist, right?"

"Yeah, I guess."

"Do you think she makes things out of yarn and popsicle sticks herself and exhibits that shit at gallery shows?"

"I doubt it," Johnny said. "I really don't worry about it that much."

There was a clay pot sitting in the corner. It was a square metal box on wheels. Inside was a big lump of brown clay, resting in slimy water. Johnny lifted the lid, coughed up a big hocker, and spat it in there. We cracked up laughing. Johnny dropped the lid back down, slamming it.

Then I lifted the lid and spat a hocker in it too. Seemed like the right place for it.

Suddenly, I heard Freddie speak up. He said, "Miss Quarles, I think there's something you should be aware of."

"What is it Freddie?" Miss Quarles said. She still had her back to us.

"Johnny and Tommy are spitting in the clay pot."

Miss Quarles whirled around and caught me with the lid up. She blew her top, and screeched at me. "Now I'll have to throw the whole batch out! And you're going to pay for it!" She was coming for me fast. I was scared she was going to scratch at me with her long red fingernails.

"Uh, I was just getting out a piece of clay to play with," I stammered.

"Yeah," Johnny said. "We just got bored with the linoleum."

That satisfied her. Amazingly, I thought, though I was learning that teachers usually accepted what they wanted to hear. She stopped coming at me and calmed down. "I'm sorry I yelled at you," she said. She walked over to where I was standing. "Feel free to use the clay. Just be sure to clean up your mess," she said. "And next time, ask me first."

Miss Quarles stood over me as I reached down into the water and got a lump of the clay. I carried the lump back to my table and sat down and pretended to work with it. All I did was make a mess. The table and my hands were soon slimy with brown gunk.

Johnny didn't want any part of it. He didn't bother to get a lump for himself. He sat beside me and messed around with his linoleum some more.

I glared at Freddie as I worked on the clay. "I'm gonna get that little asshole," I said.

"Ah, leave him alone. Nothing happened to us," Johnny said.

"Still, you can't go around ratting people out." As I've mentioned, I felt very strongly about this issue. In fact it came close to an obsession with me. And at this new school, I felt I had to make it clear that that kind of behavior just wouldn't be tolerated.

"He's just trying to get us back for the thing with the shoe," Johnny said, unconcerned. Johnny obviously didn't feel as strongly about it as I did.

"You mean he hasn't gotten over that yet? That was a week ago. He's got to learn to get over it."

I glared at Freddie some more. Freddie tried not to look at me. I made a dog out of the clay. Or some kind of animal, you couldn't tell what. It looked pathetic. I put it on some paper towels and carried it over to the shelf where pottery sat to dry.

Miss Quarles didn't pay any attention to what I was doing. She didn't care to look at my dog. She already knew that I couldn't do anything artistic.

I washed my hands at the sink. Then I got a bunch of paper towels out of the dispenser and dried my hands.

Then I thought, why did I bother washing my hands? I went over and handled the lump of clay again. I mashed it up so it looked even less like a dog. My hands were dirty again but not as dirty as before, so I took a pinch of clay from the dog and smeared that around in my hands. As I did this I glared at Freddie and waited for my chance.

It came, sooner than I expected. Miss Quarles left the class on an errand. As soon as she had closed the door behind her, I walked over to Freddie's table and stood behind him. He was carving his linoleum square. He had carved a palm tree and a sun on it.

"That's pretty good, Freddie," I said.

"Thank you very kindly," Freddie replied.

"Why'd you tell on me, Freddie?"

He didn't answer. He just went on carving.

"Do I need to repeat myself? Why'd you tell on me?"

"Because that's just gross!" Freddie blurted out.

"You must have a death wish," I said.

Freddie didn't answer, and tried to ignore me, working away at his linoleum.

I poked him hard in the back, leaving fingerprints from the clay.

"Cut it out!"

"Who's gonna make me, Freddie? There's no teachers around now." I poked him again.

"Don't touch me!"

I continued to poke and prod Freddie, getting clay all over his nice green polo shirt. Freddie wasn't pretending to work on his linoleum anymore. He was staring down at the table and clutching his knife tightly in his fist. But he was still trying to ignore me, and he was doing a pretty good job of it. Once again, I had to hand it to him there.

While I paused for a break, wondering what to do next, Johnny walked up and said, "Just let it go, for God's sake."

"The hell I will."

"It's just not funny anymore," Johnny said. "Don't you get that?"

"Ah, it's a little bit funny," I said. I was determined, desperate even, to make it funny.

I turned my attention back to Freddie. Maybe I just wasn't being annoying enough, I thought. I screwed around with his ear, tugging at it and flicking it. He hated that. Then I wiped clay in his hair, mussing it all around.

Suddenly Freddie shot around on me with the knife, but I got my arm up and blocked his lunge. He cut me on the arm, but it was a very slight cut. "Ha!" I said, as I grabbed Freddie's hand and wrenched away the knife, flinging it to the floor. Then I hit him. And I hit him again and again. But Freddie covered his head and buried it on the desk, so I was just punching him in the arms and back, and couldn't get any licks in on his face.

Miss Quarles burst through the door, and came rushing up to us. "Tommy! What in God's name!? Have you lost your mind?! Fighting in the middle of class!"

"But Miss Quarles, Freddie stabbed me!" I held out my arm to show her. It was about a half-inch cut. It was bleeding, just a bit, but enough to alarm Miss Quarles. Her jaw dropped when she saw it. "I think I need medical attention," I said.

Miss Quarles ignored me. She turned to Freddie. "Freddie, is this true?!"

Freddie was shaken and terrified. He stammered out a denial that was barely coherent.

Miss Quarles ran to the next classroom and got a male teacher to help her escort Freddie to the principal's office. When Freddie saw how he was being treated, he totally lost it. He started blubbering and crying as the man led him away.

I went to the nurse's office. The nurse said my cut was superficial. She put a Band-Aid on it. But I had to go to the emergency room to get a tetanus shot. The nurse drove me there in her car. Of course it was great to get out of class, get some fresh air. They didn't have any tetanus medicine there at the school. Not so many knifings in those days.

When I got back I had to meet with the principal. By this point Mr. Snyder was wise to my tricks. I didn't have a clean slate with him anymore. My slate was pretty dirty. He let me into his office and showed me a chair. Then he sat down as well. "Freddie Baldwin is very upset by this whole ordeal," he said. He crossed his hands in front of him on his desk.

"So am I," I said.

"Although we cannot get Mr. Baldwin to settle down enough to confirm it, we suspect it was you who precipitated this incident."

That was reasonable enough, I thought. After only a week, he knew me pretty well. "I didn't do anything," I said. "I was just walking by when Freddie lunged at me and slashed my arm." I stood and held the injured arm across the desk for Mr. Snyder to see.

He didn't seem too impressed by my wound. He just shrugged his shoulders. "Any idea as to why Freddie may have done this?"

"Well, earlier he accused me of spitting in the clay pot. But it's not true. I don't know how he got that idea."

Mr. Snyder was satisfied that he wasn't going to get any useful information out of me. He dismissed me with a wave of the hand.

"There sure seems to be a lot of sympathy for some guy who goes around stabbing people," I said as I left.

Johnny acted like he was glad to have me back, but I could tell he was more than a little ambivalent. He seemed to get into our old pattern of troublemaking for a while, but not like before, and I sensed his heart wasn't really in it. I didn't know him like I used to. We had grown apart in many ways. Johnny had formed new friendships of which I had no part, and which I threatened to disrupt. He didn't seem that eager to renew our friendship on the same terms as before. I had sensed this from the beginning, and it wasn't long before it was made even more clear.

One day soon after the linoleum knife incident, I was in shop class messing around with a hand drill. There were several different drill bits, and I tried out a few of them, but drilling through scraps of wood got old after a while. I picked up the smallest drill bit of them all. It couldn't have been more than a couple millimeters in diameter. I fixed it into the drill and looked around for something to try it out on. There was a full bottle of furniture glue sitting on a table. I grabbed it and drilled a tiny hole down toward the base of the bottle.

Several people had watched me do this, including Johnny. "You're an idiot," he said. "Riley is gonna make you pay for that." Coach Riley was also the shop teacher.

"Fuck it, man. He'll never know it was me. He probably won't even use it for a month or so. And then he'll just think the bottle is defective."

The coach came into the room and grabbed the glue bottle off the table. He said he was going to demonstrate how to glue together a gun rack he had made. He took a long piece of finished wood in one hand and applied the glue along the length of a groove that had been cut out of the wood. A thin ribbon of glue snaked out of the hole I had drilled and coiled up on Coach Riley's wrist. I had to stifle my laughter. It was several seconds before the coach noticed it.

"What the hell?! Goddammit!!!" He figured out what had happened, since the drill was still sitting on the table. "Who did this?" he asked.

Everybody shrugged their shoulders.

Then one of the retards told him. I hadn't counted on that. There were several retards in the class, but nobody paid much attention to them. I don't think they were really retarded, but they were sure stupid. They only had shop at our school, and the rest of the day they spent somewhere else, in some vocational program.

The retard who told was named Orville. He was fat and had buck teeth. He not only told who had done it, he explained in detail how it had been done. He was grinning like a moron, and seemed very proud of himself, like he'd just figured out something that no one else knew.

"Orville is confused," I said. "He must have just seen me holding the drill near the glue or something, and now his imagination is running away with him."

The coach didn't believe me. "You can't just go around destroying other people's property," he lectured me. "That glue cost seven-fifty, and I want the money right now."

"Why don't you just put a piece of tape over the hole?" I said. "It'll be as good as new."

The coach didn't go for that. I had to agree to bring in the money tomorrow. It pissed me off because I didn't even have that much and I was going to have to steal it from my parents.

When the bell rang for the end of the period and Coach Riley went into his office, I started shoving Orville around, warning him not to rat me out again. He was too stupid to know what he was doing, and I realized this. If I could teach him a lesson, fine. But mainly I was looking at the bigger picture. This was a big school and people didn't all know me yet. I felt like people needed to be put on notice.

Then, before I knew what was happening, Johnny grabbed me from behind, pinning my arms behind my back. "Hit him Orville! Hit him!" he yelled, laughing.

Orville didn't know what to make of it. He just stood there with a stupid look on his face. But then something clicked in his tiny brain and he came up to me and punched me in the stomach.

It hurt, and it made me mad as hell. Johnny had relaxed his grip and I shook him off. I came at Orville as he backed away. I backed him up to the wall and swung a right at his face. But he was quicker than I thought. He ducked and my fist smashed into the wall.

"Shit!" I danced around shaking out my injured hand. "Shit! Shit! Shit!"

While I was recovering, Orville ran out the door. I went after him, but I lost him in the halls. Goddamn him, I thought. I looked around for him for a while, but I still didn't know the layout of the school well, so I soon gave up. I stopped and checked out my hand. It was swollen and sore, but nothing was broken.

I didn't see Johnny either. I didn't see him for the rest of the day.

41

I brooded over the incident all that night, not getting much sleep. The next morning I was still angry and confused. I hardly noticed the spring dew soaking my jeans as I trudged across the field towards the school. I didn't know what I was going to do as I came up the stairs.

Johnny was already sitting in the Core classroom, and he started snickering when I walked into the room. I felt like busting him upside the head. Instead I just gave him a dirty look as I passed. There were several classes taking place in the auditorium. I took my seat with my class on the other side of the big room.

Johnny had been trying to teach me a lesson. That much, at least, I saw clearly. It had pissed him off for me to be making fun of the coach, and also for me to be picking on Orville, who everybody knew was just plain stupid and couldn't help it. Well, I'll show him, I thought.

Halfway through the period the teacher stopped paying attention to what my class was doing, so I was able to get up out of my desk and wander around. Johnny's desk was up against one of the tall bookshelves at the rear of his class. Nobody else was sitting near Johnny. He was partly hidden from the rest of the class, and actually out of the class area. Johnny was bent over his desk concentrating on an assignment in his vocab workbook. So he didn't notice when I snuck across the Core room to the opposite end of the bookshelf next to him.

Johnny's teacher didn't see me either. She was working at her desk at the front of the class. Some of the people in the class were laughing and joking around. I grabbed a desk and pulled it over to the end of the bookshelf. Then I stepped onto the seat and stood up.

On top of the bookshelf from one end to the other were stacks of dusty old workbooks. Johnny still hadn't looked up. I shoved the books hard from my end, sending two of the stacks crashing down onto Johnny's head and desk.

It made a hell of a racket. Must have been twenty or thirty workbooks. I slipped away behind another bookshelf and out into the hall.

Everybody turned around to look at Johnny. There were workbooks on his desk and on the floor all around him. The teacher's head shot up. "Johnny!!! What are you doing back there?!"

"I didn't do it, Miss White!" Johnny said. He was stunned and disoriented, and not yet able to figure out what had happened.

"Other people in this class are trying to do their work," the teacher said. "Pick up those workbooks and don't touch them again. One more outburst like that and I'm sending you to the principal's office."

While Johnny was picking up the workbooks, I stepped around the corner where he could see me. I pointed at him and laughed. Now he got the picture!

As soon as the period was over, Johnny left the classroom quickly. When I entered the stairwell, he was hiding around the corner and he jumped me, slamming me into the wall. I pushed off the wall and drove Johnny back across the stairwell, slamming him into the opposite wall and breaking his hold on me. Then I swung with a right, and Johnny ducked. This time it was like a slow motion replay. Not again, I thought, as my fist approached the wall. Twice in two days! I was able to take a bit off the punch this time, but the wall was rough concrete. It scratched and bloodied my hand and hurt even worse than before.

Now I was really mad. I ducked down, grabbed Johnny around the waist, and lifted him off the ground. But my head slid off to Johnny's side and when we went down I cracked my skull on the stone floor, breaking Johnny's fall and only hurting myself. But I didn't knock myself out. I held onto Johnny and managed to sit on top of him and get in a couple of decent punches to his face.

Like I said, Johnny had been trying to teach me a lesson. It was a lesson I was determined not to learn, but even so, I think I could have let the matter drop if not for one thing. And that was seeing Johnny sitting there at his desk actually doing his school work!

What I realized then was that there was a difference between Johnny and me. For me it was a matter of principal not to do my work, but for Johnny that had just been a pose. One of the reasons why Johnny left Catholic school was that he couldn't keep up. Here at the public school, the kids were more on his level. It pissed me off to discover this, and to see him actually fitting in. It felt like a betrayal this time for sure. He was pitiful, a dumbass like all the rest. There he was scribbling away in his workbook like it meant something. Like he liked it, for God's sake! I punched him all the harder for that.

Before I could do much damage, the janitor grabbed me off of Johnny. "You boys are going straight to the principal's office!"

I couldn't think of any way out of it. I was ready to go. But Johnny brushed past the janitor and into the hall, saying he needed to wash his face in the bathroom. "Yeah, me too," I said, and I followed Johnny. The janitor went with us and stood over us as we turned on the water at the sinks.

Johnny looked at his lip in the mirror. It was swollen and bleeding. He splashed some water on it. "Look what you did to my lip, you asshole."

"Well, look what you did to my hand." I was at the next sink running water over my hand.

"You did that to yourself," Johnny said.

"Plus, I cracked my skull on the floor."

"Serves you right. You need to learn how to fight."

"Look who's talking," I said.

Johnny splashed some more water on his lip, grumbling curses under his breath.

The janitor saw that we were friends, and so he decided not to take us to the principal after all. We walked out of the bathroom and went our separate ways.

42

Later that day I was eating lunch, sitting alone at my table. At one point I noticed that Dick Morgan was glaring at me from across the cafeteria. I started to get nervous. Morgan was a big guy, much bigger than me. He was the center on the basketball team. I tried to ignore him, but every time I looked up he was still glaring at me. Then he came over to my table. "I'm gonna kick your ass," he said.

"What for?" I asked. I was puzzled.

"You *know* what for! Meet me behind the field house after school!" he said. Then he turned and stormed off.

I suspected that Johnny was behind this, but I couldn't figure out why Morgan would take up for him. As far as I knew they didn't even know each other. Morgan was more my friend than Johnny's. I had played on the same basketball team with him a couple of years back. I still spoke to him once in a while when we passed in the halls.

Whatever Morgan's problem was, I wasn't going to run away. When the final bell rang I figured I'd just as soon get it over with. As I came around the field house I saw Morgan. Sure enough, Johnny was with him. "I'm gonna kick your ass!" Morgan yelled when he saw me.

"You already said that once, you moron," I said as I walked toward him. I coughed up a hocker and spat it at him.

It went right in his face. And it made him so mad he didn't even bother to wipe it off. He bellowed like a bull and charged me and tackled me. We wrestled in the grass and dirt, struggling for the advantage. Finally, Morgan pinned me. He sat on my chest, holding down my arms. But he didn't punch me. Instead he spat in my face. I had a burst of new energy and I got an arm free to shield my face, and was able to twist around half-way onto my stomach. But I couldn't get away from him. He was too strong. He kept spitting in my hair and he even blew his nose in my hair. But at least that was better than in my face.

"You give!? You give?!" Morgan said.

"Yeah, yeah. Let me up," I said.

"Say it!"

"Alright, I give!"

Morgan gave my head a shove into the ground, using it to lift himself off me. Without another word, he walked back toward the school.

I got up and dusted myself off, and wiped the spit and snot from my face and hair. Johnny was laughing. I walked away from the school and into the subdivision. Johnny followed me. He was walking beside me on the opposite side of the street. We walked for a while without saying anything.

"You didn't look so tough against Morgan," Johnny said finally.

"I should kick your ass again!" I said.

Johnny wasn't worried. He knew I was in no mood for fighting anymore. And since he was across the street from me, he had a good lead and would have been able to outrun me. "I laughed my ass off when he blew his nose in your hair!" he said.

"Yeah, very funny," I said. "But what I want to know is, how the hell did you get Morgan involved in this?"

"I told him you were going around the school telling people he was a fag."

43

After that, things cooled off between me and Johnny. He had his new life, and I had been thrust into a new situation and there were new people for me to get to know as well. I found that it wasn't that important to keep up the friendship with Johnny anymore. It wasn't like we just dropped each other, and in fact we talked to each other every day. I wasn't mad at him, and I don't think he was mad at me either. But there was a distance between us that hadn't been there before. It was unwelcome to me in a way, but it didn't seem unnatural. I had other things on my mind, chief among them girls. I didn't feel so burdened by my history here, not by *The Sexbook*, or even by Sheila. So maybe I did have a clean slate, in a way. Though I was still scared of the girls, and hesitant to approach them, I was always checking them out. And, as I was to find out shortly, at least one of the girls was checking me out as well.

There was a teacher at the school named Robert Doyle Jr. The name was unfortunate, because he didn't look real old. He looked like a teenager to begin with, and so naturally we just called him Junior. Even some of the students looked older than him. Besides that, Junior was a geek. He was tall and skinny and had greasy hair and coke-bottle glasses, and he had one leg slightly shorter than the other and walked with a limp. He wore a pocket protector in his shirt pocket and had a calculator strapped to his belt. He was the math teacher, which maybe explains the calculator. And he absolutely hated being called Junior.

We teased him a lot. We yelled shit at him in the hall. We started a thing where we would yell at him about beating off. For some reason, he just seemed like somebody who would do a lot of beating off. "Beat off, Junior!" I would yell at him. "Beat your meat, Junior!" somebody else would yell. We wouldn't say it to his face, but just yell it at him behind his back when the halls were crowded. Junior did his best to ignore it.

People started doing it in his class sometimes too. It was a big class, held in the cafeteria. When we were supposed to be working silently somebody would call it out, often loud enough to be heard throughout the class. Junior couldn't figure out who was doing it since the class was so big. It was fun to do it at a real inappropriate time, like in the middle of a test. It was fun to call it out when the class was silent, or when Junior said something stupid. It was best to say it in a funny voice. That got the biggest laughs.

Junior just laughed about it, or once in a while made a remark about how stupid we were. "I can't help but be humored by this adolescent fixation on bodily functions," he said one time. But it went on for a couple of weeks, and you could tell he was getting sick of it. There was a discipline problem in the class to begin with. Nobody had much respect for Junior. He had a couple of college students to help him monitor the class, but they were girls and they weren't much help.

Math class was the last class of the day. Sometimes it got me thinking about jacking off so much that I had to run home after school and jack off myself.

The class was so huge that instead of a blackboard Junior wrote on transparencies and projected them onto a big screen at the front of the class. He spoke into a microphone so the whole class could hear him. Junior couldn't control much in the class but he usually kept an eye on his equipment so nobody could mess with it. Junior was very particular about his equipment.

It was a beautiful day in early May and everybody was feeling kind of rowdy, ready to get out of class and run wild. We had just got back the tests we took a few days before. Everybody was up at the front of the class asking questions about their tests. It was chaos up there, with people standing in a long line to talk to Junior, and other people milling around. I went up there too, though not to ask a question. I thought the joke about beating off was getting old and needed to be infused with new life. I waited for my chance, when Junior had his back turned and there were people blocking his view. Then I grabbed the microphone and turned it on and said, "Beat, Junior, beat!!!" I yelled it over the microphone in a long, low voice.

Then I turned quickly away and hid in the crowd as the whole room cracked up laughing.

Junior was enraged. He charged to the microphone and started looking for the culprit. The people standing by the microphone all said it wasn't them. By this time I was strolling back to my seat, acting like I was just minding my own business.

But I hadn't counted on the teaching assistants. One of them had seen me and she pointed me out to Junior. "You! Donaldson!" Junior yelled after me. He came after me fast and had such a maniacal look on his face that I thought he was going to kill me. I broke into a run and sprinted through the cafeteria.

Junior ran after me. He ran as well as he could with his bad leg. He chased me out of the cafeteria. I was half-way down the hall before he got out of the cafeteria. "You come back here!" Junior yelled after me.

There was no way he could have caught me. But I stopped. What was I going to do, run all the way out of the school? I was in his class and I would have had to go back and face him eventually anyway. I figured I may as well get it over with.

Junior slowed down and walked toward me deliberately. I had on a flannel shirt and when he got up to me he grabbed me by the collar and slung me against the lockers on the wall. He shook me and banged my head against the lockers. He was up in my face. "You little son of a bitch!" He was ripping my shirt. "Don't you ever call me that again!"

"OK!"

"Don't you ever say that to me again!" He was slobbering and spraying spit in my face.

"Alright!"

"You hear me?!" He banged my head against the lockers.

"Yeah! Yeah, I hear you!"

Junior let go of me. He turned away and walked back into the cafeteria.

I tucked my shirt back in my pants. My shirt was ripped near the collar and it had lost a couple buttons. I walked back into the cafeteria and went back to my table. I shared a table with four girls. If you were a troublemaker they put you at a table with people who wouldn't encourage you. These girls were the studious type. I plopped down in my chair and exhaled loudly. I was rather shaken. "Damn, that was a bitch. I thought that motherfucker was gonna kill me. He slammed my head against the wall," I said. "Did you see that shit?"

"No, you were out in the hall. We only saw him chase you into the hall," Mary Beth said. She was the prettiest girl at the table, and the one I talked to the most.

"He's a fucking nut. Don't let him hear you call him Junior."

"I have no intention whatsoever of calling him that," Mary Beth said.

Mary Beth had something to tell me. She waited awhile before she told me, allowing me to calm down a bit. She had a note for me, and she handed it over. "I would have given it to you earlier, but you were too busy," she said.

It was from a girl named Clair. The note said she liked me and wanted me to meet her outside after school. It said she and some of her friends were going to the park and she wanted me to come along.

I was still shaken from the encounter with Junior, and when I got the note it made me feel even more nervous. But I sure as hell wasn't going to miss out.

Part Five

44

It's probably no surprise when I say, I liked to show off. And when it came time for impressing girls, this talent came in handy. It was bullshit like the thing with Junior that must've attracted the attention of Clair. I assume it was that anyway. I liked to think I wasn't bad looking, but Clair was out of my league in that department. Clair was a real piece of ass.

Clair was Harold's little sister. I had never thought that much about her, and had spoken to her only a few times. She didn't live with Harold and his mother in the farmhouse. Their mom and dad were divorced and she lived with her dad. She was in seventh grade. I had always thought of her as a little kid before, but now she had obviously grown up. Now I started thinking about her differently.

Like I said, Clair was pretty. She wore her light brown hair in a shag cut. It was real cute. She wore it shorter than most of the girls. Most of the girls had long, straight hair. She had a nice body and she wore jeans and T-shirts.

The note said to meet her after school out behind the field house. When math class was over I went right out there. I saw Clair and went up to her.

"What happened to your shirt?" she asked.

"Junior did it," I said. She had Junior for math too, only not the same period. Everybody had Junior. "It's no big deal," I said, and I told her the story. I was a little bit ashamed of it because I thought it made me look like a wimp.

She didn't seem to care, and that put me at ease. "There's this trip today," she said. "We're going out to the park, and I was just wondering if you wanted to go along."

"Sure, I'll go. What's it for?"

"It's for this counseling group I'm in. Father Poole runs it," Clair said. The counseling group was for kids who were disciplinary problems. They had been assigned to it for missing too much school or for other offenses. Clair didn't say what she was in there for, but I think it was for cutting class and for not doing her school work, and probably, when you get right down to it, for coming from a broken home.

For some reason I hadn't been assigned to the group. Maybe I hadn't been there long enough and they still held out hope for me.

"Who else is going on the trip?" I asked.

She named some kids who I thought were pretty cool. They weren't friends but I liked them. I still hadn't been fully accepted at the school, and they were in a group I wanted to be included in, basically rebels and outcasts like me. That made the trip sound even better.

"So what do you do in this counseling group?" I asked.

"Oh, nothing. It's a bunch of bullshit, but we get together and do something fun once in a while."

"OK," I said.

"But you have to have your parents' permission," Clair insisted.

"Ah, they don't care."

"Still, you'd better call them. Father Poole won't let you come along if you don't have your parent's permission."

"Let's just tell him they gave their permission. He's not gonna call or anything, is he?"

"I'm not going along with that. Then your parents will blame me for it if anything happens," Clair said.

"Do you think I'm gonna get bit by a snake or something?"

"No, but you just have to call."

"OK," I said. I went back inside the school and got on a pay phone and called my mother. I didn't think anything about it. I was too excited about Clair to think of what my mother would say. Clair stood there while I called her.

"Mom, I met this girl and she invited me to come along on this field trip after school. I was supposed to call you and ask your permission," I told my mother over the phone.

I didn't think there was going to be any problem, but my mother flipped out. She started asking a bunch of questions about the trip, totally interrogating me. "Now just who's sponsoring this trip?" she asked.

"I don't know, some counseling group. Don't worry, there's a priest going along."

"A Catholic priest?"

"No, I don't know what he is. He has the black clothes and the collar, but he's not Catholic. Episcopalian, I guess."

"Hmm, I don't know about that. I don't think you'd better go. I don't want you getting involved in any cults."

"I don't think it's a cult. What do you think they're gonna do, kidnap me and lock me in the basement of the Episcopal church?"

"I would have to know more about this group before I let you get involved," my mother said.

"They broke off from the Catholic church during the Reformation," I said, sarcastically.

"You know what I mean!"

"I'm not getting involved in anything. I'm just going to the park."

"No, you can't go."

"Mom, I'm doing you a favor. I didn't have to even ask you. I could have just gone. You don't know where I go half the time anyway."

"But you *did* ask. And I said you can't go. You are not to go," my mother said.

I hung up the phone. Clair was still standing there. "She said it was OK," I told Clair. "Let's go."

We got on the bus, which was already half-filled with other kids. Then the priest got on and started up the bus and drove. He didn't care whether my parents gave their permission or not.

It was warm and the sun was shining. We drove the five or six miles to the park with the windows down. I was growing my hair as long as I could get away with, and it blew back in the wind. Somebody had a radio and he turned it up loud. We sat together in a seat and Clair's friend sat in the seat in front of us. I talked to the two girls as we drove. I talked and joked around with some of the other people too. I felt good. I felt like I was fitting in with the cool kids in the school.

Before we turned off the main road we stopped at the store for some snacks and some cokes. I bought a pack of cigarettes.

The park was down a long country road. We drove through woods already thick with greenery and came out in a clearing. There was a large lake in the middle of the clearing. There were picnic tables and basketball courts near the lake. Not many people were there since it was a weekday, so we had the park to ourselves.

Some kids played Frisbee. One guy had brought a basketball and he and a couple of other guys shot baskets. A couple of losers had brought along homework and sat at a picnic table and worked on it. Some of the kids sat at picnic tables near the lake and smoked cigarettes. The priest didn't care if we smoked. That was one of the things that made it cool to go on the trip. The priest was a cool guy, almost like a hippie. He sat at one of the tables with some of the kids who wanted to talk to him. He was dressed in black, but very casual, and he wore sandals and had a mustache and wore his hair sort of long. I never figured out what kind of a priest he was. Like I said, he looked Catholic but he wasn't.

Clair's friend went off and left us alone. We walked around and smoked cigarettes. We went down and looked at the lake and then walked into the woods. The tree leaves and the smaller plants were almost full-grown, though still a pale, spring green. The air was fragrant and fresh. There was a little bridge that went over a creek and we sat down on the bridge and dangled out legs over the edge. The water trickled by a few feet below us.

We smoked cigarettes and talked about who we knew at the school. One of the girls who had gone to my Catholic school was on the trip with us. I had known her at Mother Goose, but she had left the school a few years before. I never talked to her anymore, and in fact I wouldn't have even thought of her if she hadn't been on the bus with us. But as it happened, I had a good story about her to tell. "You know Sandy Grimes?" I asked.

"Yeah," Clair said.

"She had sex with this guy in the fourth grade."

"The fourth grade! No way! How do you know?"

"It was a friend of mine who did it with her, this guy named Gerald. They did it standing up in her bedroom closet while her mother was downstairs cooking dinner!"

"I can't believe that," Clair said. But she believed it. It was the standing-up-in-a-closet part that did it. Nobody could make that up. "That's so funny," Clair said, though she wasn't really laughing.

"I know it," I said.

I reached in my shirt pocket for my cigarettes, but Clair grabbed the pack out of my hand. "Hey! Give me those back!" I said.

"You've had enough," Clair said. She put the pack in the pocket of her shirt.

I tried to grab them out of her pocket, but she crossed her arms over them. I still tried to get in there but she turned and rolled over away from me. We wrestled around in the dirt on the bridge, both of us laughing. Clair didn't care if she got a little bit dirty. She was a big girl and she wasn't delicate. I tried to get her to uncross her arms. I tickled her in the stomach and she squealed. She tried to knock my hands away and I knocked the pack out of her pocket onto the bridge. We both made a grab for them but I got them first. She tried to grab them back but I jumped up and ran away from her off the bridge. "Ha!" I said. I lit one up.

Still laughing, we came out of the woods. We went over to a picnic table where some girls were hanging out and talked to them for a while. After a while I got bored and went to play basketball with some of the guys. Clair stayed there and talked to her friends.

We were just fooling around, shooting the ball. We weren't playing a game or anything. A guy named Hank stood off to the side of the court, watching us play. I thought Hank was a really cool guy. He was the biggest guy there, but he wasn't interested in sports. After a while he called me over. He had brought along a joint and we went over by the woods and smoked it, me and him and a couple of other guys. I still didn't know what I was doing with the joint, but nobody said anything otherwise and I was just happy to be included. I don't know if I really got a buzz this time or not. I was feeling great to begin with, after all, and on top of that it just made me feel kind of lightheaded.

After we smoked the joint me and the other guys wandered back to where the girls were sitting. We sat down and talked to them. Hank was talking to Clair. He was kind of flirting with her and she was flirting back. But I didn't care. I wasn't jealous. I was flattered that he would take an interest in her. Anyway, she wasn't really my girlfriend yet, so what could I say?

Hank was sitting down and Clair was standing up. She stood leaning on the table, with her arm propping her up on the table. The way she was standing, with her legs crossed, her thighs were pressed together. Hank had a brown paper bag from the store. He wadded up the bag and stuck it between her thighs.

Clair's face got red. She got kind of mad, but I didn't know what to make of it. She looked at me like maybe she wanted me to kick Hank's ass or something, but it didn't seem called for. Maybe it was something sexual, but I had no idea what it meant. I just couldn't put my finger on it. She didn't like it, apparently, but what was I supposed to do? I couldn't do anything to Hank anyway.

Clair was only mad for a moment. She left the bag there for a moment and then took it out and threw it at Hank and called him an asshole. Then we all laughed about it.

Father Poole told us it was time to go, so we got ready and went to get back on the bus. Clair got on before me, since I was fooling around and talking to some of the guys. While I was standing there, Sandy Grimes came up to me. She cornered me and got me alone by myself. She was upset. She was almost crying. The story about the sex in the closet had already got back to her! "Why did you tell that story?" she asked.

"I don't know," I said. "Why not?" It occurred to me that this rumor might have been why she left Mother Goose. But I had only wanted a story to tell. That was all that had seemed important to me at the time. I hadn't given a thought as to who it might hurt. That could be said of a lot of the things I did at the time. I shrugged my shoulders as I walked away from Sandy and got on the bus.

Of course, fourth grade was also the year of *The Sexbook*. And when I think about it, what Gerald and Sandy had done had been part of the inspiration for the project. So maybe, without realizing it, in some weird way I was trying to pay her back. It was proving harder to put that incident behind me than I thought it would be.

Clair had got the very back seat in the bus and saved me a seat beside her. Clair's friend left us alone and on the drive back we sat in the back of the bus and kissed.

45

It turned out my mother didn't care too much about me going on the field trip to the park. There were worse places I could be, that's for sure, even if the priest wasn't Catholic. She was just suspicious about me going out with a girl. She talked it over with my dad when he got home from work. The idea of sex totally freaked my parents out. While we ate dinner they interrogated me about Clair. I was as vague as possible and didn't tell them too much about her. I didn't tell them she was Harold's sister. They knew Harold, and they knew who his mother was and where they lived, and that wouldn't have been a good recommendation for Clair. She had the same last name as him, Smith, but they didn't pick up on that.

After supper I went up to my room as my parents talked it over. Then my dad came upstairs and knocked on my door and came into my room. I was listening to the radio, and he turned that off.

It was uncomfortable for him. "Tommy, I want to talk to you about something," he said.

"Yeah?" We didn't talk much. It was just as uncomfortable for me. I was sitting on my bed with my back propped up against the headboard.

My dad stayed standing. "I know you've got to that age where you're going to start thinking about girls."

"I already *have* started."

"You know you have to be careful," my dad said. "You can't go getting her pregnant. Do you know about that?"

"Yeah," I said. He seemed to me to be getting way ahead of things. I wasn't ready to do much more than kiss.

"You know about that?" he repeated.

"Yeah, I know all about that."

"Because someday you'll want to get married and raise a family, but you don't want to have to get married when you're fourteen."

I had to smile because the idea was so absurd. "I'm not planning on it," I said.

"But you know what I mean. You may have to get married if you get her pregnant."

"I won't get her pregnant."

My dad seemed ready to leave. Then he said, "Religion is another thing to consider. If you marry a girl who isn't Catholic then you'll have trouble when it comes to raising the children."

"I don't think I have to worry about that yet," I said.

46

Now I had a girlfriend. That certainly took my mind off Johnny, and off everything else, actually. Now I didn't care what Johnny was doing. I was high as a kite.

After school the next day I met Clair outside. We held hands and walked through the neighborhood to the springhouse. The place was surrounded by lush, tall trees. We looked over the edge to where the water trickled over the rocks below. We sat down on the floor behind the wall on the inside of the springhouse where we couldn't be seen. We kissed and fooled around. Clair was sweet and nice, and sexy.

Clair had a job babysitting after school. It was in the same building as the apartment where she lived with her dad. Sometimes she did it in the middle of the day when she was supposed to be in school. She got the lady she was babysitting for to call in for her and pretend to be her mom and say she was sick. Nobody cared at the public school anyway. A couple of times I cut school and hung out with her and the kid and we played records and ate the food in the refrigerator.

The rest of the school year went by quickly. I felt lucky to have found a girlfriend without really trying. I felt that otherwise I may never have found one. I was less angry, and I stopped picking on kids. The whole time I was with Clair I don't think I picked on anybody. It was something I only realized later, after it was over. I still caused my share of trouble, but hey, old habits die hard.

Then school ended and it was summer. Me and Clair walked around the neighborhood holding hands. One time we walked over near my house. I showed Clair my house but I told her we didn't want to go in there now because my mother was bound to be there.

"Let's go in and meet your mother," Clair suggested.

"You don't want to meet my mother. That's the last thing you want to do."

"I want to meet both your parents."

"Well, suit yourself. My dad won't be home."

My mother was surprised that we showed up. She was polite, but I don't think she liked Clair very much. "You want a coke or something?" she asked me.

"You want a coke, Clair?" I said.

"Sure, I'll have one."

"Have a sandwich if you want. I just bought some lunch meat at the grocery," my mother said.

My mother was doing some ironing in the family room. She went back to it while I started getting the stuff out of the refrigerator and Clair sat down at the table.

My mother could see us through the doorway. She seemed nervous. I don't think she knew quite what to make of this new development. She peeked her head around the corner and said, "Don't stand there letting that cold out. Get what you need and close that door." I tried to ignore her. A minute later when I was making the sandwiches she said, "Don't use up all of that mayonnaise. And keep that bread sealed up or it'll go stale."

"It's not gonna go stale while we're sitting here," I said.

"Oh, yes it will. It only takes a minute," my mother said.

This was pretty standard for my mother, though it annoyed me more than usual that day. We finished our sandwiches and drank our cokes and got out of there. We had only been in the house for about ten minutes. "I'm sure glad to get the hell out of there so I don't have to listen to that bitching anymore," I said. "See, I told you she was a bitch."

"I didn't think she was that bad," Clair said.

We walked up the old main street into the little town, holding hands. I showed Clair all the places where I used to hang out with Johnny. We walked by the house where the old lady lived, though I didn't mention that me and Johnny had teased her. We crossed the road by the fruit stand where me and Johnny used to steal fruit. I was proud to be walking with a pretty girl. When we were crossing the road a carload of guys drove by and they all stuck their heads out of the car and whistled at Clair. She was wearing cut-off jeans and had a great ass.

47

Strangely enough, once I started spending time with Clair I tended to run into Johnny more than ever. It was partly because she was Harold's sister, and Johnny had started hanging out with Harold again. But there was more to it than that. Johnny was attracted to Clair. He would have been crazy not to be. But I didn't think much about it. I didn't care so much whether Johnny was around or not, but since I seemed to run into him a lot now, we started hanging around together again. Now it seemed the balance had shifted once again, and he needed me more than I needed him.

One day in early summer a bunch of us were at an apartment a few buildings down from Clair's building. Me and Clair were there. Johnny was there. Harold was there. The guys who lived in the apartment were a few years older than us, out of high school. They were Harold's friends. We were sitting on the couch talking. The stereo was on and we were listening to music and drinking beer.

"I have to go babysit now," Clair said. She got up to leave. "Wait about a half an hour and come on over," she told me. "I should have the kid in bed by then."

I waited slightly longer than that, then I took the last swig of my beer and got up off the couch and said, "I'd better get out of here."

"Yeah, you better do what your little girlfriend says," Johnny said.

Everybody laughed.

I laughed too. "Yeah, I'd better."

"Don't be such a wimp," Johnny said. "Here, drink another beer." He handed me a beer out of the sack beside his chair.

"I'll take it with me," I said.

"Don't be so pussy whipped," Johnny said.

What the hell did he know about it? I went out the door with the beer. Johnny was jealous, I realized. He didn't have a girlfriend yet and I could tell that he thought he'd really missed his chance. He'd been around Clair more than I had, probably. No doubt he had run into her a lot over at Harold's house. He thought it could have just as easily been him with Clair. When I got outside I stuck the beer down my pants so nobody would see it while I walked through the parking lot.

The kid was in bed. Clair had put an Elton John record on the stereo. I came in and we sat on the couch. After a while I put my arm around her. Clair had on a flannel shirt. I pulled it away from her body and let it fall back. I tried to grab her breast but she swatted my hand away. "So, you do it when you're drunk," she said.

We went back to the bedroom and laid on the bed. It was twilight and a cool breeze blew in through the curtains. Clair got in first and she was on the wall side, then I got in after her. We kissed and hugged, and then I unbuttoned her shirt. I was nervous but the beer helped. I felt her breast on top of the bra, then I got my hand under the bra and felt her breast under her bra. I tried to reach down her pants but she grabbed my hand and pulled it out. She said she was on her period.

We started kissing again. The room had become dark while we were lying there. What little light there was filtered in through a part in the curtains. I tried to get down her jeans again. I was buzzed from the beer. I didn't care that it was her period. That didn't bother me. I wanted to feel her pussy, but she wouldn't let me. I tried once more but she swatted my hand away again. "I have other things," she said. But that was all I had in me. I was drunk and tired and I gave up easily. I rolled away from her onto my back. I still had my arm around her and we lay there together on the bed and snoozed.

Somebody knocked on the door. Clair knew it was her dad, so she sat up quickly and shoved me out of the bed. "Oh shit! He'll kill me if he finds you here!" She buttoned her shirt and tucked it into her pants as she pushed me into the hall. "Quick, get in the kitchen and hide!"

"What for?"

"Shhh! Be quiet! He'll hear your voice. He doesn't like me babysitting. He says I'm too young. And he told me I'd better not bring any boys over here."

"Just tell him I'm the kid's uncle."

"Shhh! Quick, get in here and hide behind this wall!" She pushed me toward the kitchen.

"What's wrong with the bedroom?"

"He might look in there. He's not gonna look in the kitchen. Get in there and be quiet. I'll get rid of him fast."

I went into the kitchen and leaned with my back against the wall inside the door. The light was on. Clair reached in and turned it off.

Then Clair went to the door and opened it.

"What took you so long?" her dad said. I heard him come into the living room.

"I was just in the bedroom, putting the kid to bed," Clair said.

"Well, I just stopped by to see how you were doing. You doing alright?"

"Yeah, I'm fine."

"Not having any problems with the kid or anything?"

"No, not a thing."

"So you were able to get him to bed OK?"

"Yeah. Be quiet. Don't wake him up."

"You doing your homework?" Mr. Smith asked.

"I'm getting ready to," Clair said.

Hiding in the dark in the kitchen, I felt like an idiot. I didn't think we were doing anything wrong and I didn't like to hide. I didn't like to be put on the defensive. He doesn't have any proof that we were doing anything, I thought. We could have just been sitting and talking. What if he walks in here and catches me? That's gonna look pretty suspicious. Then it really *will* look like we're doing something.

"You need anything?" Mr. Smith asked.

"No, I'm alright," Clair said.

"I'm right upstairs if you need anything."

"No, I'm OK, really."

Neither of them said anything for a moment. Jesus Christ, I thought, why doesn't he leave? I heard the floor creak and it sounded like he was walking around. I thought, oh shit, any minute now he'll step around the wall and catch me.

"Anybody else in here with you?" Clair's dad asked, suspiciously.

"Just the kid. Who else would there be?"

"You don't have any boys in here, do you?"

"Yeah, ten of them. In the bedroom. Come on, dad!"

"Mind if I have a look?"

"Sure. Better check under the bed."

I seriously thought he was getting ready to search the house. I figured it would look worse if he caught me hiding, so I stepped around the wall and walked into the living room.

It was the first time I had seen Clair's dad. I looked him over. He had a slight build, and was only a little bit taller than me. "Hi," I said.

He looked puzzled. "Hi," he said. He looked back at Clair.

"We're not doing anything," Clair said. "He just stopped by to get a drink of water. He just walked in a minute before you did."

"You better get him out of here," Mr. Smith said.

"He's leaving right now. I'm just saying goodbye to him."

"I'll talk to you later, young lady. We're gonna have to have a talk about whether or not this babysitting thing is gonna work out," Mr. Smith said. He gave me a very dirty look on his way out.

"You idiot! Why did you come out?!" Clair screamed at me when her dad had gone.

"I thought he was gonna come in and catch me."

"No, he wasn't. He was getting ready to leave."

"Well, he sounded like he was gonna search the place."

"He was joking! Now I'm in big trouble!"

"It didn't seem like he cared," I said, more hopefully than anything else.

"Oh, you don't know him. He's not gonna say anything in front of you."

Clair was running around the room freaking out. "Now he's not gonna let me babysit anymore! That's the only way I've got of earning any money, and now you've ruined it. Thanks a lot!"

"I'm sorry. I thought he was gonna catch me," I said again.

"But he wasn't. He was leaving," Clair repeated.

"How was I supposed to know that?"

"You didn't have to know anything. All you had to do was stay in there."

"Well, he left. He didn't run me off or shoot me or anything, so probably he doesn't care."

"Oh, he's watching for you. You have to get out of here right now!"

"What's the big rush?"

"Go! Go! Get out of here!" Clair grabbed my arm and pulled me and then pushed me toward the door. "Maybe if he sees you go he'll let me babysit again. Hurry up and go and he'll see you're gone."

I slipped away from her. "Let me get my beer out of the refrigerator." I had put it there earlier.

"Hurry! Hide it under your shirt. We don't want my dad to see it."

48

I walked around to the front of the building so Clair's dad could see I had gone, but I didn't see him looking out the window. I didn't feel like going home yet, so I went back around the building and walked through the parking lot to a playground on the other side of the complex. We hung out there sometimes because it was secluded. I was going to sit there and drink my beer.

But there were some guys already there. They were quiet and I couldn't see them in the dark, so at first I didn't know who they were. Taking a chance, I went into the playground anyway, and when I got close I saw that it was Johnny and Harold. Johnny was sitting on the end of the sliding board and leaning back with his hands behind his head. Harold was sitting on a bench on the far side of the playground. They were both in the shadows.

They were drunk. They were drinking from a fifth of bourbon that Harold had in a brown paper bag. Johnny was really trashed. He was lying on the sliding board, but he wasn't quite passed out. He saw me walk up, and when he recognized me he said, "You in there getting some of that young pussy?" He was slurring his words.

"Shut up," Harold said.

"In there getting some pussy," Johnny mumbled.

"Don't pay any attention to him," Harold said. "He's wasted."

"It takes more than that to bother me," I said. In fact, it pleased me to see Johnny bitter like that. There were still some hard feelings between us.

Harold gave me a drink off the bottle. I sat down on the bench and opened up my beer and we drank that too. Johnny lay on the sliding board with his eyes closed.

"You better try to get home," Harold told Johnny.

"Give me another drink," Johnny said. He got up and staggered over to the bench and fell into Harold.

Harold pushed him off. "No, you've had enough."

Johnny didn't say anything. He stumbled over to the swing set and leaned against the bar. Nobody said anything else for a while. Then Johnny said, "Fuck you both. I'm going home." He staggered through the gate and out of the playground.

49

We stayed out on the playground and drank until late. Then it got chilly and started drizzling, and I didn't feel like walking home in the rain. Harold said it would be OK to hang out in his dad's apartment for a while. He said his dad and Clair would be asleep by now.

Mr. Smith wasn't asleep. He was up watching TV in the living room. But he didn't pay any attention to us when we came in. We went into the kitchen and got some cokes and ice out of the refrigerator and mixed drinks. We sat at the kitchen table drinking.

After a while Mr. Smith got tired of watching TV and came into the kitchen. Harold didn't bother to hide the liquor bottle. "Hey Pop, this is Tom," Harold said.

"We met earlier," Mr. Smith said. He saw the liquor and grabbed the bottle off the table and took a swig. "Ahh! Where have you been all my life?"

"I thought you were on the wagon, Pop," Harold said.

"Does it look like it?" Mr. Smith took another swig.

"Why don't you get yourself a glass, old man?" Harold said.

"That's what the bottle's for."

Mr. Smith hung around with us for a while. He told us dirty jokes and drank some more liquor straight out of the bottle. He's not a bad guy, I thought. He never did sit down but he did finally get himself a glass. We smoked a bunch of cigarettes, smoked the whole kitchen up. Harold and his dad smoked the same brand, Marlboro.

After a while Mr. Smith got tired of talking to us and went back into the living room. He took a glass of liquor with him and went to sleep watching TV. His head fell back and he started snoring. We could hear him all the way into the kitchen.

I looked at the clock over the stove. Somehow I hadn't noticed it before. "Shit! It's one o'clock! I gotta get out of here!"

"Don't worry about it. You can spend the night here," Harold said. "There's an extra bedroom. We can crash out in there."

"But I need to call my parents, and it's too late. They'll be asleep."

"What are you worried about? Tell them in the morning."

Harold went into the living room and got a bag of reefer out from behind the stereo where he had hidden it. He had been waiting for his dad to fall asleep so he could get it. "I don't like to carry this around with me since I'm on probation," Harold said as he dumped the bag out in the middle of the kitchen table. It was more pot than I'd ever seen before, close to an ounce. I grabbed a big bud and looked it over. Harold started cleaning the seeds out of a small sample of it. "Let's smoke some of this now that he's passed out," he said.

"What if your dad wakes up?"

"Ah, he don't give a shit. Just as long as you don't do it right in front of him."

"This seems like pretty much right in front of him," I said.

Harold got out a rolling paper and sprinkled some reefer in it and rolled up a joint. "You worry too much, you know that?"

We smoked the joint. This time Harold showed me how to smoke it properly, how to suck the smoke deep into my lungs and hold it there. I was already drunk as shit, and now I got completely wasted. My head was reeling.

Mr. Smith made a loud snort and woke himself up. He woke up in a bad mood and came into the kitchen grumbling. He smelled the smoke and saw the pile of reefer sitting in the middle of the table. "What the hell is this?" he said. "It smells like a goddamn opium den in here!"

"You've got your drugs confused, Pop," Harold said. "Maybe you should take a course or something."

"I'm getting pretty sick of your shit, Harold. You better clean up your act or you're gonna wind up in prison." Then he looked at me and said, "I'm getting pretty goddamn sick of seeing your ass around here too."

He turned back to Harold. "I tried to teach you, Harold, but now you're old enough and you can do as you please. But you're not taking me down with you. That stuff is still illegal. This is my house and I don't want it in here."

Harold ignored this. He didn't look at his father. He looked away from him, staring off into space. Then he took a swig off his drink.

"You still sitting here, Harold? Get that shit out of my house!"

Harold still didn't look at him. "Suck my dick, old man," he said.

Mr. Smith sprang on Harold and grabbed him by the neck and choked him. The chair came out from under Harold but he caught himself and didn't go down. At first it surprised Harold, but then he fought back. He grabbed his father and drove him back across the kitchen and slammed him against the metal pantry cabinet.

Clair heard the racket and came running into the kitchen. She just had on a T-shirt and shorts. "Harold! Leave him alone! Get out of here! Get out of here!" She ran right up on them. I thought she was going to try to physically separate them, but they quit struggling and let go of each other right away.

"Yeah! Get out of my house, you son of a bitch!" Mr. Smith said, pointing at Harold. "Both of you sons of bitches!" He pointed at me too. I had got up from my seat and was standing.

Harold got his reefer off the table. He swept it into its bag. "Let's get the fuck out of here," he said.

It wasn't raining anymore but the roads were still wet. We walked down the wet, black road without saying anything. I was impressed that Harold had dared to stand up to his father like that, though I also felt that there was something sordid in the whole situation. It was Harold who finally broke the silence. "I'll kill that old bastard one of these days."

The excitement had straightened me up momentarily, but now that it was over I was twice as wasted as ever.

"You oughta come stay at my house. You're pretty fucked up. You can't even walk straight," Harold said.

"No, I may as well go home," I said. We had come to the street where I had to turn off.

"Suit yourself," Harold said.

It took me awhile to get the door unlocked because I was so drunk. I couldn't get the key in the lock, and I dropped my keys several times. My dad was waiting right inside the doorway for me. He had been waiting in the dark. "Where have you been?!" he said.

"I was over at Clair's house. I was gonna spend the night but then I decided to come home."

"What!? Her parents let you stay over there with their daughter!?"

"No. I was staying there with Harold."

"Harold? Harold who?" Then it dawned on him. "What's he doing over there?"

"He's her brother. You didn't know that? That's where their dad lives."

I was standing there swaying the whole time I was talking to him. My head was swimming and I was slurring my words. All I wanted to do was get upstairs and go to bed. "I'm going to bed," I said. I tried to slip by my dad and get to the stairs.

My dad grabbed me by the arms and slammed my head against the wall, lifting me off the ground. I bit my tongue and saw stars. It almost knocked me out. "You're drunker than a sea cook!" he said. He slung me over onto the staircase and I scrambled away from him up the stairs. I went in my room and struggled out of my clothes, then flopped down in bed and passed out.

50

The next day my dad decided on my punishment. He woke me up before he went to work. He made me sit up in bed when he talked to me. I felt like shit. My head was throbbing and I could hardly even understand what he was saying to me. He told me not to go out that day. It sounded like a reasonable penalty. He said something about how he wasn't through with me yet, but I wasn't listening too closely. I just wanted him to leave me alone so I could go back to sleep.

When I woke up at noon I felt OK, though I had the sinking feeling that I was still in trouble. I had offended against my dad's two main prohibitions, alcohol and sex. Even if the sex was mostly in his own mind. When my dad got home from work he grounded me for a month.

I didn't go down for dinner. I stayed up in my room and played records. I called Clair and talked to her for a while and told her I was grounded. My dad was full of shit, I said. He was overreacting. He was overreacting mainly to the fact that I had a girlfriend. He wanted to keep me away from her. I told Clair that I wasn't going to put up with that shit.

The thing that bugged me worst was the prospect of not seeing Clair for a month. She was the only thing good in my life and I wasn't about to have that taken away. Nothing else mattered. So I decided to run away from home. Later that night while my parents were watching TV I stuffed some blankets and pillows under my covers to make it look like I was in bed. My parents were staying up later than usual to prevent me from going out. They were watching for me to try and sneak out the front door.

I went down the hall and knocked on my little brother's door and got him up out of bed. The chimney ran up the side of the house outside my brother's window and the bricks sloped up to the window. I had thought about it before as a way to get out. I told my brother not to tell and he lent me five dollars. We opened the window and took the screen out and hid it in the closet. I was able to climb down the bricks without too much trouble.

I went by Clair's apartment and threw rocks at her window, and when she opened it and stuck her head out I told her I was running away. I told her I was going over to my cousin's house to stay. He was the one who lived in the Hippie Shack. Clair couldn't sneak out of her apartment past her dad, so I said goodbye and she went back to bed. Everybody else had gone to bed too, and nobody was out. I walked around the neighborhood for a while, trying to stay off the main roads and hiding when a car came by.

I really did intend to go over to the Hippie Shack and ask my cousin if I could stay there for the night. But then when I got there I couldn't get up the nerve. I fooled around in the woods for a while and then stood there looking at the house. The lights were on, but I couldn't tell if there was anybody home or not. I didn't know what I was going to say if my cousin wasn't there. I didn't know what I was going to say anyway. For all I knew, he would call my parents. I didn't know if I could count on him. Even though he was hippie, I didn't know if I could trust him. Maybe my parents had already called there looking for me.

So instead I went into a shed in back of the house. It was filled with old farm junk, and with leaves and dirt that had blown in through the doorway and the busted-out windows. There was a raised shelf and I brushed the dirt off of it as much as I could. I got up on it and stretched out and tried to sleep. I laid on my stomach so I could hold onto the shelf and not roll off. I was right by a window where I could raise up and see the house.

The shelf was very uncomfortable, hard and rough. I tried to shift around and get comfortable without making too much noise.

After about an hour it sounded like some people had come home. I raised up and looked. They turned on a bunch of lights and then turned on the stereo. They played their music loud, and they played it long into the night, into the early hours of the morning. They played Pink Floyd's *The Dark Side of The Moon*, over and over. When it got to the end of one side it would be quiet for a few minutes and then somebody would flip the record over. It was a good album, my favorite, as I mentioned before, but I didn't feel much like hearing it just then.

It started raining. The rain came in through the cracks in the roof of the shed. It made a racket on the tin roof. It came in through the broken windows and made the place cold and damp.

I never was able to sleep. As soon as the sun came up I got up off the board and came out of the shed. I walked through the wet weeds and came out on the old main street and walked up into the little town. There was nobody out this early.

I was cold and hungry and wanted to get something to eat. None of the stores were open yet. The first place I found open was the Burger Chef. There wasn't anybody else in there except the manager. There weren't any customers. I went up to the counter and ordered a hamburger and a coke but the manager said they didn't serve hamburgers that early. All they served for breakfast were sweet rolls. I had a sweet roll.

I hung out in the Burger Chef for a while but I was afraid to stay there for too long. When I left the Burger Chef I walked down a country road that curved back around by Harold's house. I sat on the front porch until I heard somebody moving around inside, then I went around to the back door and knocked. Harold's mother was up, and she let me in and I sat down at the kitchen table. Harold wasn't up yet. His mother went upstairs and told him I was there.

Harold came downstairs in just his underwear and sat down at the table. He didn't say much. He was still waking up.

"Put on a shirt, Harold," his mother said, but Harold ignored her.

I didn't say anything about sleeping outside. I told Harold I had spent the night at my cousin's house. "I felt like I'd better leave before my parents thought about calling him," I said.

Harold's mother made me breakfast. She cooked bacon and eggs and toast. Harold and his mother had coffee, but I didn't drink coffee. "Your mother called here looking for you last night," Harold's mother said. "Your mother and father are very worried about you. Maybe you could stay here for a few days if you're having trouble at home. But you have to call your parents and let them know you're OK first."

"I'm gonna call them later on," I said.

Harold's mother had to go upstairs and get ready for work. When she came back into the kitchen she had on a dress. She was a tall woman, so maybe that's where Harold got his size. She was even taller now in her high heels. "You shouldn't do this to your parents, especially not to your mother. She's worried sick."

Harold's mother was ready to go out the door. "I'm not gonna tell on you, but you have to call your mother. Promise me you'll do that," she said.

"OK," I said.

Then she went out the door. I heard her car start up and drive down the gravel driveway.

I hung out with Harold for the rest of the morning. We sat at the table and smoked cigarettes.

"You can't stay here. My mother will rat you out," Harold said.

"She said she wouldn't."

"She will. And they'll figure out about your cousin eventually, if they haven't already, so you can't stay there. Do you have any money?"

"I've got about seven dollars."

"I can lend you some. I don't have much on me now, but if I can move this ounce I can probably lend you about twenty bucks. I'll have to go out and it'll take me awhile to sell it off. I was gonna sell it in joints. But I think nickels and dimes is the way to go to move it faster."

"OK."

"Now we've got to figure out what we're going to do with you," Harold said. He paused to think about it, and lit another cigarette. "You should leave town. They won't catch you then. That'll make it a lot harder for them anyway. I've done it before. I've got friends in Florida if you want to go that far, and I can call them and tell them you're coming. It's easy to hitchhike to Florida."

I didn't say anything. It sounded like a lot of trouble. It seemed to me that Harold was going way overboard with this.

"Or if you don't want to go that far, you can go to Cincinnati. I know some people there too. But they'll probably catch you there. You'll have to be real careful. I recommend Florida. If worse comes to worst you can sleep on the beach."

"Couldn't I just stay around here?"

"No way. They'll find you immediately."

It got to be noon. I got up from the table and went over to the phone on the wall. "I'm gonna call my parents now."

"No, you don't want to do that." Harold said.

"I may as well," I said.

"What for?"

"I promised your mother I would."

"So what? Don't listen to her."

I got on the phone and dialed the number. "They could be tracing this, you know," Harold said.

I talked to my mother, and then my dad got on the phone too. He had stayed home from work to look for me. And then just like that, my parents gave in. I had worried them good enough. My mother said to just come home and I wouldn't be grounded anymore. I hung up the phone. "That's it. I'm not grounded anymore," I said.

"Good. So what are you gonna do now."

"I guess I'm going home."

"Don't tell me you're giving up already!"

"I'm not giving up. They gave in. I got what I wanted," I said.

Harold shook his head in disgust. "Pathetic," he said.

51

When I woke up it was already getting dark. I still felt groggy, but good. I had slept through dinner, but my mother had saved some food in the oven for me and I wolfed it down. It was fully dark now, and I went outside. It was a cool summer night. Though I regretted that I had lost Harold's respect, I didn't worry too much about it. I thought he was being childish. And after all, I had won! I went over to see Clair where she was babysitting.

The kid was already in bed. Sitting on the couch in the living room, I talked to Clair about running away. "They weren't gonna tell me I couldn't go out," I said. I was proud of myself. "They gave in," I said.

"So what are they gonna do to you now?" Clair asked.

"Nothing. That's great, isn't it?"

Clair wasn't as happy about it as I was. She was mad at me. She had gotten in trouble too. Her dad was making her give up the babysitting job. She was only allowed to keep babysitting until the people she was working for found somebody else.

"That sucks," I said. "I don't know what he's so upset about."

Her dad had also decided that he didn't like me very much and didn't want me coming around anymore. But I wasn't worried about it, because as long as Clair could go out he couldn't stop us from seeing each other.

"You jerk! You got me in trouble!" Clair said. "It was your fault and you're not even getting punished!"

She punched me in the arm. "It's not fair!" She tried to punch me again, but I grabbed her arm. Then I grabbed her other arm and we wrestled around. I pulled her down to the floor and we wrestled around on the rug. I got on top of her and started tickling her. Then she rolled over on top of me and started tickling me.

Then we started kissing. But I was still just playing around, like a kid. It was innocent on my part. I wasn't getting aroused.

Clair started unbuttoning my pants. "Hey, what are you trying to do?" I said. But I didn't try to stop her. I didn't care, I just let her do it. It took her awhile, since my jeans wouldn't just come right off. She got my belt unbuckled, then she undid the button of my pants, and struggled to get the zipper down. My jeans were tight. She tugged my pants down over my ass, then she got to her feet and pulled at them. She pulled down the pants and the underwear came with them. She pulled them both down together until they were around my ankles. Then she looked at my dick. It wasn't hard.

"It's so little!" she said. And she giggled.

I was so embarrassed that I didn't know what to say. I reached down and grabbed my underwear and my pants and pulled them back up.

52

The next day Clair called me and told me to come over to where she was babysitting. I tried not to think about what had happened the night before. It was much too embarrassing to think about, really, and so for the most part I had put it out of my mind. I was eager for things to get back to normal and I thought it was a good sign that Clair had called me. She had sounded a bit strange over the phone, but I thought that was only to be expected. It was hot outside, in the nineties.

Clair let me in from the porch. Johnny was there. When I came in through the sliding door I saw him sitting on the couch. I thought that was kind of odd, but it didn't necessarily have to be bad. We all hung out together sometimes, and he could have just stopped by.

I didn't see the kid. He must have been back in the bedroom.

Clair plopped down on the couch next to Johnny. I didn't sit down. "Hey, how you doing, Tommy?" Johnny said.

"Hey Johnny. What are you doing over here?"

"Ah, we're just hanging out."

I noticed that they were sitting pretty close together. Clair scooted even closer and put her hand on his leg. When she did that I saw that they had written each others' names on their jeans with a ball point pen. "You see that?" Johnny said, indicating the writing. He put his arm around Clair.

"We like each other. We're going together now," Clair said.

"Oh yeah?"

"What do you think about that?" Johnny said.

I didn't know what to think. I just kept looking at the writing on their jeans, thinking I had somehow misunderstood. I didn't say anything.

"We just wanted you to know," Clair said, smiling wickedly.

"What are you gonna do about it?" Johnny said, a little nervously. I think he expected me to fight him.

I took a moment to consider Johnny's question. I looked at Johnny, and at Clair, and at the writing on their jeans. I remembered when Johnny was just the new kid and not yet Johnny to me. We were standing in line for something in the classroom and I was a few places back. A kid tried to butt in front of Johnny and Johnny jumped on him and got him in a headlock and twisted his head around until he begged to be let go. And I remembered one of the first times I came to his house and he showed me how the trees in the little grove of woods in his back yard were all chopped up. He said when he felt frustrated he came back there and chopped at them with a hatchet until he felt better.

"I don't know," I said finally. "Nothing."

"We don't need you here," Clair said when she saw I wasn't going to fight for her. She had an angry expression on her face.

"What did you call me for then?"

"We just wanted you to know," she said again.

"Is that all you wanted to tell me?"

"Yeah, that's it."

"I guess I'm leaving then," I said. I turned to go. I walked to the sliding door and tried to get out but the door didn't open easily.

Then Clair attacked me. She jumped on my back and started hitting me, raining down blows on my head and back. "You fucking bastard!" she yelled at me. A few months before I would have thrown her off me, maybe even hit her back. But now I had no desire to do that. Ducking my head to avoid her blows, I tried to get away from her but I couldn't get the door open. It was stuck in its track and it wouldn't slide open. I kept pulling at the door and Clair kept hitting me and yelling at me until finally I got it open and stumbled out onto the porch in a blast of hot air and sunlight.

Clair didn't come after me. She stood there in the doorway, her hands on her hips, scowling. As I walked away from the building, I felt disoriented, confused. I wasn't sure what had just happened. I only knew that I had lost my best friend and my girlfriend, both at the same time. Wandering down a stretch of fresh blacktop in a new, near treeless part of the suburb, I began to realize that I had left behind a large part of my childhood too, back there with Clair and Johnny, but that, strangely, I was no longer so attached to the idea of preserving it.

Acknowledgements

Thanks to my wife Debbie Martin for all her work in helping me perfect the manuscript for *Lords,* and for her continued support. Thanks also to Jacob Smullyan at Sagging Meniscus for a great editing job, and for starting this much-needed press in the first place; to Royce M. Becker for a superb cover design; to Rita Barros for a fine author's photo; and to Sandy Jimenez, who has once again outdone himself on the excellent book trailer (he produced the trailer for my previous book, *The Chintz Age,* as well).

Ed Hamilton was born in Atlanta, Georgia and grew up in Louisville, Kentucky. He has a bachelor's degree in psychology from the University of Kentucky and a master's degree in philosophy from the University of Louisville, where he wrote his thesis on Ludwig Wittgenstein's *Tractatus Logico Philosophicus*. Ed is the author of *Legends of the Chelsea Hotel: Living with the Artists and Outlaws of New York's Rebel Mecca* and *The Chintz Age: Tales of Love and Loss for a New New York*, which was on the Small Press Distribution Best Sellers List for the better part of 2016, and was also named to *LEO Weekly*'s Ten Best Books by Kentucky Authors list for 2016, and was a New York Public Library Recommended Read for May/June 2016. His short fiction has appeared in dozens of small journals and anthologies, beginning with *Exquisite Corpse* in 1993, and including: *The Journal of Kentucky Studies*; *Limestone: A Journal of Art and Literature*; *Pikeville Review*; *River Walk Journal*; *SOMA Literary Journal*; *Bohemia: Waco's Art and Literary Journal*; *Footnote: A Literary Journal of History*; *No Umbrella*; *Omphalos*; *Somewhere, Sometime: Lowestoft Chronicle's 2014 Anthology*; *Experienced: Rock Music Tales of Fact and Fiction* (anthology); *Lumpen Times*; *Modern Drunkard*; and in translation in the Czech Republic's *Host*. His non-fiction has appeared in *The Villager*, *Chelsea Now*, *Huffington Post*, and *Living with Legends: Hotel Chelsea Blog*. *Lords of the Schoolyard* is his first novel. Ed lives in New York City.

www.edhamilton.nyc | edham1@yahoo.com